# A MOTHER'S LAST WISH

JO BARTLETT

Boldwood

First published in Great Britain in 2025 by Boldwood Books Ltd.

Copyright © Jo Bartlett, 2025

Cover Design by Head Design Ltd.

Cover Images: Shutterstock

A CIP catalogue record for this book is available from the British Library.

Paperback ISBN 978-1-80483-991-1

Large Print ISBN 978-1-80483-992-8

Hardback ISBN 978-1-80483-993-5

Ebook ISBN 978-1-80483-990-4

Kindle ISBN 978-1-80483-989-8

Audio CD ISBN 978-1-80483-998-0

MP3 CD ISBN 978-1-80483-997-3

Digital audio download ISBN 978-1-80483-996-6

This book is printed on certified sustainable paper. Boldwood Books is dedicated to putting sustainability at the heart of our business. For more information please visit https://www.boldwoodbooks.com/about-us/sustainability/

Boldwood Books Ltd, 23 Bowerdean Street, London, SW6 3TN

www.boldwoodbooks.com

*For Anna and Harry, who I couldn't bear to leave, and for all the other mothers who so desperately wanted to stay, but who didn't get the chance, especially Danni, Nicky and Ali xx*

# 1

## LOUISA

I've always been sure I'd know if something life changing was about to happen, even before it did. Last month I watched a documentary about people who claim to have a sixth sense, and one woman described getting an intense pain at the precise moment her son's car made impact with a tree hundreds of miles away. When I turned to my husband and said, 'That's just like me,' he laughed so hard he nearly choked on his beer. It earned me the nickname of Psychic Sue for the rest of the weekend, despite the fact my name's Louisa. I suppose Tom might have a point, I've never had a premonition of that magnitude, but I can predict the weather. It started when I was twenty-six and broke my big toe tripping up a kerb after a few too many drinks celebrating a promotion. I still get a dull ache in it every time it's going to rain and, if my toe is capable of insight like that, I'd definitely know if the results of the scan I've had were going to throw up anything serious. But there's nothing warning me of impending bad news, not even a twinge in my little finger. The other symptoms I reeled off to my GP were all very common too: lack of energy, indigestion and a marked increase to the middle-aged spread I'd been hoping to stave off for a few more years. I'm just feeling my age, that's all, with the kind of nana-worthy complaint that a woman in her forties can apparently expect.

I'll no doubt be given a list of things I can no longer eat. So I might not mention to the doctor that the only reason Tom is with me is because we're going straight out to eat after my appointment, to celebrate our anniversary. It's a lunch-time date, but that's how we roll these days. With two children under seven, we're both too exhausted for evenings out, and this way we don't have to worry about getting a babysitter. It's not a sacrifice that bothers me in the slightest. I hate the cliché of what I'm about to say, but my children really are my whole world. Even now I'm focused on them, rather than the appointment, wondering how much longer it's going to be. We should have gone in almost an hour ago, and at this rate I'm going to have to ask Sophie, one of the other mums I befriended on the school and nursery run, to pick them up if we still want to go out to celebrate. We help each other out whenever the need arises, so I know Sophie won't mind. Despite that, I can feel my agitation building as the hands of the clock continue to move round, and Tom isn't doing much to help.

'You can go if you want to; we can always take a rain check on lunch.' I whisper the words as he taps his fingers against his thigh, one by one, for what feels like the millionth time. We're sitting in a soulless hospital corridor, facing a row of innocuous-looking consulting room doors, and I'm starting to wish I hadn't had the bright idea of trying to squeeze lunch in. Tom doesn't do well with waiting around. He's always been a go-getter, filled with boundless energy and enthusiasm. It's how he's made such a success of his career. You don't become a groundbreaking journalist by sitting around contemplating your navel. He's willing to take the sort of risks that still make my breath lodge in my throat, even after almost fifteen years together, and he's travelled to countries most people have never even heard of. The problem is, somewhere along the line, he's completely forgotten how to sit still. When he tries, he's like a caged animal, and right now it's driving me mad.

'You know I don't like you coming to hospital appointments on your own. Not after what Holly went through.' Turning to look at me, Tom cups the side of my face with his hand, and for a moment I forget my irritation. His eyes were the first thing I noticed all those years ago; they're the colour of the sky on a summer's day, and they're every bit as striking as they were back then. When he looks at me, he usually makes me feel as if I'm the only person who exists to him, but right now Tom can't sit still for long enough. He's moved on to foot tapping, and I know without having to ask that he's thinking about all the things he could be doing if he wasn't here with me. But he doesn't want to be one of *those* men. He's thoughtful and kind, and the sort of husband I know for a fact that a lot of my friends wish they had. He doesn't need to explain why he feels the need to be here, I understand only too well, but he does it anyway. 'We both know it's going to be gallstones, but it still kills me that Holly was on her own when they told her she had breast cancer.'

'Me too.' I've never shaken off the guilt of that. Holly's my twin, and I should have been with her, but her husband was supposed to go, so I didn't. I had no idea he'd let her down at the last minute and left her to face the devastating news alone.

'I know how traumatic that was for you both and how hard it is being back in the hospital where she had her treatment. So, I'm here to distract you, and who wouldn't be distracted by a prime hunk of a man like me.'

He's laughing before the words are even out, and I can't help joining in. Tom's laugh is one of my favourite sounds, and his restlessness is already forgiven. His complete inability to take himself too seriously is one of the things I love most about him, and he has no idea just how attractive other people find him. Tom's mind is always on other stuff. For him there are only really three things that matter: work, the children, and me. I try not to think about what order he'd place those things in, because it doesn't really matter. I'm just forever grateful to be in his top three.

'Just try not to distract the doctor too much with your overwhelming good looks.' Shaking my head, I laugh again, but there's a hollowness to the sound this time. Ever since Holly's diagnosis I've found it difficult to spend time in a hospital environment without dread creeping in. It's as though it's an echo of the terror that I might lose my sister. I was there with her for every treatment and I'm so grateful that it was a success, but I can still picture the fear and sadness etched on her face as she went through each stage. I don't want to think about that, so I focus on the children again instead. Just picturing their faces lifts my mood. 'What do you think the chances are of the kids eating anything if I have to ask Sophie to pick them up and give them some dinner?'

'Not good.' Tom shakes his head, and I know he's right. Stan, who's four, is going through a phase of refusing to eat any food that isn't beige, and for Flo, who is two years older, it's all about texture. If something hits her tongue that doesn't feel right, she's capable of projecting the offending item across the room in a way that would give that girl from *The Exorcist* a run for her money. Tom says I spoil them, and I know he's right, but I want them to be able to look back on the happiest childhood possible. If that means cooking three different dinners every evening, that's what I'm going to do.

I don't think Tom always understands and I'm not sure a person like him, whose childhood was so opposite to mine, ever really could. He was the centre of his parents' existence, a late baby born after they'd given up hope of it ever happening. His argument that he always ate the same thing as his parents might be more persuasive if I didn't know that they chose to eat the things their son enjoyed. He didn't have to slot into their lives, or way of doing things, because they built their world around him. Of course I've told him about my childhood, and the fact that more often than not Holly and I would cook for ourselves. On the occasions when one of our parents did cook, we had to eat what we were given, or there'd be trouble.

Even now I can't look at a plate of spaghetti without picturing it being hurled against the wall, the sound of the plate shattering almost ringing in my ears at the memory, just because I'd prodded at the sauce with my fork and asked if there were mushrooms in it. I'd been almost certain that my mum, Mandy, was going to hit me at the time. She had a vicious temper when she was drinking and her eyes had blazed as she looked at me, her hand drawing back in readiness to slap me.

'Look what you made me do, you little—'

'It's okay Mum, I'll clear it up.' Holly had stepped in between us. We couldn't have been more than about ten, because we were still at primary school, but she put herself in the line of fire to save me. She risked getting hit and while it had happened to us both before, this time her quiet calm seemed to quell Mum's temper, rather than inflame it further. Mum had just scowled at me instead.

'Don't think I'm making you anything else, you ungrateful little shit.' She'd turned then and slammed out. I'd known where she was going, straight downstairs to the pub she ran with my father. An environment that created the perfect storm for two functioning alcoholics, or at least they gave a good impression of functioning for their customers. Propping up the bar and acting the jovial hosts was the easy part for them, it was dealing with their twin daughters that seemed to push them over the edge. Dad had always been a drinker and, although that resulted in some less-than-textbook parenting from him too, he was more predictable. Alcohol didn't give him the kind of temper it gave my mother, so he was neglectful but never abusive. Sadly, they did a good enough job of functioning to fly under the radar, which meant Holly and I were left in their care when we'd have been much safer with my father's parents, our beloved Nan and Gramps.

Looking back, the strangest part is that Holly and I were protective of Mum and Dad, helping them cover up their short-comings and wanting to stay with them, despite their behaviour. I think we always hoped they'd change one day, but they never did. I know my grandparents were riddled with guilt when they finally discovered the full extent of what we'd been through. Nan told me before she died that she'd been certain Mum was going to be good for Dad. They'd been worried about his drinking for a couple of years before he met her, and they'd tried to help him, but he'd always insisted he was in control of the alcohol, rather than the other way around. Mum had confided in Nan, when she and Dad first got together, that she was sure she could change him. Instead, she was the one who had changed and started matching my father drink for drink.

Nan said she thought Mum probably had postnatal depression when her drinking first started and that it wasn't picked up back then the way it would be now. Giving birth had brought the demons of her own difficult childhood to the fore. She'd lost her parents, who'd had problems with alcohol too, without ever having resolved the issues between them. I wonder now if that's why she was attracted to Dad in the first place, seeing him as her second chance to save someone after being unable to save her parents. But it wasn't to be, and Mum developed a habit of self-medicating. The two of them enabling one another, white-washing over the resulting behaviour as if it was nothing.

Unlike Dad, who to this day still doesn't think he's got a problem, Mum has made several attempts to quit drinking in the past, but they never last. The day after an outburst, like the one with the spaghetti, she would always apologise, promising it would never happen again. Until the next time. It was the narrative of mine and Holly's childhood, and I thank God every day that we had one another. It saved us both. It's made us incredibly close too, and she understands my parenting decisions way more than Tom ever really will. He knows all the stories, but he didn't *live* them, so he could never hope to fully comprehend what that felt like, and I don't try to make him. I just put up with an occasional eyeroll or comment about over-indulgent parents not always being the best thing for kids instead. It might be true that there's a line you can cross where you do too much for your children, but if there's such a thing as making them too great a priority, I know which side of that line I'd rather be on. All I want to do is be there for them when they need me, including when they finish school today. *Come on, just call my name already.*

Looking around I realise how selfish I am for being impatient. There are four consultants seeing patients for different clinics, all using the same waiting area. And it's obvious some of the other people waiting would give anything to have problems as minor as mine. There's a man in a wheelchair at the far end of the corridor, with the kind of hollowed-out cheeks and sunken features that tell their own story. He's wearing a bright yellow jumper, which only emphasises the greyness of his skin and guilt washes over me. I'm wasting the consultant's time. Someone could email me a list of the foods I need to avoid or let me know if my name is going on a waiting list for gallbladder surgery. There are so many patients who need the doctor's time far more than I do. I'm fidgeting almost as much as Tom now, barely fighting the urge to forgo my appointment altogether if it helps someone else get seen sooner. Someone who's actually ill. It's only the thought of Tom's reaction that's stopping me. What happened with Holly seems to have given him a bit of health anxiety and my attempts to put off the scan did not go down well, so I went ahead with it. When I got a call saying one of the consultants, Mr Whitelaw, wanted to see me about the results, my heart sank. I haven't got time to be laid up after surgery, even for a few days. Tom's job takes him away a lot of the time, and there are big changes ahead for the children's schooling. So if this can be managed with diet, I'll give that a go first, even if it means giving up all my favourite food.

Looking up, I catch the eye of the woman who's sitting next to the man in the yellow jumper and another wave of guilt prickles my skin. She looks exhausted, and incredibly sad. Without knowing anything about him, it's obvious the man in the yellow jumper has had to face unimaginable things, and that the people who love him have too. I don't know if the woman is his partner, a relative, or a friend. But it's clear from the way she adjusts his position in the wheelchair to make him more comfortable and helps him take small sips of water from a paper cup, that she cares for him very much. Everyone needs someone like that, but when I catch the woman's eye again, it hits me how hard it must be to face losing the person you love, and I remind myself of just how much I have to be grateful for. Although it's not something I've ever taken for granted, especially after Holly's diagnosis.

Ever since Stan and Flo came along, the idea of mine and Tom's mortality has been something I've tried not to think about too much, but his job doesn't make that easy. The thought of what it might do to my babies not to have their dad around has stopped me sleeping far more times than I can count, especially when he's doing an investigative piece on people known for employing extremely violent tactics. I can't imagine a life without Tom, and I don't want to, but in the run up to our wedding he forced me to talk about it and to make the promise that if his job ever ended up making him pay the ultimate price, I'd allow myself to eventually move on and meet someone else. My attempts to write it off as something that would never happen just seemed to upset him and he even said he didn't know if we could get married if I couldn't promise him that. The idea of me and any kids we might have being on our own forever, was just too much for him. In the end, I agreed just to give him the peace of mind it was obvious he needed. The irony is, when I asked him to make me the same promise, he shook his head.

'You're not going anywhere; I couldn't be me without you.' He kissed me then, and I knew he meant it. Tom's a brilliant man, but I've always been the glue that holds everything together while he's away, and I'm the one who organises whatever he needs for his latest adventure. Everything from visas to blister plasters, his head is always too caught up with the chase for the story. He adores the children, but he wouldn't have the first clue where to start if it was all suddenly to fall to him. We're a team, but I need to be on top form to keep family life running the way it's supposed to. There are probably lots of people who think our set-up is old fashioned, but it works for us, and it makes us both happy, which in my book must mean it's the best thing for the kids too. The truth is, it's never just down to me, even when Tom's away. With Holly taking such an active role in our lives, we've always been a team of three. Thankfully he's never seemed to resent the fact that Holly and I come as a pair, perhaps because it takes the burden of guilt off him when he's away so much, but they've always got on incredibly well too. Today, though, it's just the two of us.

'Louisa, do come in. I'm very sorry to have kept you waiting
for so long.' Mr Whitelaw is staring at me as I look up, and I can't
help wondering why he's only using my first name, as if we're old
friends. We've never met before, yet he sounds almost avuncular,
and the expression on his face is sympathetic. It's only as I walk
towards him that I see the details written on the name plate on
the outside of his door.

Mr Whitelaw, Hepatobiliary Surgeon

I glance at Tom, wanting to ask him what hepatobiliary
means, but he doesn't seem to have seen the sign. When I got the
call asking me to come in to see Mr Whitelaw, I didn't think to ask
what his specialism was. The woman on the phone didn't seem to
know much. The information that had come with the invitation
to attend the scan mentioned something to do with checking liver
function. Hepatobiliary sounds a bit like hepatitis, which I know
has something to do with the liver and that at least one form of
the disease can be pretty serious. The thought makes goosepim-
ples break out all over my skin and it's as if the atmosphere has
completely changed, the way it does when the sun goes behind
the clouds and there's a sudden drastic drop in temperature.
When I turn to look at Tom to see whether he's realised this
might be more serious than we thought, he's smiling. As I look at
Mr Whitelaw again, my breath catches in my throat. I still have
no idea what hepatobiliary means, but I've just seen a word I
understand only too well.

The woman standing next to Mr Whitelaw is wearing a dark
blue uniform, and the sight of her name badge makes nausea
swirl in my stomach. The words 'Macmillan Cancer Support' are
written in green above her name, spelling out her role and why
she's here. I've had regular mammograms ever since Holly was

diagnosed with breast cancer and I've always been clear. Surely the kind of scan I had couldn't pick that up anyway. There must be some kind of mistake. I can't need a cancer support nurse, I've got two young children. Inside I'm screaming at her to go away, but the scream never leaves my head and Tom's still smiling. He has no idea what's coming and, if I just turn around, I can break into a run and get back to the car where the words I know Mr Whitelaw is about to say can't reach me. If I don't hear them, they can't be true. Yet, somehow, when Tom takes my hand, I find myself following him further into the room.

Maybe I'm wrong. Nothing life changing can happen here, it looks so ordinary. There are photographs of Mr Whitelaw's family in a heavy wooden frame on his desk; three children, two parents, and a black Labrador. It's just the sort of dog Flo would go crazy over. She's been begging us to get one almost from the moment she could talk, and I've always said we'll do it one day, when the time is right. I make myself a promise as I hold my breath, waiting for Mr Whitelaw to speak. If he says I'm okay, or that this is all just a blip, something that can be easily sorted, then we'll get a dog. If this moment has to be life changing, I'm going to make sure it's for all the right reasons. There'll be no more putting things off until 'one day' any more. All I want him to say is that whatever is wrong is an easy fix, but it feels like my heart might stop as Mr Whitelaw gestures towards the seats opposite his desk.

'Please sit down, Louisa. Is this your husband?' When I nod in response, some of the tightness in Mr Whitelaw's expression relaxes, but it has the opposite effect on the muscles in my jaw, which suddenly feel as if they might snap. 'It's good you've got someone with you. This is Mira, one of the nurses from the Macmillan team.'

I don't even turn my head as he indicates the nurse now

sitting to his left. I haven't gripped Tom's hand this hard since I gave birth to Stan.

'Has the scan shown something serious?' Even as I say the words, I'm willing Mr Whitelaw to shake his head. All it would take is a very slight movement from the left to the right and back again, but instead he draws in a breath so deep it makes it feel as though he's stolen every bit of oxygen in the room.

'I'm so sorry. It's cancer.'

The scream that's been trapped inside my head from the moment I spotted the nurse comes out as a shout, a single word 'No!' bouncing off the walls with the force of the denial. Except it's not coming from me, it's Tom who's shouting and, when I turn to look at him, I know what he's thinking, because I'm thinking it too. This is the worst possible thing Mr Whitelaw could have said. Except when my eyes meet the doctor's again, I realise he's nowhere near finished yet.

# 2

## LOUISA

Tom hasn't been able to look at me since Mr Whitelaw said the word 'cancer'. He's tried a few times, but every time he does, his eyes fill with tears, and he has to look away again. Right now, he's busying himself searching for something at the back of the fridge, his head buried deep in every sense. It's hard for me to hear what he's saying, but it doesn't matter, because I know he's repeating what he must have said a hundred times already, and it's been less than four hours since I got the results of my tests.

'...we'll find the best doctors and you'll be okay. Holly was.' Even muffled by the walls of the refrigerator, I know my husband is doing his best to sound upbeat and positive. From the moment we got back to the car and he started talking, it was clear he was only prepared to focus on the best-case scenario that Mr Whitelaw had outlined. As desperate as I am to believe that Tom might be right, I know from his online profile that Mr Whitelaw is renowned in his field. He's the sort of doctor patients cross oceans to see for a second opinion, and he didn't think the best-case scenario was the likely outcome. There was a sadness in his eyes when he said that. I wish I hadn't seen it, but I did.

'I'll make some tea.' My words sound so every day and normal, and as I catch sight of my reflection in the side of the kettle, I find myself peering closer, unable to believe that I look the same as I did this morning. They must have got it wrong. Surely I should have 'likely to be incurable' tattooed across my forehead, because it feels as if those words have seeped into every cell in my body, circulating through my system, even faster than the cancer that started in my pancreas and may well have spread beyond that, given that the initial scan indicates it may already have spread to my liver. Mr Whitelaw has booked me in for a PET scan to see whether surgery is possible, but he didn't sugar coat things.

'Pancreatic cancer is horribly sneaky, because the symptoms often don't appear until it has begun to spread, which means the chances of it being in other parts of the body are much higher. If that is the case, surgery won't be advisable, unless we can significantly shrink any tumours we find.'

Even now I still can't believe the word cancer applies to me, let alone the likelihood that it's spread. I can't be ill, there are too many people who need me. I haven't thought about how I feel yet, not really, and I suspect it's my brain's attempt to protect me so that I don't collapse at the enormity of what we've been told. It means the news hasn't really sunk in yet and Mira said that's quite normal. She took us to another consulting room after my appointment and told us she was there if we had any questions. I had so many things to ask, but I couldn't find the words and I just stared at her blankly, still waiting to wake up and discover it had all been just a bad dream. Mira explained that I might be numb for a while, and that shock could delay the reaction to news like this. She had kind eyes and a soothing voice, but when she gave me her details to contact her whenever I'm ready to talk, I wanted to tell her that she'll never see me again.

I'm not the sort of person who has a cancer support nurse in the contacts on her phone. I'm Louisa, or Lou to those closest to me. I'm a very occasional freelance writer, a wife, a daughter of dysfunctional parents who need me more than I need them, a sister, and a friend, and most of all Mummy. It's the name that means the most to me and I felt my heart start to pound at the thought of one day not being there to answer when my children call out to me. I promised myself before they were even born that I'd never allow them to be hurt or let down the way Holly and I were. Every time I think about it, I feel as if I'm being crushed from the inside out. So even though I nodded as Mira spoke, I couldn't accept that anything she was saying could really apply to me, because if it did I'd be responsible for inflicting pain on my children and I can't bear that.

When I asked Mr Whitelaw how long I'll have if the results of the PET scan reveal the worst-case scenario, he couldn't answer. Or he wouldn't. I'm not sure which and I don't want to know. The whole conversation is something I wish I could wipe from my mind, but it's playing on an endless loop through my head. Every time I asked the doctor a question, I braced myself for the worst, and each time Mr Whitelaw delivered. The cancer in the pancreas was large enough to see on the CT scan and leave absolutely no doubt about what it was. There are also suspicious areas in my liver and some other possible areas of spread, and yet it still didn't feel as if he was talking about me when he delivered blow after blow. I keep putting my hand on my torso wondering if the tumour is growing beneath it. Surely, I'd be able to sense it, if something like that was taking over my body bit by bit. I want to believe he's wrong, or just being pessimistic and trying to prepare me for the worst, but Mr Whitelaw doesn't seem like a man who is prone to being over dramatic, just someone who's honest even when it hurts.

'I wish I could give you better news, but it appears to be a highly aggressive cancer.'

When Tom asked if they'd be able to operate, I wanted to snatch the question back and beg Mr Whitelaw not to answer. I knew exactly what it would mean if he said no and I wasn't ready to face that. I'm still not.

'Like I said, we'll need to do the PET scan so we know the full extent of any spread. That will allow us to select the right type of chemotherapy for the type of tumour, and to see whether surgery is an option. However, pancreatic cancer is often quite difficult to treat...' Mr Whitelaw didn't look me in the eyes, and the numbness that Mira described meant I barely even reacted. I couldn't grasp the implications of what he was saying, at least not for myself; all I could think about was Flo and Stan. I couldn't imagine how my babies could survive without me, and all my terror in that moment was reserved for what my diagnosis means for them. My primary purpose is to give the children the best possible childhood, but losing me would rip their worlds apart and it's completely out of my control. My throat burned as Mr Whitelaw paused, and I could barely breathe. All I wanted to do was run, so I could get to Stan and Flo as quickly as possible, but I was rooted to the spot. So it was left to Tom to ask all the questions.

'But the chemo can cure the cancer, right?'

Mr Whitelaw pulled a face and bile rose in my throat as my children's faces swam in front of my eyes. He was handing me a death sentence, without saying a word. That was when he shifted in his seat, giving the kind of response a politician might when they're trying to avoid giving a straight answer to a question. He talked about treatment 'options', which could help slow down the growth of the tumours and alleviate some of the symptoms, but he never once mentioned the possibility of a cure. I looked at

Tom, willing him to say something that would convince me I'd misunderstood, and that the voice in my head telling me I wouldn't get to see the children grow up had it all wrong. My mind went to the strangest of places, panicking about who would know how to make Stan's toast the way he likes it if that happened (with just the right amount of honey), or whether Tom would remember to check the class WhatsApp group for the latest information about what was going on at Flo's school. My heart hurt at the thought of their little faces if those little routines, and a thousand other things they'd always been able to rely upon, suddenly changed. Stan and Flo couldn't lose any of the things they took for granted. I had to have misunderstood, but when I turned to Tom, he looked broken, and I knew there was no mistake.

'If the extent of the tumour and any subsequent spread makes the cancer inoperable, we'll be able to treat it, but we won't be able to get rid of it completely.'

'It'll be incurable?' Tom's question seemed to pulsate through my veins.

'I'm afraid so, but we'll know more about our options when we get the results of the scan.' Tom clenched his fists in response to the doctor's words, and for a moment I thought he might actually throw a punch, but he didn't move, and it felt like no one in the room knew what else to say. My husband was furiously wiping away tears, and that's when I asked Mr Whitelaw how long I had left. I had to know and, in that moment, I would happily have made a deal with the devil if he'd guaranteed I'd be around to see both children leave school.

'A prognosis is always very hard to give but around 10 per cent of patients can become disease free, if it's caught early enough. If not, the outcomes depend on so many factors, including how you respond to the treatment and most importantly the size of the tumour and extent of the spread. For those patients whose tumours can be surgically removed, up to 50 per cent will survive for at least five years, when surgery is combined with six months of chemotherapy.'

'And if I can't have surgery.' I held my breath, but I should have known I wouldn't be able to pin him down.

'I don't think it would be helpful for us to talk about that until we know more about what we're dealing with.'

Part of me is glad that he refused to tell me just how bad it might be, because I need to hang on to hope. But I can't be like Tom and bury my head, pretending it's all going to somehow be okay. I know Mira is right and that my muted response won't last. I'm winded every time I think about the children and the strangest part is how easily I can visualise their pain if they lose me, and how much that hurts, yet I can't picture myself dying, even as part of that. It's not because I'm some selfless, earth mother, it's because the idea of me not being around just seems impossible. As stupid as it sounds, I've always been here, for every moment of the life I've lived, so it's impossible to imagine a life without me in it. But what I can picture all too clearly is what it's like for a child without their mother around, because I've lived that experience already, when Mum was trying to get sober and would disappear for months on end so that she could 'get well'.

Our paternal grandparents became mine and Holly's safety net, they were our contingency plan and our happy place, providing respite at the worst of times, when Mum was absent and Dad seemed to sink even deeper into the well of his addiction. Mum boomeranged in and out of our lives and every time she came back home, she and Dad swore to my grandparents that they were making a go of it this time. Sometimes she managed to stop drinking for several months, but she always gave into temptation at some point. Anything could trigger a relapse, from a row with a friend, to a final demand for an overdue bill. My grandparents kept hoping that each time would be the one where things finally came good, and much later they confessed that they didn't know for a very long time quite how bad things had become, mainly because Holly and I covered for Mum and Dad a lot.

When my grandparents finally realised how bad things were, they tried to persuade our parents to sign over custody, but my mother told them that she'd fight until her last breath to keep us. We were all the family she had, after all. So I know she loved us, she just loved booze even more, and nothing has changed in the two and a half decades since Holly and I left home for university at eighteen, and never again lived full time under our parents' roof.

Understanding the impact of an absent mother is why, right now, all the impact of my diagnosis is focused on Flo and Stan. I know at some point the shock will wear off and, when it does, I've got to be ready. I need to have as many plans in place as possible, in case I don't have the strength to make them if the cancer is incurable. I've got to hold the family together and prepare them for what's to come, the way I always do. Except this time, I'm going to need help, and there's only one person in the world who I can be completely honest with.

# 3

## LOUISA

The need to tell Holly what's going on has been burning in my chest, but I've been struggling to work out how to do it. Maybe there was a part of me that hoped we'd suddenly become telepathic, the way twins are supposed to be, but that's something we've never been able to claim. We're fraternal twins, and therefore no more alike than any other pair of siblings might or might not be. In our case, it's definitely the latter, but the differences between us are probably why we get on so well. If we were more alike, we'd almost certainly clash more, but instead we've always been good friends. Although it turns out we've suddenly got a lot more in common than I thought we had. When my sister was diagnosed with breast cancer eleven years ago, I was devastated and I wanted to do whatever I could to help. I hosted bake sales, ran a half marathon, and even shaved my head to support her, but I still never imagined something similar happening to me. Maybe I'm paying for that arrogance now, but it felt like my role was to be there for Holly.

Holly's cancer was detected early, and the tumour in her left breast was removed with clear boundaries. There was no need for a mastectomy, and the chemo she had was preventative. A year later, it was almost like it had never happened, at least for the rest of us. But it brought up issues in Holly's life, and she discovered the hard way who really cared for her. I told her that was probably no bad thing. She must have hated me, back then, for how simple I tried to make it all sound, and for my insistence that we focus on the positives. Part of me hates myself too, now that I understand what it's really like to hear the words *you have cancer*. I was just trying to stay upbeat, thinking that encouraging her to look on the bright side would help, but sometimes it's far more helpful to acknowledge just how crap the situation is. Life isn't all sunshine and Hollywood endings; sometimes the worst really does happen. Holly's been well for over a decade, and now it's my turn to look to her for support, only I'll be asking so much more of her than she ever did of me.

I think part of the reason why I'm struggling so much with what to say is that I know Holly's instinct will be to focus on the cancer and to work out ways we can 'fight this', a phrase I'm already starting to loathe. It's not like anyone just rolls over and gives into this shit, is it? But sometimes people don't stand a chance and, if I turn out to be one of those people, I don't need another relentlessly upbeat cheerleader, telling me that if I just focus positively enough, I'll find a way to prove the statistics wrong. Tom has already taken that role and run with it. After his initial shock on the day of my diagnosis, he now seems to refuse to accept anything that Mr Whitelaw said about what the scan indicates, and what it will mean if they're right. He spends hours every day googling my type of cancer and researching new drug trials or treatments under development. He seems genuinely convinced I can be cured, and I hope to God he's right. But sometimes, in the three days since the diagnosis, his blind optimism has made me want to scream. The chances are it's *not* all going to be okay, and I'm terrified that means nothing for our children will ever be okay again. At one point yesterday, when Tom showed me yet another 'miracle cure' for cancer being touted online, the only thing that stopped me ramming his teeth down his throat with my fist was the fact that Stan was in the next room watching the *Paddington Bear* movie.

I know it's early days, but if he really wants me to focus on trying anything and everything to get cured, he should know me well enough to realise I'll need a plan in place first in case none of the treatments work. I've been that way for as long as I can remember, and having a contingency plan is the only way I feel safe. A therapist would probably tell me it's what comes of having alcoholic parents who preferred propping up the bar of the pub they ran, rather than spending time with their children. Thank God we had our grandparents, they were the first back up plan we needed in order to survive our childhoods and maybe that's what triggered the rest.

I thought all of that had taught me how to cope with trauma, but my reaction to my diagnosis is still muted. Like Tom, I've done my share of googling and even though I know it doesn't look good, most of my emotions seem to have been replaced by what feels like a core of tightly packed cotton wool. I'm not happy, or sad; I don't seem able to feel anything much at all, and when I googled 'why haven't I cried since my cancer diagnosis', the internet told me I must be in shock. The only times I've cried have been when I've looked at my children. That's when the gut-wrenching fear hits. The terror I feel about their future, if I'm no longer around to make sure they're okay, makes it hard to breathe. I've never had a panic attack before, but that's what it feels like, as if the walls are closing in on me and there's nothing I can do to stop them. The longest I've ever been away from the children is two nights, and the thought of never seeing them again is too overwhelming to even be able to imagine, like the concept of a black hole and every bit as dark.

Tom adores them with all his heart, I know he does, but he's always been able to compartmentalise, to go to work and focus on that, assuming all will be okay with the kids while he's gone. The love I have for them is different; they are never truly off my mind. When they were born, I felt so grateful to have the option of putting my career on hold, and ensuring that my children had one parent whose primary focus was them. The panic closes my throat when I think about them being sidelined in any way. Without me around, I know Tom might not have the choice. He'll have to work, and it's his passion, his raison d'être, but that never mattered because the children were my reason for being, and every time I look at them the gut-wrenching horror of the changes ahead of us hit me all over again. I've managed to hide it from them so far, thank God, and it's made me grateful that the rest of the time my emotions seem to have been deadened.

'You look so well.' It's something he says at least ten times a day, as if to convince himself that Mr Whitelaw somehow got it horribly wrong, that he picked up the wrong scan results and someone else is blissfully unaware that they're probably on borrowed time. I understand why Tom is clinging on to that hope. But when I look in the mirror, there's a definite difference in how I look. All the spark has gone out of me, the circles beneath my eyes are darker, and even my bones feel tired, but I don't look like I'm dying. No one has told me I am, and even when he was outlining the worst-case scenario, Mr Whitelaw was careful not to use the D word. But if they can't cure the cancer, there's only one way this is going to end, and I'm terrified of my children's security being ripped away from them. Nothing in the house happens if I don't make it happen. Without me the children won't get to nursery or school on time, let alone have whatever they need for their latest art project, charity fundraiser, or *world-something-or-other* day. No one in the family will have their birthday remembered, immunisations will be missed, and none of the bills will get paid. Stan won't be able to come to his mummy for the cuddles that make everything better, and there'll be no one who can spot that look in Flo's eyes when something is worrying her, and who can find a way to make everything right in her world again.

If I think about all the milestones I'll miss it kills me. When the children were born those things flashed through my mind like memories that hadn't even happened yet. I pictured first days at school, and now I'm not even certain I'll get there for Stan, never mind live to see all the other things I imagined. I pictured teaching them both to drive, in the same way I've taught them to swim and ride a bike. I saw myself being filled with pride, but a mess of soggy tears at the same time, when I dropped them off to start university, and being even more emotional watching them graduate and eventually leaving home for good. I thought about their wedding days, and becoming a grandmother, but none of those things are going to happen unless there's some kind of miracle. I'd swap seeing any of those milestone moments for all the ordinary days in between, as long as it meant I got more time with my children.

When I looked in on them last night, their blissful ignorance broke my heart. Flo had her thumb in her mouth, her beautiful blonde curls fanning out around her head like an angel's halo. Her biggest concern right now is moving on from infants to juniors at the village school, because it means I won't be able to walk her all the way into her classroom any more. She's struggled with being separated from me ever since starting school and just last week she made me laugh and cry when she said she didn't know how she could make it through the whole day at school without seeing me. How can I possibly tell her that she might have to get through the rest of her life without me? I can't even contemplate having to explain that to her, because I can't bear the thought that I won't get to see my baby girl grow up, or be there for her when she needs me, like I swore I would. Every time I even think about it, I want to claw at my throat, because I forget how to swallow. I have to press my hand against my neck to remind myself how to do even the most basic of things.

The feeling only gets worse when I think about Stan. He's such a mummy's boy, partly because Tom is away for work so often, and whenever anything in life upsets his delicate equilibrium, which is pretty much an hourly occurrence at four years old, it's me he turns to for comfort. Tom and I joke that only Mummy will ever do. It's going to break his heart if I suddenly disappear from his life. All the joie de vivre my son carries with him will be dimmed. My little boy won't be the same child he was before this happened, and the idea of that changing who he is breaks my heart too. Stan should be able to rely upon me, to know that I'll be there to read *The Gruffalo* just the way he likes it, doing all the silly voices that never fail to make him giggle, and to provide the soft embraces he needs at the end of the day, almost as much as I do. Stan should be several decades away from having to face anything like this. I'm terrified that losing me will rob both him and Flo of their childhoods, and that all the happy memories I've worked so hard to create will be completely wiped out.

I need to make a plan to somehow soften that blow, if the worst does happen. I've got my PET scan tomorrow and if Mr Whitelaw doesn't think the cancer is operable, I may need a biopsy further down the line to see what kind of chemo is most likely to help. If the tumour can be resected, they'll do the biopsy after it's removed, which is the outcome I'm desperately hoping for. I made the mistake of reading some online forums so I know what to expect. I went down a rabbit hole about pancreatic cancer and the survival rates if it turns out to be stage four. Stan's only three months away from starting school, but in the worst-case scenario I won't be here to see that day. I can't afford to let my thoughts spiral like that, so I'm focusing on planning for every possible outcome and I think the adrenaline of that is what's carrying me through.

That's why I need Holly. I can't do it without her. Ever since they were born, the future has been all about Flo and Stan, and I've got no idea how to ensure that a future without me can still be a happy one for my children. Like me, Holly understands what it feels like to have an absent parent, and it means I can trust her to put herself in the children's shoes, and not keep up a relentless stream of platitudes, insisting it'll all be okay – as Tom has. I need someone I can talk to about the *what-ifs*, and my sister is the only person for the job.

I know it's a lot to put on Holly, but I don't have a choice. I can't even think about breaking the news to my parents. They've never been able to cope with the usual stresses and strains of life without going on a bender, and I know they won't be able to handle this without sliding into oblivion, courtesy of however many bottles of vodka that takes. I'll have to tell them eventually, but I want to have a treatment plan when I do. If the tumour is operable, the prognosis will be far more hopeful, at least in terms of surviving the next few years, and I need to be able to dress this up in the best possible light for my parents. It's not lost on me that I have to shelter them from the harsh reality in the same way as I'm doing for my children.

I should be able to turn to Mum and Dad, to offload some of the burden and to share my fears about what I'm facing. But I can't do that; I've never been able to lean on my parents in that way, and I can't rely on them to be there for Stan and Flo when

I'm gone either. Mum came home for good after she finally gave up trying to get sober, and my parents are still together. They both drink far too much, and their house is like something out of one of those hoarder shows on TV. There's no way on earth I'd ever allow the children to stay with them. In fact, I've never even taken them there. We always meet in a park, or at the zoo. Somewhere neutral with no access to alcohol.

Tom's parents died before the children were even born, so we've had no support from grandparents, which is something most of my friends rely upon and take for granted. I know I'd have felt the gap far more if it hadn't been for Holly, but she's been incredible from day one and I wouldn't swap her support for any other kind I might have had, if things had been different with Mum and Dad. Holly has been my built-in contingency plan since day one, and she's the only one I'm letting in on the secret.

I can't risk telling friends, because they're bound to discuss it. The last thing I want is someone else's child hearing about my cancer before my own children do, or worse still, telling them about it. Even my oldest friend, Joanna, who I've known since primary school might mention it to her parents and it could get back to Mum and Dad that way. I can't take the chance of any of my family hearing about this second hand and spiralling in ways I just don't have the energy to deal with right now. I wish no one I love had to be told about my diagnosis, but the only thing I can do in the midst of this hell on earth is to attempt some damage limitation and keep my circle as small as possible.

I've been trying to think of a way of telling Holly that won't devastate her, but three sleepless nights haven't delivered the inspiration I hoped for. There isn't a good way of saying this and time is running out. Tomorrow morning I'm going in for the PET scan and I want Holly to know before I go, so I suggested we meet up for a coffee. Except now I'm here I can't stop shaking, and I'm worried she'll guess that something awful has happened, before I even try to find the best way to explain.

'Well, this is an unexpected treat!' Holly kisses me on both cheeks as she comes into the room and runs a hand through the dark curly hair that tumbles down past her shoulders. Whenever Flo and Stan draw pictures of their family, they add a series of circles to represent Holly's hair, whereas my straight blonde hair is usually a row of spikes depicted with the aid of a yellow crayon. It always makes us laugh and, in Flo's last picture, we looked like Louis the Thirteenth and the scarecrow from *The Wizard of Oz*. Holly put the drawing straight on her fridge, in pride of place nonetheless, and I know she loves the fact that in every family scene the children draw, Auntie Holly unfailingly has a place. I smile at my sister now, wishing that the reason I suggested meeting up was as simple as the one I'm about to give.

'I thought we'd have a grown-up get together for a change. You grab a seat and I'll get the drinks.' My voice sounds the same as always, not like the voice of a person who's about to deliver bad news and suddenly I'm still not certain I can do it. I'm scared that Holly's response will be what breaks through the sense of disbelief that's been protecting me so far, and I'm almost as afraid of my reaction to that as I am of hers. For now, all I can do is keep up the act that everything's normal. 'What can I get you? Latte and a bit of carrot cake?'

'Perfect. We really should do this more often.'

I'm already desperately wishing that we had. Now that there's a good chance my time might be more limited than I ever imagined, I've got so many regrets. All I want is to have more time with the people I love. It's not that I haven't spent lots of time with Holly, but I should have spent some of it in a different way. She's always slotted into my life, rather than the other way around. I told myself it's because she's single and doesn't have children, and that it's easier for her to be adaptable, but I'm already wishing I'd done more. Even something as simple as enjoying coffee together. Most of the time when I have a latte, it's accompanied by the sound of noisy four-year-olds, in the soft play centre near our house. I don't regret any of those moments with Stan and Flo, but I should have prioritised Holly too, instead of asking her to meet me at Mr Happy's Fun Factory, for what I told myself was quality time together. No wonder she thinks meeting in a real coffee shop is an unexpected treat, but it's not the only reason guilt is gnawing at me as I queue up to place our order. I haven't even given Holly a hint about why I wanted to meet, and it feels so cruel to spring this on her when she's clearly thrilled we're having some time together, but I think part of me wanted to leave the option open to chicken out of telling her at all. I silently will the barista to take longer than he should to make the drinks, but he's far too efficient and, no matter how slow I try to make the walk back to the table, I'm suddenly face to face with my sister.

'Thanks, sis.' Holly narrows her eyes as I set down the coffee and cake down in front of her. We're no closer to being telepathic than we've ever been, but she knows me better than anyone. Even Tom. 'Why haven't you got anything to eat? Please tell me you're not on a diet, there's nothing of you.'

'I'm not on a diet, I'm just not hungry.'

'Have you had breakfast?' She's holding my gaze and, when I shake my head, she sighs. Holly is only twenty-three minutes older than me, but she has always mothered me, right from when we were small. From the age of six we were left to entertain ourselves in the flat above the pub, far more often than was good for us. It was Holly who'd make us toast, if we were both getting hungry and neither of our parents had thought to feed us, and who'd tell me a story to calm me down if we'd watched something on TV that we shouldn't have done. It's why I always knew she'd make an amazing mother, and why, until now, it's been the biggest sadness of my life that she never got the chance.

Holly reaches out and puts a hand over mine. 'I know you're busy with the kids Lou, but you need to look after yourself, because if you don't you'll get sick and who's going to look after them then?'

Holly's words are like a punch in the gut. She's verbalising all the things I'm most afraid of. *Who will take care of my children if I'm not around?* Tom will be there for them, but he can't do this alone. How can he possibly be everything they need when they've been so used to having a mother figure at the forefront of their lives? Will Holly step up to the plate? Is it even fair of me to ask that of her? It seems ironic that just lately I've tried to encourage her to broaden her horizons, because I was desperate for her not to miss out on the chance of finding someone who loves her the way she deserves to be loved. Only now I want her to put her own life on hold indefinitely, so that she can become a stand-in mum to Flo and Stan if the worst does happen. That's not fair, I know it isn't, but I still want her to promise me she'll do it, if I need her to. Except, as I look up at her now, my carefully prepared speech has fallen out of my head. I spent most of last night thinking about what to say and how to say it. I don't want to make things sound hopeless, but I don't want to gloss over everything in the way Tom is insisting on doing either. Only now that I'm here, all of my plans have been forgotten and I fire the words out like bullets. 'I've got cancer.'

For a second or two what I've said seems to hang in the air between us, and then her face falls as the reality hits home.

'You can't have.' She gets to her feet, shaking her head, almost like she's angry at me, but I know the rage she's feeling isn't really directed my way. 'You had all the tests when I was ill. There's no faulty gene and you have a mammogram every year.'

'It's not breast cancer, it's in my pancreas.' Every time I think about that the absurdity hits me. I've done all I can to protect myself from the risk of cancer, especially the kind my sister had, but the type I've got very rarely affects someone like me, a relatively young woman, who doesn't smoke and with no family history of diabetes, let alone this kind of cancer.

'Can't they just take the pancreas out?'

'Technically yes, but if they do I'll be diabetic.'

'That's okay, that's manageable.' God, I wish it was as simple as Holly is making it sound. 'I know you must be scared, but thank goodness it's not an organ you need to survive, like your brain or your liver. When they take it out, it will all be okay, you'll see.'

Holly has gone from terror to relief in seconds. As she sits down again and picks up her drink, her whole expression changes. She's had a reprieve from her very worst fears, and I hate the fact I've got to reverse that again. Taking a deep breath to steady myself, I pinch the skin on the back of my hand in the hope that the physical sensation will somehow distract my emotions for long enough to let me get through this. 'It might not be that simple if it's spread. If the tumour is too large to be operable, or has already spread elsewhere, the only thing I'll be offered is palliative chemotherapy.' I don't even get the chance to tell her what the implications of that are, before she jumps back to her feet, the coffee cup slipping from her grasp. It's amazing how far a small amount of liquid can spread, and the tables on either side of us are caught up in the splash zone as Holly bursts into tears.

'Oh darling don't worry, it's just a bit of coffee. Everything will dry off; there's no need to get yourself upset.' The kindness of one of the ladies on the table to our right only makes Holly sob even harder. I'm not sure if the stranger has been listening to our conversation, but she's the one who has to offer comfort as my sister continues to cry. I don't know what to say, and Holly just keeps repeating the word sorry, over and over again.

My sister has always been the strong one and seeing her break down like this is terrifying, because it suddenly feels much more real and some of the numbness that has been carrying me through has worn off. She's been my mother figure, the person I could go to for a solution to fix any problem, but I'm going to die, and she knows it. That's something not even she can fix. My children losing their mother has been my entire focus since I was told I had cancer, but, as I witness Holly's meltdown, the realisation hits me that I'm not just losing the chance to see them grow up. I'm losing everything. I'm desperately trying to cling on to the sliver of hope that I'll somehow get more time. I'd give almost anything for the numbness to return, so that I can bury my head back into the sand that was protecting me from reality and focus on making things right for the children. It's bad enough that I'm leaving them; I can't let them down before I go. I need to stuff my own emotions back inside, and I'm going to have to ask Holly to try and do the same. The trouble is, I've got no idea if that's even possible.

The other customer is making soothing sounds and gently patting Holly's shoulder, still believing the apology is directed at her, but I know it isn't. My sister is sorry because she's terrified that there's nothing she can do to change what I'm facing, but she's wrong. She might not be able to do anything about the cancer, but I know she can help in ways I haven't even thought of yet and I need to be able to talk to her properly, so we can work out what they are, together. I've never needed her more than I do right now, and somehow we're both going to have to find a way to cope with our emotions, because I've got a terrible feeling we might not have much time.

# 4

## HOLLY

Even as the coffee shop staff swung into action, replacing the spilt coffee free of charge, and giving the lovely lady who got soaked a complimentary muffin, I still couldn't stop crying and I hate myself for it. I should have been the one comforting Louisa. Not letting a stranger comfort me, while she sat there alone. All I could do was keep repeating an apology for failing her at the worst time in her life, and sorry will never be enough to make up for that.

It took at least ten minutes for me to regain any kind of composure and when Lou suggested we go back to my place, I didn't argue. It's only a two-minute walk from the coffee shop and we didn't exchange a single word on the way. I was frightened that if I spoke, I'd start crying again and I know that's the last thing Louisa needs. A counsellor once told me to put an elastic band on my wrist and to ping it every time I feel anxious. As soon as we walked through the door to my place, I found one in the drawer of the hallway table and put it on. I'm twanging it now, over and over, and it's reminding me how to breathe in and out. I'm certain I'd have stopped by now without it.

'I'm an idiot, Lou. I'm making this all about me. I'm so sorry.' I'm still apologising as we sit down on the sofa, facing one another again, like we were less than fifteen minutes ago at the coffee shop. It's such a short space of time and yet everything's changed. My whole world has been spun on its axis and nausea is swirling in my stomach. I can't even begin to imagine how Louisa feels.

'I shouldn't have blurted it all out like that, but Tom won't accept what the doctor is saying about how likely it is to have spread and what that means. He just keeps saying that anything other than beating this isn't an option, and I know he thinks that's helping, but it isn't. Of course I want that, but I need to be able to talk about all the what-ifs and he won't let me.' Lou reaches out a hand to me and I want to take it and never let go. If I hold on tightly enough, she won't ever be able to leave me. I've got to find a way to keep her here and I'll do whatever it takes. We're twins and if there's any part of me they can use to make her better, it's already hers, even if it compromises my own health. No question. I want to tell her that I agree with Tom and that getting rid of the cancer is the only thing we should be focusing on, but I know Louisa. She'll need to have a Plan A and a Plan B in place, if she's going to be able to do anything other than be paralysed by fear. She's always been that way, needing a safety net for life because of the way we grew up. On every trip we've ever taken together, Lou has mapped out alternatives – a different way to the airport in case a road gets closed, an alternative flight we can book if we miss our planned one, and other hotels nearby if the one we've booked turns out to be a hell hole. It's the only way she can relax, and it's one of the quirks that makes her Lou. It's ironic that when we used to talk about starting families, she was the one who had an alternative path mapped out in case it didn't happen. In that scenario, she'd concentrate on her career, travelling as widely as she could and writing about her experiences. I was the one with no Plan B, yet it was me it never happened for, and maybe I should have learnt from Lou's example a long time ago.

Having a plan mapped out for if they can't get rid of the cancer will help her to focus on the treatment, and I need her to do that. I'm really not sure I can survive without her; she's been my other half since before we were even born. The thought of being without Lou is something I can't get my head around, but somehow the aching void it would leave behind already feels heavy in my chest, as if someone has placed a slab of concrete on top of me. Would there even be a Holly without Lou? Being her twin sister is who I am and, if I allow myself to imagine that no longer being the case, something akin to terror washes over me, making my skin prickle in response. She can't die, I won't let that happen, because if she doesn't survive I'm not sure I will either.

It's easier to focus on the anger that is welling up inside me at the injustice of all of this. Lou does all the right things to keep herself fit and healthy, to make sure she's around for the kids in a way our parents never were. She puts the children first in every-thing she does. If anyone should be facing a diagnosis like this it should be Mum or Dad, who've abused their bodies for years, pouring so much alcohol into them that it's become poison. Yet it's Lou who's been handed this terrifying diagnosis, and she's handling it the only way she can. I'll play along with the Plan B because I know that's what Lou needs from me, but I'll speak to Tom later and let him know that I agree with him. We'll exhaust every option before we even think about acceptance, because I know Tom can't live in a world without Lou either. But it's the thought of Stan and Flo losing their mum that hits me like a knife to the heart, and there's a physical pain in my chest when I look at my sister.

'This can't be happening to you, the kids...' I'm failing her already and the tears are streaming down my face, as the words get lodged in my throat.

'Holly don't cry, it's going to be—' She's about to say it's all going to be okay, but she stops herself and another piece of my heart breaks at the realisation that she doesn't want to lie to me. It's a pact we've always made with one another, and I trust Lou more than I trust another living soul because of it. Only just this once I wish we didn't have to be so honest. My own cancer diagnosis taught me lots of lessons I never wanted to learn, and I know that when the cancer has spread, it isn't good news. Even in the best-case scenario of an eventual cure, this is going to be brutal. Another painful lesson I learnt was who I could rely on, and that list turned out to be far shorter than I ever expected, but Lou's name was right at the top. I need to repay that now, so I squeeze her hand even more tightly than before, making a promise to my sister that I'd rather die than go back on.

'I'm here for whatever you need. Every step of the way.' *Right until the end.* The last four words remain unspoken, and I don't think I could say them out loud if my life depended on it. I'm not ready to face that possibility, even if my sister needs to believe that I am.

'Do you promise?' Louisa holds my gaze with such an intensity that I find myself thinking about all the times we played stupid staring games as kids, locking eyes until one of us burst out laughing. Only now there's nothing to laugh about, so I nod slowly instead.

'Anything.'

'Thank you.' Louisa closes her eyes for a couple of seconds and, as her tears come at last, I have to dig my nails into the palms of my hands to stop myself from crying again too. I can't keep doing this; I've got to try to be the strong one now, or at least pretend I am, otherwise Louisa won't be able to let her guard down. She'll feel like she's got to keep holding it together, like she has since my diagnosis and the domino effect it had on the rest of my life. When we were kids, I relished being the big sister and looking out for Lou. But all of that changed when I was ill, and if she hadn't helped me up from the pit of despair I fell into, when the future I'd thought I was building disappeared almost overnight, I might not be here now. So, I've got to be strong, even if it feels like I'm dying inside.

'What can I do to help? Just tell me and I'll do it.' I'm already thinking about how I can arrange to take some extended time off work, but I'll quit if I have to. The only thing that matters now is Lou.

'I don't know how to tell the kids, but I won't be able to avoid it once the chemo starts.' Her words make the breath catch in my throat and I can't stop myself from picturing Stan and Flo, the children I love as though they were my own. People might think I can't say that and truly understand what it means, because I don't have children of my own, but I know what's in my heart. I'd do anything for them, and the thought of not being able to protect them from the hurt that's coming their way is agony. I can see it's unbearable for Lou too. She looks exhausted, but I've seen that kind of tiredness in my sister before, borne out of a chronic absence of sleep when the children were tiny. The thing I've never seen before is the naked fear in her eyes, and I'd give anything to take that away. Whatever the next scan results show, we just need to find a treatment that works. There are probably things her doctor hasn't even heard of yet. They're always coming up with amazing new treatments in the US and, if anyone can find out about them, Tom can; he breaks news for a living. But just because I'm going to cling on to hope for a miracle with both hands, it doesn't mean I can't help Lou with what she's facing right now too.

'I can help you work out how to tell the children; we'll speak to the specialist nurses about how best to handle it, but you don't have to do any of this on your own. I'll be there and so will Tom.' Even as I say the words, I wonder if this will end up being the first lie I'll tell my sister. I love Tom, he's a great guy, and from the outside it probably looks like he's the family's provider. But he's the first to admit that he's nothing without Lou. She's the one who's supported him and who makes sure the children never feel like they're missing out, despite how often he's absent. That's an incredibly difficult trick to pull off, and one that no one managed for us, despite how hard our grandparents tried to make up for our mother's absence. I've got no idea how Tom will react to that support disappearing, let alone how he'll respond to the progress of Lou's cancer, and the prospect of her dying, if the worst really does happen. There's a chance he might bury himself in the work he loves to avoid having to face losing the woman he loves even more, and I'm in no position to promise her that he won't. But she's far from stupid and what she says next makes it clear that she understands that too.

'I'm not sure Tom will be there, not in the way I need him to be, or the way the kids do.' As Lou shakes her head, her sadness is palpable. 'Almost the first thing you mentioned was Stan and Flo, and they're all I've been able to think about since the consultant told me just how serious this is. I might get five years, maybe even more, but I might not even get two. I'm far more scared of leaving the children behind without me than I am of dying, and I've barely slept since my diagnosis. Every time I shut my eyes, they're all I can picture.'

'Oh Lou.' It's impossible not to cry, and I let the tears flow as I wrap my arms around her. She already feels thinner and more fragile, which makes this feel even more real. The idea of Lou having to leave the children is agony, and even as I try to find the words to comfort her I know it's futile. There are no words capable of doing that. It's like trying to find specks of dust in the pitch black, and nothing I say will make the prospect any less painful for either of us. I want to scream at the top of my voice about how unfair this is, and to thump my fists against the wall, but I can't let her see how scared and angry I am. I'm having to fight the urge to bundle her into the car and keep driving until we're hundreds of miles away, as if getting away from here will somehow allow us to escape from the horror of her diagnosis, but I know it won't. All I can do is be here for Lou and wait for her to tell me what she needs.

We don't speak for a long time, just cry together, but typically it's Lou who manages to get herself together first and breaks the silence.

'It's okay. I'm going to do whatever it takes to be here for the longest time possible, but if I'm going to have the energy to do that, there has to be a Plan B.' I knew this was coming and I almost want to smile at Louisa's words, because this feels comforting and predictable in a way that nothing else does right now But I can't smile, because my lovely sister has cancer, and I'm already scared that if she doesn't get better, I might never smile again. So instead, I say what I know she needs to hear.

'I've already told you I'll do anything I can.' I've got no idea where this is going, but it doesn't matter. I made a promise to give Lou whatever support she needs, and I meant every word.

'Do you remember when the kids were born and we made a will, we asked you to be Flo and Stan's legal guardian if anything happened to us?'

'Of course I do.' I'd felt so honoured when they'd asked and I hadn't needed any time to think; it had been the easiest yes of my life. I couldn't love Stan and Flo any more than I do and, if the unthinkable had happened, I'd happily have given my all to raising the kids, but I've always known I'd never do as good a job as Lou.

'And do you remember the night we met up to ask you if you'd do it? It took both of us to finally get Tom to discuss what would happen if neither of us were around any more, even then it was like pulling teeth.'

'I remember.' It wasn't something I could ever forget. I felt like I'd got to know my brother-in-law a whole lot better that night, and it had shown me just how much he loved my sister. Ever since they met, he's been open with her about the risks that come with his job, heading off to war-torn countries, where the prospect of a safe return is never a given. Before they got married, she told me that he made her promise that she'd be open to finding love again and starting over if anything ever happened to him. The night they asked me to be the children's guardian, she tried to turn the tables on him, but no matter what she said he wouldn't even discuss the idea of starting a new life without her.

'It was so easy for us to pick you as the children's guardian and I knew if anything happened to us, the kids would get all the love they need from you. There was never anyone else in the equation for either me or Tom, because you've loved the children like they're your own from the moment they arrived and I'm so grateful for that.' Louisa gives my hand another squeeze, and I want to tell her it's me who should be grateful, because Stan and Flo saved my life. Five rounds of failed IVF treatment before my breast cancer diagnosis left me with nowhere to put all the love I'd stored up for the moment I held my baby in my arms, a moment that never came. So I poured all that love into my niece and nephew instead. They filled the gap my ex-husband had left behind too, and they don't care that I've got wonky breasts or scars on the outside. It's because of them that I've got far less scars on the inside than before they were born, which means any idea Lou has about being grateful to me for loving them is ridiculous.

'They're everything to me.' Our eyes lock for a moment and I know what she's thinking, that the children are everything to her too, but she's having to face leaving them behind. She doesn't have to tell me that it's the prospect of doing that that scares her more than death, because I can see it in her eyes. My heart is breaking again for Lou, for the children, for all of us.

'I know and that's why it was so easy to choose you to raise them if we both died. But I never thought about making a plan for the children if Tom was left on *his* own to care for them. I need you to promise you'll always be there to make sure they don't miss out because I'm not around. He'll be brilliant in lots of ways, but there are things he'll have no idea about, and there's no way of knowing what outside influences he might listen to. You know me better than anyone, and you'll know what I would probably have done or said in any situation that might arise.'

'It's not going to come to that; you're going to be okay.' I can't help myself, because I can't bear the thought of her thinking like this, but Lou shakes her head.

'Please Holly, I need to know you'll do this for me if I'm not here, and that you'll do whatever it might take to fill in the space I leave behind.'

It's the last half of the sentence that floors me, and suddenly I'm not sure I can make the promise after all. It would be like accepting that it's inevitable Lou won't survive until the kids have grown up, and it feels as if she's already giving up on any hope of the best-case scenario, where the cancer can become just a horrible memory, like it is for me. I can't give up on that, I won't. Except Lou is still watching me, waiting for my answer, and I know she needs me to do this in order to face whatever tomorrow's scan might reveal. So I look her in the eye and make another promise.

'Okay.' It's just one little word, and I've got no idea how big its connotations might be. All I know is that what we both need right now is hope and faith. Hope that doctors can either cure Lou's cancer or keep it at bay for decades, and faith that it will somehow be okay for Stan and Flo if they can't. I push down the fear that is making my heart thud against my rib cage, and force myself to silence all the what-ifs that are clamouring inside my head, about how any of us will carry on without her. We have to find a treatment that works, because the alternative is unthinkable and, if I let myself truly go there, I'll be no help to Lou or the children.

# 5

## LOUISA

Sometimes when I wake up, I forget about the cancer for a moment or two. It's like waking from a bad dream that leaves a lingering sense of dread, which is swiftly followed by a wave of relief when I realise it was all in my head. Only now the wave of relief never comes and instead the sense of dread settles in my stomach like a rock I have to carry round all day. I'm getting quite good at painting on a smile and the circle of people who know about my diagnosis remains very small.

The PET scan is done and it's being analysed so that my fate can be decided. I've got an appointment with Mr Whitelaw to discuss the results, plan the chemo and talk about whether or not he'll operate. I'm trying to hold on to the hope that he will, but when I went in for the scan, I kept looking at the technicians' faces and I swear to God I could see sympathy in their eyes. I wanted to ask them if my body had lit up like the Blackpool illuminations, with horrible pockets of cancer being detected way beyond the point where it had first started, but I'd already been told I wouldn't be getting any results today. So instead, my mind went to the place where it has done for as long as I can remember, and I imagined the worst. I guess that's what happens when you spend years desperately hoping that you won't come in from primary school to find your father spreadeagled on the sofa, with a three-quarters empty bottle of vodka tipped on to its side, only to discover he's exactly where you didn't want him to be. Or when you pray for your mum to come back and make everything okay, but time and again she doesn't turn up because she's either trying to get sober, or failing horribly and on a bender of her own. I know only too well that the worst can happen and that more often than not it does, so it's hardly surprising that my mind goes to those places when the future's uncertain.

Talking about agreeing a chemo schedule once the results are analysed didn't help either. I know it's inevitable, whatever the scan shows, and that I shouldn't worry about losing my hair in the midst of all of this, but I'd be a liar if I tried to pretend I don't care about that. I don't want to look in the mirror and see an unavoidable reminder that I've got cancer, and I don't want my life to change in all the ways it's going to. Very soon I might not even be up to doing this, something as simple as taking my son for his weekly swimming session, but I've got to keep trying to live in the moment and carrying on as normal for as long I can, otherwise I'm as good as dead already.

Pulling my swimming costume up and adjusting the straps, I look over at Stan, who's splashing in the water that's collected in the gulleys of the changing room meant for drainage. I won't be able to get in today because I couldn't even have a canula fitted without it becoming more complicated than it should have been. The site where the cannula was positioned is red and painful, and when I saw my GP this morning, she suspected it might be infected and she didn't think swimming was a good idea. Instead I plan to sit on the side and let my legs dangle in the water while I watch Stan, which is the next best thing to getting in with him.

Holly is taking the afternoon off work so she can be the designated adult he needs in the pool. I could just have sat this one out, but the voice inside my head that refuses to shut up just lately keeps reminding me that I don't know how many more of these I'll get to go to, so I'm not missing out on watching my little boy swim, even if I can only sit on the sidelines.

Stan loves our swimming sessions and it's precious time on our own while Flo is at school. Will I be able to swim in the midst of chemo? Will I even want to? I'll probably have to wear a swimming cap to stop what's left of my hair from floating off and scaring the other children, or horrifying their parents. Shaking my head, I attempt to shake out the thought at the same time. It's a new habit since my first meeting with Mr Whitelaw, and I suspect it's not a particularly healthy one. I have a feeling I should be confronting all the emotions that I've pushed down since my diagnosis head on. I still haven't allowed myself to think too much about what might happen if we run out of options on the treatment front. Instead, I'm focusing on two things: the first is the main piece of advice contained in one of the leaflets I was given about living with cancer which is to plan my days the way I always have done, and to set up events to look forward to. I've got to do that, if I'm going to prevent the cancer from taking my life long before it might eventually do. My second focus remains the children. All the websites on how to live with a diagnosis like mine tell me to spend time with the people I love, so that's what I'm doing. But that's always been my priority anyway.

'Are you two ready?' Holly calls out from the cubicle next door, bringing me back to the present, and Stan's head jolts up in response.

'Let's go swimming!' His excitement is palpable and those are the words we always shout out as we're about to head into the pool, so I respond the way I know he's expecting me to.

'Yeah, let's go swimming!' As I step out of the cubicle, the smell of chlorine hits me and a wave of nausea makes my stomach roll. Maybe I should have sat this one out, but feeling so nauseous brings home how difficult it might be to come along once the chemo starts. For now, I'm determined to make the most of still looking like the mummy Stan has always known, and focusing on finding something to enjoy in every day, just like the websites tell me to, even if that feels impossible.

\* \* \*

After the session finishes, Serena, one of the other mothers from Tots and Tigerfish – the swimming group Stan and I have been coming to since he was six months old – suggests going to a cafe. The children all go to Little Acorns nursery which means I know the mothers reasonably well and, like any group, there are some I like better than others. Two I'm a bit closer to, because they have children in the same year as Flo at our village primary school. There's also one mother I knew long before the school runs even began, Billie, but she's my least favourite of the whole group and, as I queue up for coffee, I tell Holly to nab us a seat at the opposite end of the cluster of tables from her. At first, my sister protests, telling me I should be the one sitting down while she queues up, but I shoot her a look that tells her this isn't up for discussion. Shrugging, she knows when she's beaten, and she puts Stan in a highchair. It's a struggle to fit him in it and we won't be able to for much longer, but if we don't contain him in, he'll be doing circuits of the coffee shop in minutes, zooming around and pretending to be a plane, or a dog, or something else noisy and fast that presents a serious risk of knocking other people's drinks on the floor.

Holly has taken a colouring book out of her bag, and Stan is already furiously scribbling over one of the illustrations with a crayon. My sister is often better at entertaining the children than I am, and never resorts to letting them watch cartoons on her phone, the way I've been known to do, particularly when Stan is in one of his bouncing off the walls moods, and we're in a public place. He never minds if there's no volume on the phone, and I figure it's better for him to watch a few cartoons than to disturb everyone else around us. But with Auntie Holly in charge, he's being entertained and creative all at the same time. She puts me to shame, but never deliberately, and she has no idea just how great she is.

My strength has always been in making sure there is a schedule of activities for the children, or that I've brought all the supplies needed for a planned craft session. I panic when it comes to making stuff up on the spot, because it reminds me of the chaos of family life with my parents, where no plans or schedules were ever stuck to. It's funny that I was the risk taker when it came to choosing a career, and that Holly was the sensible one, but the stakes were far lower, and a Plan B for my career felt easy to come by. When the children came along, I wanted them to have a structure they could rely on, to give them the security I'd never had, and I think I lost some of my ability to be spontaneous as a result.

Holly's such a contrast to Billie, who makes sure everyone knows what a wonderful mother she is, or at least thinks she is. I have my own opinion on that, which I keep to myself, but I've seen the expressions on the faces of some of the other mothers, which tells me I'm not the only one. She's holding court now, and Serena is queuing up to get both of their orders. Billie isn't the sort to queue, and she has this air of entitlement that somehow persuades other people to do stuff for her. It's fascinating to watch, but there's never been any chance of me falling under

Billie's spell. She's fake and everything I don't want to be as a parent. Given the choice, I'd avoid her completely, but in a village the size of ours it's almost impossible. What makes it completely impossible is that she's married to Tom's best friend. Despite that, Billie is the last person I'd want to confide in about my diagnosis. She'd fawn all over me, but she's an emotional vampire and she'd make it all about her. There'd be posts online about her 'special friend with cancer', and how hard it's been on her to support me while I go through treatment. She's the sort to set up a GoFundMe page I know nothing about, anything that makes her the centre of attention, and she's got form for it. When Serena lost her unborn baby last year, anyone would have thought it was Billie's bereavement the amount she posted about it online. But when we set up a schedule in the WhatsApp group to organise a rota to pick up Serena's little boy from nursery while she was still in hospital, and look after him until his dad got home, Billie was suddenly far too busy to help out. She's completely self-absorbed.

'Three weeks in Bermuda. I can't wait!' Billie's voice carries to where I'm standing, and I deliberately take a long time deciding what I want to order. It's clear she's dominating the conversation, and I'm in no hurry to go over to the tables, even if Holly and I are at the opposite end to her. She'll want to make sure we all hear whatever it is she has to say and, if I try to ignore her, she'll focus on me all the more. She's thick-skinned enough not to pick up on something as subtle as body language. What amazes me, is the fact that some women in our group seem to hang off her every word. When I turn, I catch Holly rolling her eyes, long before she notices that I'm glancing in her direction, and I immediately love my sister just a little bit more.

'We're staying at a hotel in a private cove, with its own harbour. Jonathan wants to treat me for our tenth anniversary. Nothing but the best for his princess, he said, and who am I to argue?' Billie gives an affected laugh, which sounds about as melodic as fingernails down a chalkboard, and I can't stop myself from responding, as I walk towards the tables.

'Are you taking the children?' I know the answer, even before Billie wrinkles her nose.

'God no, it's not a holiday for children. They wanted to go camping.' Her disgust deepens at the very idea. 'Matilda, our au pair, and her boyfriend Scottie are going to take them. She works for us two days a week usually, when she's not at the language school, but she's happy to do some extra days to cover the holiday. So it works out perfectly.'

'That's kind of her and how nice that you're all getting to do what you want.' Serena hands Billie the mocha she queued for as she speaks, and I have to take a sip of my far-too-hot coffee to stop myself from responding with greater honesty than would probably be acceptable. Billie is warming to the theme that's she doing everyone else some kind of favour by leaving her children behind in the care of an au pair they barely know.

'Matilda has been dying to see more of the UK while she's here and of course she's only been with us a month, so she's still terribly keen to impress.'

'And how long have you known Scottie?' I keep my tone light, but I exchange a glance with Sophie. Her son is in Flo's class, so I know her a bit better than most of the others and I think we're on the same wavelength. She doesn't let me down, pulling a face, as we all wait for Billie to respond.

'We've only met him once, but he seems very enthusiastic about camping with the children.'

'Is he DBS checked?' I nearly choke on my coffee, as Holly pipes up. She's not just baiting Billie, she's genuinely concerned.

'I'm sure there's no need for that. Matilda wouldn't get

involved with just anyone; she worries about the children far too much for that.'

'At least someone does.' I mean to keep the words inside my head, but somehow I say them out loud, and Billie raises her perfectly laminated eyebrows.

'Not everyone prefers the company of their children to their spouse. Some of us put our marriages first, but then maybe that's why Tom works away so much these days. According to Jonathan, he never used to be like that.' The grating laughter is back and then she blows me a kiss. 'I'm only joking, Louisa. I'm sure your marriage is a happy one. I guess you and I are just very different.'

It's intended as another jibe, I'm almost sure of it, but she couldn't have paid me a greater compliment if she'd tried, and I blow her a kiss in return. It's only as I look at Holly again, helping Stan choose the right felt-tip for the next picture in his colouring book, that I realise the other implication of her statement about not everyone preferring the company of their children to their spouse. I know it's normal and healthy for parents to need time together away from the kids, and whenever Tom and I have done that I've valued the chance to just be a couple again, but I've always been desperate to get back to Stan and Flo too. I've never thought to ask Tom if he felt the same, because I just assumed he did, but maybe he was taking my lead on that.

I'm not naïve enough to think Tom will stay alone forever if I die and I wouldn't want him to. But what if the woman he ends up with feels the same way as Billie, and the children are pushed further and further down their list of priorities? What are the chances of a stepmother feeling that unbreakable bond to Stan and Flo, one which means they always come first? Step parenting is not something I've experienced from either side, but memories of the girlfriends my dad had when he and Mum were apart are coming back to haunt me. Suddenly the only image of a stepmother I can conjure up is the one from fairy tales: the wicked stepmother determined to force a wedge between her new husband and his children. I know I'm being irrational, but panic is coursing through my veins and my desire for a Plan B that I can somehow control, even when I'm no longer here, is stronger than ever.

# 6

## TOM

The only way I've managed to continue my career, without it making me feel like the entire human race is doomed, is to believe that the good in the world still outweighs the bad. Since Lou's diagnosis, that's been so much harder to do. Despite the hours I've put into searching for a possible cure for every stage of pancreatic cancer, I haven't been able to find a single doctor or trial that suggests she can beat this if it's reached stage four. I've been accused of being a workaholic more than once in the past, but I've never put anywhere near as much effort into a work-related project as I have into this. I can't sleep anyway, so I've spent long nights on the computer, praying that the next click will lead to something – anything – that might make this all go away, even if the scan results don't bring good news. Sometimes I've read until I literally can't see straight any more. The idea that someone as good as Lou could be struck down like this has shaken my belief system in a way that nothing else ever quite has. I know it's because it's personal, and that there are horrific injustices and terrible tragedies every single day, but this is Lou, and it doesn't seem possible that this is happening to us.

I know she doesn't believe it when I say it, but I fell for her the moment we met. The only stumbling block was that I was already engaged to Abigail at the time. Unbeknown to me, Lou had spent a lot of time in the village where I grew up when she was a child, but I was thirty when our paths crossed for the first time, and she was twenty-eight. It was at an open day at Castlebourne Hall, the only venue in the village that hosted wedding receptions. My then fiancée, Abigail, insisted we go along and even now I feel guilty that I agreed, when I knew my heart wasn't in it. My parents were already way past retirement by then, having had me more than two decades after they married. They were desperate to see me settled and Mum had said more than once, 'I just want to see you happy before I go.' She'd had pneumonia and sepsis the winter before, and I'd been terrified that I was going to lose her. It was in the wake of Mum's illness that I proposed and I regretted it almost immediately; Abigail didn't want the same things out of life that I did, and her primary goal seemed to be to try and change me into the person she really wanted me to be, frequently suggesting that I might want to consider a job in PR instead of journalism, because it would give us more security. But despite my doubts, once the proposal was out there and she'd accepted, it was as if we'd got on a train that had already left the station and there was no turning back.

I'd met Abigail at university, and we'd stayed in touch after I left. It was never a grand passion, because our focus was all work, work, work when we got together. She was a lawyer by the time we'd drifted from friendship into a relationship, and I think, looking back, that it only happened because we were just there, in one another's lives at the right time, or the wrong time, depending on how you want to look at it. Our relationship was part of Abigail's ten-year plan. She had a vision for everything, from when she'd be earning a certain salary, to the optimum time to have a child, with minimal impact on her career trajectory. She wanted to be married by the time she was thirty-two, and there I was, convenient and someone Abigail could mould into what she wanted, or at least so she'd thought.

It's quite sad that we both seemed so willing to settle for almost good enough, each of us for very different reasons, but the truth was my only real passion back then was work, and I wasn't even sure I believed in the kind of love that could eventually become more important than anything else. That was until I met Lou, and a feeling I'd never had before hit me with a force I wouldn't have believed possible. Here was this woman who was everything I'd never even realised I wanted, but there was a problem, a big one. Lou was at the open day too, which meant she had to be planning a wedding as well. It was ridiculous to be so crestfallen that this complete stranger had promised to marry someone else, especially as my own fiancée was sitting right next to me, clutching my hand. I didn't know a single thing about Lou, but it still felt like a catastrophic loss that I'd never know what it was like to hold her hand instead, or to share a private joke that only we knew the punchline to. She was as beautiful then as she is now, her golden blonde hair making it feel as if the sun had come out in the room, and the twinkle in her amber eyes when she smiled that made me want to discover all the things that brought her happiness. But it was more than that; there was just something about her that I couldn't put my finger on. Even after almost fifteen years together, I still can't define it with any kind of accuracy. I just know she's my favourite person on earth.

Watching her now – brushing Flo's hair and still managing to comfort Stan, who somehow bit his own thumb while eating his toast – I want to freeze time. This is what perfect looks like to me now, and the chaos of family life beats any high point I've had in my career, hands down. My dream once was to get in front of the camera and make the kind of documentaries that have the power to change hearts and minds. But I'd swap everything I've achieved in a heartbeat, to keep what I've got in this room right now whole and intact, and unchanged by the injustice of Lou's cancer diagnosis. I've never known pain like it, and nothing I try – even attempting to bury myself in work – can begin to alleviate the agony of the prospect of losing Lou. Almost as bad is the utter helplessness I feel. Everything I've achieved is meaningless, because I can't change the one thing that really matters, and it's hard to find a point to anything any more. I want to grab people by the scruff of the neck when they complain about the mundane, trivial stuff in life and remind them how bloody lucky they are to have their health. If I don't manage to keep a lid on it, I'm going to end up getting myself into trouble and the last thing Lou needs to worry about is me falling apart, on top of everything else. So I paint on a smile when I think that's what she needs to see, and hope it isn't obvious how destroyed her diagnosis has left me feeling.

'Can you get that, please? It'll be Holly. You know she's like clockwork.' Lou returns my smile as she looks over, the sound of the doorbell a reminder that time always runs out eventually. I can't freeze it, or stop the days from passing so damn quickly. I haven't been able to do a single fucking thing to change this situation, and in another ten minutes I'm going to have to drive my wife to the hospital to discover just how bad things are. What Mr Whitelaw says could be the difference between the possibility of a complete cure, or as little as months if it's as aggressive as pancreatic cancer has the potential to be, and I'm honestly not sure I can face it. As I walk to the door, I think about begging Holly to leave. If she isn't here to take the kids to school, we can't go to the hospital, and Mr Whitelaw can't give us worse news than we've had already. I want to keep hoping for the best, but it's getting harder to do that, and the last thing I want is for Lou to see me losing hope.

'How is she?' They are the first words out of Holly's mouth as I open the door. She keeps her voice low, mindful that Louisa could overhear; we both know how much she hates being the focus of anyone's sympathy. She can't stand the thought of anyone pitying her, and I'm convinced that's why she hasn't once shown any sign of feeling sorry for herself yet either. All she's talked about so far is the impact of all of this on the kids. Never mind what she might have to go through, and the strong possibility she might be robbed of decades she should have had. I can't believe she isn't sad about that, because I'm heartbroken about what's being taken from *all of us*, not just the kids, and I'm bloody angry too. When I phoned Holly, the day after Lou told her about the cancer, Holly said she thought that focusing on the kids was Lou's way of coping, until the PET scan told us more. We're almost at that point, and Lou is still being so stoic it scares me at times. I'm terrified that when the reality finally hits, she'll fall to pieces and there'll be nothing I can say or do to put her back together again.

I'm so scared of losing her; she's my best friend, my confidante and the person I long to come home to whenever I'm away. I can't even imagine what it would be like to know I can never come home to her again. She's the best mother the children could have asked for, and she makes it so easy for me to be their dad. I know she does all the heavy lifting on that front and the kids would be every bit as lost without her as I would. She's irreplaceable and I can't accept the possibility that she's dying. What scares me almost as much is the idea of the light going out inside her, and of us losing her long before she's gone. How can someone be expected to continue embracing life and be the person they've always been, if they've been told they're dying? Lou is perfect, at least to me, and I wouldn't change a thing about her. But even if the news is the best we could hope for, I know this is going to change her, and she'll never be the same again. I don't want this to be our life. I don't want any of this, I just want things to go back to the way they were. I can't tell anyone any of this, though, not even Holly. I have to pretend to be strong.

'You know Lou, she's carrying on as if I'm about to give her a lift to a check-up at the dentist.' I kiss Holly on both cheeks, glad that she's here, despite the circumstances. I discovered the first day we met that she and Lou came as a pair. When the organiser of the wedding fair had asked each person to tell the rest of the group a bit about why they were there, my heart had felt as though it was soaring when Holly had said she was there with her sister, Lou, because her fiancé hadn't been able to make it after something had come up at the last minute.

Maybe we should have known that Jacob would never prioritise Holly, but it was another couple of years before we found out just what a waste of space he would turn out to be. I barely gave Holly's fiancé a thought back then, all I could think about was how happy I was that Lou wasn't the one getting married. And by the time we left Castlebourne Hall, I'd fallen in love. What I didn't realise was that Abigail had fallen in love that day too, with the venue. When she tried to pin me down to choose a date to get married, things came to a head. She'd been so angry she threw her engagement ring at me, and said if I couldn't choose a date then we might as well split up seeing as I clearly wasn't on board with the plans we'd made for everything we wanted to achieve in the next few years. I didn't say that all the plans had been hers, because it was like I'd been handed my pass to freedom. The last thing I wanted to do was hurt Abigail, but I'd never loved her in the way I should have done. Meeting Lou was like a wake-up call to stop sleepwalking through life; I felt guilty, but I couldn't let something that felt so life changing just pass me by.

Once Abigail had made the decision for us to split, I didn't hesitate to get in touch with Lou, finding her on Facebook and explaining what had happened. I knew there was a chance she might not want to see me again given that I had a fiancée when I met her, but it wouldn't have changed the relief I felt about Abigail calling off the engagement. Ending it the way we did meant she believed she'd had the choice about whether we stayed together or not, and that she'd chosen to finish with me, which tempered my guilt a bit. It was the least I could for her in the circumstances, and I've never told anyone how happy I was that she called time on our relationship, not even Lou. Once or twice she's questioned how I felt about things ending with Abigail, and every time I tell her that I've never loved anyone like I love her. It's true; no one I've ever met can compare to Lou. She's my everything and it's a cliché, but I mean it when I say I'd die for her. I wish we could swap places, because I'd rather be facing my own mortality than hers.

'Are you nervous?' Holly's question jolts me back to the present and her chin wobbles as I nod in response. She's as terrified as I am about what today might bring, and she reaches out to squeeze my hand. 'I'd better go through and take over getting the kids ready for school.'

Letting go of my hand, she brushes past me in the corridor and a chorus of cheers go up to greet her arrival. I can already hear Flo and Stan competing for her attention; they adore their auntie, and I understand why. I've never for a moment resented that my wife and her sister came as package deal. With anyone else it would have been easy to feel irked that she's always around, but not Holly. She's so different from Lou, in almost every way. She's got dark curls, and blue-grey eyes, and she's always been sensible, wanting to lay the foundations for her future. Holly qualified as an accountant and saved hard to ensure she and Jacob would have everything in place by the time they started their family. It was a contrast to Lou, who'd started her career on a wing and a prayer writing travel pieces to bring in the next pay cheque and seeing how far that windfall could carry her until she sold her next piece. It was the only time in her whole life that she didn't plan things with military precision, because it was also the only time in her life when she didn't have responsibility for someone else.

Lou never returned to the family home after university and both she and Holly had distanced themselves from the day-to-day drama of their parents' lives. She'd told me once that her job as freelance travel writer had given her a freedom she'd never dreamt possible. Deep down, though, she'd still had a Plan B, and every year she'd complete an application to go back to university and do a PGCE so that she could become a teacher if that next journalism job didn't materialise. She'd never had to take up her place and it was the freest she'd ever been, but as soon as the children came along she reverted to needing plans in place for every possible scenario. There were back-up plans for everything, from who she could call upon to pick the children up from school or nursery if she ever found herself running late, to the life insurance policies she insisted we take out on the same day she discovered she was pregnant with Flo.

I sometimes wonder if Holly feels bitter that things fell into place so easily for Lou when we finally got together. We moved in together quickly, married five years later, and then had two babies in quick succession as soon as we decided to start trying, while Holly's life slowly fell to pieces. But if it's ever bothered her, she's never let it show. Instead, she's worked hard in her career and volunteered at every opportunity she got, to express gratitude for having survived cancer, despite what the fallout from her illness cost her. She fundraises and advocates for others who aren't as lucky as she believes she was, but it seems like a bitter irony that despite all her selflessness and gratitude, cancer might be about to take something she loves from her all over again, in the worst possible way. Through every bit of trauma she's endured, Holly has still been the most wonderful auntie and sister anyone could ask for, and she's been the best sister-in-law I could ever have wanted too. Right now, I've got no idea how I'd cope if I didn't have her to talk to; she's the only person in the world who understands what I'm feeling at the prospect of losing Lou. And all those things are part of what make Holly my second favourite adult in existence. It also means that I feel slightly less alone than I would otherwise. I won't have to walk through the storm we're all facing on my own, even if the very worst happens and we lose Lou. I wouldn't say that makes things better, because nothing can, but Holly is the main reason I'm just about holding it together.

'Daddy!' Suddenly there's a tug on my shirt and I look down to see Flo staring up at me, with the same amber eyes as her mother. 'Mummy says it's your turn to put Stan's shoes on, so Auntie Holly can take him to baby school.'

Baby school is what my daughter insists on calling nursery, mainly because she knows it winds her little brother up so much. At the grand old age of four, there's nothing Stan hates more than being referred to as a baby, except perhaps having his shoes put on. Given the choice, he'd rather be barefoot, or wear wellies, and every other form of footwear is akin to a torture device as far as he's concerned, even Crocs.

'Hmm, I seem to recall I had the joy of putting Stan's shoes on yesterday. So I think it might be Mummy's turn.' I say the words as I walk back into the kitchen, and Lou gives an exaggerated shrug, the mischievous look in her eyes so much like the one she was wearing on that first day I met her.

'I've been doing some research and, apparently, I've got what they call a protected characteristic which dictates that reasonable adjustments have to be made. I'm pretty sure that means never having to wrestle Stan into his shoes again.'

'That's not fair.' I grin, despite my protest, grateful that in the midst of all of this we can still find some humour.

'What's a pro-tect-tick carry-o-tistic?' Flo wrinkles her perfect little nose as I spot Stan out of the corner of my eye, trying to hide his trainers in the dishwasher.

'It's just Mummy reminding me of all the stuff she does to look after us, so the least I can do is put Stan's new shoes on. The ones that will make him run as fast as a cheetah.' I retrieve the trainers from the dishwasher as I speak, shooting Stan a smile in the hope that the mention of running as fast as a cheetah will convince him to let me put the trainers on with less of a fight. He's got a thing about cheetahs, ever since Lou read him a story about one, and he knows there's nothing on land that's faster. But he's crossing his arms over his chest in a look of defiance that tells me exactly how this is about to go.

'Mummy's the best.' Flo puts arm around her mother's waist, and I nod in response, because I don't trust myself to speak for a moment. How can I ever face my children and tell them that their mummy has gone? I have to hang on to the belief that we won't lose her, because if we do it will be like a hand grenade going off and the beautiful life we've built together will be disseminated, our children's lives changing beyond all recognition. I'm terrified that I won't be enough for them, and that I'll let Lou down in the worst possible way by failing our children. As I swallow hard, preparing myself to respond to my daughter, I catch Holly's eye and I know she understands, her glassy eyes betraying just how hard she's finding it watching Flo cuddle up to her mum, when we both know that very soon she might not be able to.

'She is and we couldn't do without her.' Walking towards Lou, I press my lips against hers, before turning to scoop up my son, who's already wriggling to break free, desperately hoping that someone, somewhere, recognises my prayer.

# 7

## LOUISA

'I'm sorry.' As soon as Mr Whitelaw said those words, I knew what was coming. Less than half an hour ago, I still had hope. I didn't realise how much hope I'd been holding on to, until it was snatched away, and I'd give anything to turn back the clock to who I was just thirty minutes ago. Tom's constant insistence that the doctors will be able to cure my cancer has driven me insane, because it's meant a complete refusal from him to discuss what will happen if they can't. But what I hadn't grasped until this morning was just how tightly I was clutching at straws too, just different ones to Tom. I'd forced myself to be more realistic and face the prospect that they might not be able to make this go away completely, but what I've been holding on to far more than I knew, was the belief that it could be held at bay. If not indefinitely, at least for a good long while.

I should have known the cancer wasn't playing fair, given how much worse my symptoms have become. I've tried to pretend that the obvious yellow tinge to my skin could just have been down to me catching the sun, but it's in the whites of my eyes too. The pain in my side has started to make me catch my breath sometimes, and the over-the-counter medication I've been taking no longer seems to touch it. I'm losing weight too and sometimes I have to force myself to eat anything at all. Despite all of that I was still managing to cling to hope, until Mr Whitelaw told us that it wasn't good news and the look on his face made it obvious just how bad it was.

'It's moving fast and aggressively. Given the extent of the spread, particularly to the liver, surgical intervention wouldn't be appropriate at this stage.' He didn't say the word pointless, but I heard it all the same and it felt as if there wasn't enough air. There was going to be no miracle, and all my worst fears came flooding in. My children would lose their mother, and I was going to lose everyone I loved. Even as I looked at the doctor, trying desperately to find a reason to latch on to some of that hope I hadn't known I had, it felt as if my life was already slipping through my hands and there was nothing I could do to stop it. I couldn't stop the tears from coming either, and it was impossible to catch my breath to ask the doctor any of the questions that were screaming inside my head, yelling at me that there must still be something they could do, but he'd anticipated at least one of them. 'You'll need to start a course of chemotherapy to see if we can shrink any of the tumours and then we can look at whether surgery might be an option.'

'So you're saying your suspicions were right and it's incurable?' Tom's voice caught on the last word and I wanted to tell him to shut up and stop asking questions that I didn't want the answers to. No good could come from knowing just how bad things were, but when Mr Whitelaw confirmed that there was no chance of me ever being cancer free, I started to retch. I wasn't actually sick, probably because I'd hardly eaten a thing since my first meeting with Mr Whitelaw. Terror at what this meant made my stomach contract over and over again. My kids needed me to be the mum I always had been, not some shadowy version of that, dying in front of their eyes. This shouldn't be happening; it wasn't fair, and the idyllic childhood I'd so desperately wanted for them had been ripped to shreds. I was never going to be well again. I was never going to be me again, and the last shred of hope I'd had was gone.

I didn't take in much after that and I couldn't even bring myself to acknowledge Mira's offer to schedule a meeting so that we could talk through all the side effects of the chemotherapy, and answer any questions I might have. All I wanted was to get out of the hospital, so that I could breathe properly again. It felt as if my lungs were on fire after what seemed like hours in an airless room being bombarded with the worst possible news. But even now that I'm outside, it still feels as if no matter how deeply I inhale, I'll never be able to get enough air into my lungs again. I'm breathing faster and faster to try to stop it feeling like I'm suffocating, but every breath I take seems to make it worse and I've got an almost overwhelming need to claw at my neck.

'Lou, you're scaring me, shall I go and get someone?' Tom puts his hand on my arm. The fear he's just described is as evident on his face as it was in his voice. I manage to shake my head. I don't want any doctors; they can't do what needs to be done. I want to tear open my skin, reach inside and pull out all the cancer. Or just set myself alight to burn it all away. I fight to slow down my breathing, reaching out to grab the handrail on a barrier that separates the car park from the road and try to steady myself.

'Do you need any help?' A woman who looks to be in her mid-twenties stops beside us. She's heavily pregnant and a bitter stab of envy hits me in the gut as I look at her. She's got so much to look forward to, bringing a new life into the world, all her dreams for the future wrapped up in the promise of what's to come. I want to ask her if she knows how lucky she is, and to tell her to count her blessings every single day she gets to spend with the child she's carrying, because one day – without any warning – it could all be taken away. I want to tell her about my babies, how they've been the greatest joy of my lives, and how much I'll miss the weight of them in my arms, the smell of their hair when they nuzzle their heads into my neck, and the sound of their laughter. That uncontrolled, joy-filled laughter that I'm terrified will be stolen from them by losing their mum. But I don't say any of that. Instead, I shake my head and mumble, 'No thanks,' watching as she moves slowly towards the entrance of the maternity unit and a future filled with endless possibilities.

A car pulls out of a space to the left of me, another one pulling in almost straight away, and there are people coming and going all around me. Some of them look serious, some are smiling, and on the other side of the car park a shout of laughter fills the air. People are getting on with their lives, as if nothing has changed, but for me everything has changed.

I'm know I'm not supposed to give up, that I should cling on until my very last breath and hope that the chemo will slow things down and allow me to have surgery. But I'm not ready to be hopeful, and I'm definitely not ready for Tom to tell me that's what I need to be. I can't even think straight. All I want to do is to escape my own body. I hate the thought of this poison spreading inside me, turning everything toxic. It's like I'm possessed by a demon; that's what the cancer feels like, and suddenly I know where I want to be – where I *need* to be – and it's what's allowing me to breathe again.

'I'm going to St Martin's.' As I utter the words, Tom's eyes shoot open and I can guess what he's thinking: that I've really lost it now. I'm not a church kind of person, and I've only put any faith in the existence of God a handful of times in my life, but I feel in my bones that it's where I need to be, even if I have no idea why.

'I'll drive us.' I'm shaking my head almost before Tom makes the offer.

'I want to be on my own for a bit, so I can try to process everything. I just need you to drop me at the edge of the village on the way back home.'

'Lou, I really don't think that's a good idea. I can't stand the thought of you being on your own with all of this going through your head.' Tom sounds desperate and I don't want to cause him any more pain than he's already in, but I feel as if I need this every bit as much as I need the oxygen that's refilling my lungs.

'Please, I won't be long, and I promise to call if I need you.' I look at my husband properly for the first time since we saw Mr Whitelaw. He looks exhausted. There are new lines etched on his face that weren't there a few weeks ago, and a sadness in his eyes that hurts my heart. I can't think about what the weeks and months ahead might do to him, because I need to believe that he'll get through it. He has to, for Stan and Flo. Taking his hand, I hold it as if my life depends on not letting go and for a moment it feels as though it does, but then I release it anyway. Maybe it's a metaphor for the parting neither of us wants, that will come far sooner than either of us expected, and finally Tom seems to understand.

'Okay, but promise you'll keep your phone on and, if you're not back by one, I'll be coming to find you.'

'Thank you.' It's something I've said to him thousands of times, although I've never meant it more than I do right now. But as I turn to walk away, he catches hold of my wrist.

'I love you so much, Lou, you know that don't you?' His eyes have filled with tears, and I nod, not able to answer because I'm scared if I do that I'll start crying and I'll never be able to stop. 'You're the best thing that ever happened to me and the thought of losing you—'

He can't finish what he's saying and the first sob escapes as I step forward and he pulls me towards him. Within seconds my hair is wet with his tears, and he's oblivious to the people around us, but I can see the looks we're getting – sympathy, curiosity and relief on the faces of the people who pass us by, that it's not them going through whatever it is Tom and I are facing. I wish I could say something to comfort him, but it's as if I'm frozen inside. I can't allow myself to feel everything there is to feel all in one go, it's just too much. If I let myself worry about Tom as much as I'm already worrying about the children, I'm scared I'll fall apart completely. So many times, since the diagnosis, I've tried to talk to Tom about the future, and about what happens if I'm not here. If he can't accept that that I'm dying after what Mr Whitelaw has just told us, I don't think he ever will. But now is not the time to try and get him to talk. Instead, I let him cry it out, until finally it seems there's nothing left.

'You've never given me any reason to doubt how much you love me, and I love you so much too.' Even as I say the words, it's as if I'm on some kind of auto pilot. It's not that I don't mean them, but if I let myself *feel* them, I'm afraid I'll spiral out of control. Instead, I squeeze Tom's hand again, before letting it go for a second time.

'I promise I'll be back by one, I just need some space to process everything.'

He nods in response, the torment in his red-rimmed eyes making my throat burn with all the emotion I'm desperately trying so hard to contain. I feel like an unexploded bomb, where one false move could prove catastrophic and I'm just praying my instinct that St Martin's will bring some kind of peace holds true, because I've got no idea how to carry on if it doesn't.

\* \* \*

St Martin's is where Tom and I married, almost five years after we met, following in the footsteps of my grandparents, who would have been married for seventy-two years this year, had they still been alive. It would be an outright lie to say they never argued; good-natured bickering was the backing track to their marriage, but somehow it was always done with love. A typical exchange would go back and forth. Nan would complain about Gramp's complete inability to put anything away, and he'd tell her it was because he couldn't think straight, after she'd kept him awake all night with her snoring. Then she'd say, 'Talk about the pot calling the kettle black, you snore like a saddleback pig,' before doing an impression that made them both laugh. It was their love language, and I'd much rather have emulated that than the quiet distance that grew between my parents for years before they split up, then got back together, then split up, before finally getting back together again. They can't seem to stay apart, but I sometimes think it has more to do with co-dependency than love.

My admiration for my grandparents' relationship meant that choosing to marry in St Martin's had been almost a foregone conclusion. Tom had grown up in Castlebourne and I'd spent so much time here as a child, that it felt like home. Castlebourne had been mine and Holly's safe place, an idyllic village buried deep in the Kent countryside, surrounded by the vineyards and orchards of the Garden of England. We'd spend warm summer days paddling in the stream that meandered through its centre and passed by the ruins of the medieval fortress which gave the village its name.

Castlebourne is where I fell in love with Tom too. Somehow, in all the time I'd spent here visiting my grandparents, our paths had never crossed, but the moment I saw him at the wedding event, I felt a connection that seemed crazy given the circumstances. I can even pinpoint the moment my feelings changed from an initial strong attraction to something else. The wedding coordinator had got all excited about the parallels between our jobs, and she started telling me that Tom was a bit of a local celebrity, having won some awards.

'It's really nothing.' A hint of a blush coloured Tom's cheeks and looking back I think that's probably the moment I fell in love with him. 'I started off making some short documentaries on YouTube and I got picked up by the channel I work for now. It's not as exciting as it sounds and the biggest compliment I've ever had was when someone called me the Poundshop Louis Theroux.'

When Tom laughed, I did too, but despite somehow knowing how easy it would be to fall for him, I'd never cross that kind of line with a man who was engaged to someone else. It wasn't until Abigail ended her relationship with Tom that he and I got to discover just how many interests and values we shared. He tracked me down on Facebook and I'd been as surprised as I was thrilled to get his message, especially when he told me that his engagement was over.

Tom has never said anything derogatory about Abigail, just that they drifted into a relationship because they were both so busy and it was convenient. I didn't read too much into that until the last few weeks, but now it terrifies me that he could get into a relationship on that basis and, because of that, it's hard to trust that any person he brings into the children's lives in the future will be right for them. I think it's a big part of the reason why the what-ifs started as soon as Mr Whitelaw told me I had cancer, and I tried to picture my children's future with a me-shaped hole in it.

My own experiences as a child have only served to heighten the fear I've felt for Stan and Flo since that moment. Neither of my parents had any serious relationships with other people during the periods when Mum left to try and get sober but my dad came close a couple of times. One morning I went in to see him when I woke up, to discover a woman I'd never met before pressed up against him, their legs tangled together and her mahogany-coloured hair fanning out across both their pillows, the smell of stale booze and even staler bodies almost overwhelming. I had to stifle a scream at the sight of her. When they eventually emerged from the bedroom, he introduced Linda to me and Holly. She planted a kiss on my face with lips covered in a thick gloss that stuck to my cheek, even after I furiously wiped it off. She started hanging around a lot, cooking for us – if that's what you could call heating up frozen pizzas and nuggets. She wasn't horrible, but I still hated her. I hated the way she was always hanging off my father, not caring whether we were in the room when she started snogging him like a teenager in the back row of the cinema. I didn't want this strange person in my father's bed, in our flat, or in our lives. The first thing I told my mother about the next time I saw her was Linda. I wanted her to somehow make this woman disappear from our lives, and she did, by coming home for just long enough to make Linda a distant memory, before Mum left again too. But I won't be there to do that if Tom meets someone the children don't like after I'm gone.

What if the person Tom meets turns out to be like Linda, or worse still, like Billie; someone who sees their own children as little more than an inconvenience, and God knows how she'd feel about someone else's. I can't bear the prospect of a woman like that being stepmother to my kids. But even when I was focusing on my deepest fear – that my children might be unhappy – I wasn't really picturing myself as gone, not completely. I was there as an observer, at a distance, unable to intervene, but somehow still around, like I was watching on a closed-circuit TV in a neighbouring room. It's only now the doctor has confirmed there's no chance of a cure that I realise I hadn't really accepted the idea I might actually die from this. I'd focused on the horror of what would happen if I had to leave my children, but I didn't allow myself to think about the finality of it all. Part of me pictured myself as a version of my mother, coming and going from my children's lives at will. But I won't be able to do that, and I won't be able to see what's happening, not even from a distance, let alone be able to do anything about it. I'll be gone, forever, and I've got no idea how to continue to live in the meantime. Tears are choking in my throat again, because I know I have to find a way to keep living while I'm dying; I can't waste a moment of the precious time I have left with the people I love, but I've never felt so lost, or so alone. I don't even know how to begin to cope with this.

Running a hand over the flint wall of the church, I desperately try to focus on the here and now. It's something I read in one of the pamphlets Mira gave me about mindfulness as a way of coping with what's happening. I'm supposed to think about five things I can see, four things I can hear, three things I can touch, two things I can smell and one thing I can taste. But as soon as I turn to my left, I spot an overgrown grave, marked by a worn-away headstone, denoting the final resting place of someone even time has forgotten. My breathing gets ragged again and, just like at the hospital, the air won't seem to get into my lungs. Holding on to the wall, I close my eyes, concentrating on the roughness of the flint surface until the feeling of panic isn't quite so intense.

When I finally think I might be able to take a step without my legs collapsing underneath me, I move towards the heavy oak doors at the entrance to the church. Pushing inside, the coolness envelops me and immediately I feel a little bit calmer. I'm not religious and I've got no idea if there's something more than this life, but whatever atmosphere is pervading the building, it's what I need right now.

As I take a seat at a pew towards the back of the church, the simplicity of the whitewashed walls is somehow helping to quieten the racing of my thoughts. I'm still not sure why I'm here, but I know I don't want to leave. So many important moments have happened in this place. Our wedding, the children's christenings, the sad goodbyes to my beloved grandparents. Holly didn't marry in Castlebourne in the end. Jacob took her to Vegas and persuaded her that they should get married out there, without any of her family or friends to witness their big day. I know it's not what she wanted, and she tried so hard to make him happy, but in the end nothing she did was ever enough. It's so unfair that he has a child now and she never got that dream. The thought stings my eyes, but I've got to blink back the tears, I can't let them fall. I'm too afraid to cry again, in case I can't ever stop.

'Louisa.' The sound of my name feels completely out of place, in a way I don't think it ever has before. At least not to this extent. I look up to see Kate, the church Reader, concern etched on her face. 'Are you okay? You look really pale.'

I try to form the words 'I'm fine', to utter the meaningless response everyone wants to hear, even when it couldn't be further from the truth. Instead, I shake my head and something very different escapes my lips.

'I'm dying.' The blunt words make Kate gasp, but they are true even if they haven't been said to me directly. Mr Whitelaw told me that if there are things I want to do, I should do them now. The horrors of Google revealed the brutal truth that the average prognosis for someone with advanced pancreatic cancer is eight months if the chemo works, or less than four months if it doesn't. I wanted to stand up and scream, to tell him that I need at least forty years to do all the things I want to do, and even that won't be enough. I want every moment owed to me in the average life span I should surely be entitled to. I nodded along when Mr Whitelaw suggested that I should do everything I want to do before it's too late, like it was easy advice to follow, instead of being so blisteringly unfair that sometimes I'm scared the anger will overwhelm me completely. I'm holding so much in, despite blurting out the words that make Kate recoil as if she's suffered a physical blow, but she regains her composure quickly.

'Oh Louisa.' Kate is at my side in seconds, her soft voice even more gentle than usual. I've known her for years; she grew up in the house next door to my grandparents, where her father and stepmother still live. I wouldn't call her a friend, exactly, but right now I don't need the complication of someone who loves me, whose feelings I have to protect in ways that mean I can't be honest about my own. I need someone I can be straight with, but who'll care enough to want to help me, and I can't think of anyone better than Kate.

'I've got pancreatic cancer, it's incurable and aggressive too. Spreading fast.' My explanation sounds matter-of-fact, as if I'm describing a problem a work. But if I let myself connect with the meaning of the words I'll never be able to get them all out.

'I'm so sorry.' As Kate takes my hand, I almost tell her that's what all the medical staff have said, and none of them can do anything to really help me, but my bitterness at all of this is just one of the things I'm desperately trying to keep locked inside. And there are no words that can help. I'm not sure anything can, now I know just how bad things are, but that's what I need to work out. Maybe I should join one of the support groups Mira mentioned, in case someone there has the answers about what the hell to do next. Except right now I can't think of anything worse than being surrounded by other dying people. Since my diagnosis, cancer seems to be everywhere. It probably always was, but I didn't notice it before. But my new-found personal experience has only heightened the awareness that it exists.

I've read more online about cancer since my first meeting with Mr Whitelaw than I ever thought possible. Every article and blog post I read seems to shame me for being so bitter about my diagnosis. Almost every person writing about their 'cancer journey' says that they never asked, 'Why me?' but instead only thought, 'Why not me?' I wonder what makes me so different from them. The *why me* is what screams inside my head every time I look at the children, or Tom, or Holly. Or even at my own reflection in the mirror. There are people who've committed horrendous crimes, who could have been given this cancer instead. How can that possibly be fair? Maybe I'm just not as brave or as selfless as all those other people detailing their cancer stories online, but I'll never ask the question *why not me?*, because I already know the answer. I've got people who need me, the same people I can't bear the thought of leaving, and that should be enough to make it clear to the universe why it shouldn't be me. But then I guess that means it shouldn't be anyone. Most people have someone who needs them, or loves them, and those who don't have suffered more than enough already. So instead of saying any of that, I give Kate what I imagine is a more acceptable response.

'I'm sorry too.'

'Have they said...' Kate hesitates for a moment, before giving an audible swallow. 'How long?'

'No, but even if the treatment works, I've probably got less than a year.' A sob catches in my throat as the reality hits me again. 'I might not even make it until Stan's fifth birthday, and a year or two after that he won't even remember who I was.' It's a recurring thought I've had that I've tried to push down inside me so many times, but it won't go away. The idea that I might become nothing more than a second-hand memory to the little boy I love with all my heart is so agonising that I couldn't even begin to describe how much it hurts. But the thought just won't stop torturing me.

'You've got to think positively.' Kate's words are so earnest and I know she means well, but I snatch my hand away. The rage I feel about the situation is threatening to boil over and I'm not sure I even want to try to stop it.

'How the hell am I supposed to think positively about being told that I'm dying and that I'll be leaving my kids and everyone else I care about?'

'I'm sorry, I didn't mean...' Even Kate's neck has gone red. 'I just meant you can't give up hope. Miracles can happen.'

'But mostly they don't, do they? Mostly shit just happens.' I know I'm lashing out and I wish I could believe that a miracle might still happen, but I might as well have stuck my fingers in my ears when Mr Whitelaw was speaking if hoping for some kind of divine intervention is my only plan. Pretending it's not happening won't make it go away. I need to find a way to deal with it that doesn't ruin whatever time I have left. But I've still got no idea how I'm supposed to come to terms with my own death. It seems impossible. It *is* impossible. My children can't be motherless. They can't. The idea terrifies me, but so does the alternative, and I'm already jealous of the woman who might one day fill that role. I don't want them to forget me, but I don't want them missing me so much that it blights their lives either. I don't know what to do and I'm starting to panic again, my breath getting caught in my chest, as I look back at Kate. 'I'm scared.'

'Of dying?' Her voice is so quiet, I have to strain to hear, but I shake my head, trying to take a slow deep breath and release it again before I speak.

'No, yes. I mean of course I'm scared about that, but I'm more scared of what happens afterwards.'

'I believe that, after all of this' – Kate gestures around us, her face suddenly flooded by a light that seems to come from within – 'there's a joy we can never know in life, a freedom from pain and all the burdens we carry with us, and that we're reunited with all the people we've loved and lost.'

'I'm afraid I don't believe I'll be sitting up there on a fluffy white cloud having a catch up with my grandparents. I wish I did, but that just feels like bullshit to me, especially now.' I know I'm being rude, dismissing Kate's beliefs the way I am, especially given where we are, but I don't care. Maybe this is as close as I'm ever going to get to feeling what Kate describes, a freeing up of earthly burdens, including the need to politely nod along with something I don't believe is true. But she hasn't understood what I meant, and I need her to. 'I'm not talking about what happens to *me* after I'm dead. I'm talking about what happens to everyone else, to all the people I love, but most of all to Flo and Stan. It's all I've been able to think about since the moment they told me I had cancer. At first I still had hope that it might be curable, and focusing on them was a weird kind of distraction from facing the fact that I might die. Only now they're telling me there's no chance of a cure, and that dying isn't just a possibility any more, it's a certainty. I'll be gone soon and all the power I have to try and make things right in my children's lives will be gone with me. How can I accept that, and how the hell am I supposed to tell them I'm going to have to leave them? They're not nearly done needing me, and I'm not nearly done being a mother. I can't do it, I can't do it, I can't do it.'

I'm sobbing now, white-hot fear washing over me again, and I'm choking on my own tears. I widen my eyes in terror, suddenly unable to find my voice, but I'm begging Kate to help me nonetheless. My chest is so tight it feels like my heart's exploding and I wonder if a heart attack is going to take me, before the cancer even gets the chance.

'Louisa, you need to breathe.' Kate tells me what I already know, but I find myself nodding as she puts her hands on my arms, so that looking at her is almost like looking at my reflection. 'Copy me and take a slow breath in and then out again, like this.'

Kate follows her own instruction, taking one hand off my arm and then raising it slowly, before lowering it down at the same rate.

'That's it, we just need to keep breathing, in and out, in and out.' She raises and lowers her hand again in time with the words, until the feeling that I'm about to pass out finally lifts and I remember how to breathe without visual and verbal guidance.

'Felt like a heart attack.' My words are faltering and she nods.

'Panic attacks are like that. I got them a lot after I lost my mum.' Kate takes my hand again. I remember when that happened. Holly and I must have been about eleven, and Kate a couple of years older than us when her mother was killed in a boating accident. Heat prickles my skin; she must hate me for being so scornful about her views of an idyllic afterlife where she'll be reunited with her beloved mum.

'I'm sorry. What I said about after we die, I—' As I start to apologise, Kate squeezes my hand more tightly.

'Don't be sorry. I shouldn't have tried to make it all sound...' She pauses and gives a half-smile. 'I'm struggling to think of a better word than heavenly, I'm afraid. But I can't even begin to imagine what it's like to be in your situation. Losing Mum so suddenly was really hard, but at least she didn't have to grieve for what she was losing too. I wish there was something useful I could say, but it just feels like every time I open my mouth I mess up.'

'No, you don't.' I try for a smile too, but I can't quite manage it. 'And I think there is something you might be able to help me with, but it's asking a lot.'

'Whatever it is, if I can do it, I will.'

'I want you to tell me what it was like to lose your mum, in as much detail as you can. The things that helped, and the things that definitely didn't. I want to know how you felt when your new stepmum Irene came into your life, and how you think your father handled all of that.' I can see a myriad of emotions passing across Kate's face already, but then she nods. She understands why I need to know this, even if neither of us have any idea what I'll do with the information. At least not yet.

'I can do that and, if it helps, I'm sure Dad and Irene would be happy to talk to you too.'

'Thank you, I might well take you up on that.' Leaning forward, I hug Kate. She feels solid and warm, and a tiny bit of the unrelenting fear about what happens 'after' lifts a little. She's survived what Stan and Flo will have to face, and she's still here, doing good things, and living a life that gives her the kind of peace I'm not sure if I've ever really known. Whenever I see Kate, she seems happy. No, happy is the wrong word, but she certainly seems content with the life she's built for herself. That's what I want for Stan and Flo, for Holly and Tom, and for my parents, after I'm gone. Maybe Kate will prove me wrong, and there'll be an afterlife where I'll have more contentment than I've ever known too, up there somewhere on a cloud, with Nan and Gramps. But facing whatever future I have left will be so much easier, if I know the people I love most can find their way back to some kind of contentment, when they're left in the 'after' without me.

# 8

## LOUISA

I cried on the day I dropped Flo to her first day at school, thinking about how fast my little girl was growing up. Before my diagnosis, I anticipated that dropping Stan off for his first day would be even harder. The last of my babies disappearing into a classroom, where they'd spend more waking hours than they did at home during term time, where they'd start to live lives that I had no real idea about parts of, only the bits they chose to tell me about. I can already see that with Flo. When she was at nursery, and even when she first started at primary school, she'd tell me in the minutest detail about what her day had entailed. Now when I ask her, sometimes I get detailed answers and, on other days, mostly when she's very tired, she'll say things like 'not much', or even 'school stuff', like a six-year-old who's going on thirteen.

On days like that, I can picture the teenager she's going to be one day so clearly, and it's a thought that's made me want to slow time down in the past. Except now, post-diagnosis, part of me wants to fast forward time instead, so I can watch Stan transition from the little boy who tells me everything, to one who has parts of his life that are his alone, just as his sister already does. And to watch Flo become the teenager I can already sense waiting in the wings. But I'm not going to be there for either of those things, and someone else will have to be there to pick up my children from school, and to ask them about their day. I know Tom will want to be the one to do that, but I've got no idea how that will work with his job. Holly will step in, as much as she can, and when I picture her in my place at the school gates, even though it's still agony, it hurts a little less. That's all I can hope for right now, I'm starting to realise. There's no avoiding the pain that came hand-in-hand with my prognosis. The before and after of my hopes for the future are changed beyond all recognition by being told I have aggressive, incurable cancer. What I hope for now looks so different from before, but hurting a little less feels like a win and maybe that's what I need to focus on, rather than trying to orchestrate a future for my children that I can't possibly control.

'Looking good, Lou!' Billie calls out to me as I approach the school gates. I hate the over-familiarity of her shortening my name, which grates on my nerves when it comes from her mouth. 'Losing weight suits you. What is it, Ozempic?'

I have to bite my lip to stop myself from telling her exactly what's behind my weight loss, but the children are already starting to file out from the classroom and shouting, 'I've got terminal cancer, you fucking idiot,' is not something any child needs to hear, let alone Stan, who's clamped to my hip, his head on my shoulder, sleepy from a day at nursery that's left him with paint-stained hands and stray grains from the sandpit stuck to his legs. He's too heavy for me to carry, really, especially now, but I want to hold on to every moment, and to him, for as long as I can.

I ignore Billie's mention of my weight completely and address the fact that she's at the school gates at all. The days when her au pair, Matilda, or her lovely mother-in-law, Jan, pick up the children instead are always far more pleasant. 'We don't usually see you on a Wednesday.'

'I know. I should be at Pilates, but I've changed to a Thursday morning class so Jonathan's mother can't play the martyr and pick up the kids.' Billie looks like she's sucking on a sour sweet whenever she talks about Jan, but I can't help poking the bear. Maybe it's just another part of not caring what people think so much any more. Or maybe it's the anger that's constantly bubbling away inside me now.

'Jan always seems delighted to pick the children up. Almost as thrilled as they are that it's her who's here to collect them.' I don't even try to disguise the dig, but if Billie picks up on it, she's choosing not to react.

'Oh she's delighted all right, anything to get her claws into them and stay as close to Jonathan as possible.' Billie is almost snarling. 'She calls him Jon-Jon, can you believe that? Turns my stomach. Whenever she's around it's like I don't even exist, so I had to do something to reduce the amount of contact she has with the kids and, by default, with Jonathan.'

'That's horrible.' Now that cancer has tapped into my truth vein, I don't seem to be able to control it. Jan and her husband, Graham, adore their only son and his children. It's been obvious every time I've seen them together, and with Jonathan being Tom's best friend, they've been on the periphery of our lives ever since we got together.

'It is, isn't it? Fancy having a sickly name like that for your son and taking every opportunity to hang around him. Jonathan's almost as bad. Talk about an Oedipus complex.' I still don't know if Billie is deliberately misunderstanding me, or whether she really is that thick skinned, but as her son Felix comes out of the door of the classroom his face falls.

'Where's Nanny?' It would break my heart if Flo looked that

deflated that I was the one picking her up, but Billie doesn't even seem to notice.

'Nanny won't be picking you up from school any more. You've got Mummy or Matilda every day now!' Billie's doing her best to make that sound like wonderful news, but Felix's expression tells a very different story, even before he responds.

'But I want Nanny. She was going to take me to the park before we get Bella.' The whiny note in his voice earns him a sharp look from his mother, who grips his hand so tightly her knuckles turn white.

'I can take you to the park and then we can get ice cream on the way home.'

'I want Nanny.' Felix tries to pull away, but Billie yanks his arm in response.

'Well Nanny isn't here and if you keep on I'll just take you home. No park and no ice cream.' Billie yanks her son again in the direction of the playground, so I don't hear his response, but I do see the sadness in his eyes, as he turns around when they reach the school gates, no doubt desperately hoping he'll suddenly spot Jan and that they can go to the park together after all.

There's an uneasy feeling in the pit of my stomach and I hug Stan even closer to me, until I can feel his heartbeat thudding against mine. Should I call someone? Jonathan maybe, or Jan, and let them know how upset Felix was, and how hard his mother is being on him? I don't think Billie would ever cause her son any physical harm, despite her roughness, but the potential for psychological distress almost worries me more. And as Flo emerges from the classroom, her blonde ponytail swinging from side to side behind her as she rushes over to me, I realise it's not just Felix I'm worried about. The idea of Holly being the one to take my place at the school gates gave me a crumb of comfort, and I know she'd do that every day without question. But what if something puts a stop to it? What if Tom eventually meets someone who feels threatened by me, even though I'm gone? What better way to erase my existence in my children's lives than to push my sister out of the picture? Even as I reach down towards Flo, and my daughter clings to me, with Stan sandwiched between us, I shiver at the thought. I've got to do whatever it takes to stop that happening and it's time to invoke the most important Plan B I've ever had to come up with.

# 9

## LOUISA

It's been thirty-six hours since Mr Whitelaw broke the news that my cancer is incurable, and I've spent far too much of that time online. If I haven't got any time to waste, I shouldn't be spending it staring at a screen, but I'm searching for anything that might help. I'm not talking about cures that somehow my well-respected consultant hasn't heard of, but some random person on TikTok has. I'm talking about something that might help me ensure my children's lives aren't ruined by my death.

Research is something that comes fairly naturally to me, having made a living as a travel journalist. I still do a bit of free-lance writing, mainly for parenting stuff rather than travel, but nowadays people turn to Instagram and TikTok for content, far more than they do print. Having the peak of my career just before all of that hit always used to make me feel so lucky. I've always felt lucky, but it finally seems that my luck has run out.

Even before the writing jobs started to tail off, motherhood had already become my new dream. I was thirty-five and Tom was thirty-seven when we decided to start trying for a family. We'd been enjoying our freedom together, and with my childhood having been as disjointed as it was, I wanted to make sure I was 100 per cent ready to go all in. But for at least three years before we decided to start trying, I'd been having not so subtle reminders from loved ones and virtual strangers that I didn't have forever. Devastatingly, it turns out they were right, but not in a way any of us could ever have imagined back then.

*Over the age of thirty you might find it more difficult than you think to get pregnant. I hope you don't discover that something's wrong, because if you need help, you won't have much time. If I was you, I wouldn't wait around, especially after what happened to Holly.* I must have heard lines like those a hundred times, often with the best of intentions, but sometimes they were said almost gleefully, as if the person delivering them secretly hoped this wouldn't all just fall into place for me. Except my luck held. Florence arrived within a year of me coming off the pill, just in time to be guest of honour at Tom's thirty-seventh birthday, and she was joined by her brother two years later. I knew from the moment they were placed in my arms that I could never do what my mother did, and leave them. Except it turns out that I won't have a choice.

I would die for my children, but instead I'm dying for something far more futile, an overproduction of cells that's poisoning my body from the inside and there's not a damn thing I can do to change that.

Motherhood has been everything I wanted it to be and more, and I'd give anything to see it through, or even to start it all over again from the beginning and make sure I treasured every moment the way I should have done. There was a stage when Stan was a baby, when I didn't own a single item of clothing that didn't smell of vomit. Sometimes I dreamt of a quiet desk in an office somewhere, or a tube ride where no one would call for Mama's attention, and even going for a wee without the company of a toddler seemed like an impossible dream. I still wouldn't have swapped it for the world and, half an hour ago, when I looked down at my sleeping son, the ache in my chest was almost unbearable. I can't even think about how Stan will feel on the day he calls for Mama and I don't come. It hurts too much, a million times more than the gnawing fear in my gut that seems ever present since my diagnosis. It's another physical reminder that there's cancer in my body, growing untamed, and hellbent on destruction, like a weed choking all the good things it encounters. But I will take any level of pain if it means my children keep their blissful ignorance about my illness for as long as possible, and I know I might have to.

Last night sleep wouldn't seem to come at all, and I suspect tonight is going to be the same. Every time I shut my eyes, I picture my children trying to understand where I've gone and why I'm not coming back, and the thought jolts me upright, the now horribly familiar sense of panic overwhelming me each time. So I'm back online, where I spent almost all of last night, looking for something that might give me hope that it will all be okay. I searched through posts of other people with cancer until my eyes burned. It felt as though I'd read about every possible scenario, but what I couldn't find on one single site or forum, was any guidance on how to make sure my husband makes the right decisions for our children once I'm no longer around. After hours of googling, trying lots of different variations of the same question, I eventually found something: an article from a problem page, where a woman dying of a terminal illness wrote about how terrified she was of leaving her child in the care of her alcoholic husband, who had seemed incapable of being a properly functioning adult even before her illness. Tom's nothing like that and he'd do anything for me and the children. But I also know that at just forty-five I don't want him to be alone for the rest of his life. I don't want him to have to give up the job he loves either. He's going to be devastated enough at losing me. As brilliant as he is in so many ways, with his mind so often on his work, he needs someone by his side, and so do my children. The thought hurts my heart, because I want that someone to be me, but it can't be. So I need to know that when he does find someone new, he'll prioritise all the right qualities. Not just the things he might be attracted to, but far more importantly, the ones that are best for our kids.

When I couldn't find anybody online who'd asked for advice on the same thing, I decided to post an anonymous question on a discussion forum for women with cancer, called The Grapevine. Giving myself the username @worriedmum1982 I typed out my message, deciding to tell a white lie about the type of cancer I have in order to make sure the messages couldn't somehow 'out' me, or reduce the amount of advice I was offered. Most of the other women seemed to have one of three other types, so I decided to pretend I did too, a type I was all too horribly familiar with.

I've been told my breast cancer is incurable. I have two very young children and I'm trying to accept that at some point it'll be down to my husband to raise them without me. The chances are he'll meet someone else and I want him to be happy, but how can I make certain he gets it right? I guess what I'm asking is how can I have a say in who my husband's future partner will be?

It was only once I started getting replies that I realised I hadn't said enough in my post. Most of the advice was to talk to my husband, to be honest about my fears and to talk to him about what sort of qualities he thinks are important, so I could get an idea of what he might prioritise and find a way to steer him on that. It would be sound enough advice if I could persuade Tom to talk about anything apart from the treatment being some kind of miracle. Strangely for a person in a job as dangerous as his can be, he finds talking about death impossible. And he's certainly not ready to confront mine. It's only been two days since we were given the results of the PET scan and we don't know how well I'll respond to the chemo, so it's no wonder Tom thinks I'm jumping ahead of myself. But Mr Whitelaw's no-holds-barred consultations have made me face my mortality in a way I've never had to before, and I can't leave it until I'm on my death bed to have these conversations; it'll be too late by them. Although it turns out Tom isn't the only who thinks I shouldn't be having them at all. One user on the forum in particular seemed happy to give me a piece of her mind.

Wow @worriedmum1982 that's quite controlling, don't you think? Wanting to pick your husband's next partner is a pretty weird thing to admit to.

I thought for a while before I replied, and I kept my response short if not entirely sweet.

Maybe it is @booblesswonder777 but having to face up to the fact that I won't be able to see my children grow up is pretty weird too.

A response pinged back almost immediately, and this one felt more aggressive in tone.

On this forum terminal illness doesn't make you special @worriedmum1982. A lot of us are facing the same prospect, but it's no excuse for trying to control the lives of everyone around you.

I nearly fired back a two-word answer after that, but instead I closed down the webpage, trying not to wonder if she might be right. I couldn't resist going back on the forum later on, and most of the messages on the thread were supportive, saying they understood where I was coming from, and a few of them called @booblesswonder777 out on her tone. But a handful of users agreed with her, and I've been questioning myself ever since. Part of me knows I should just trust Tom to do the right thing and any attempt I might make to manipulate that is crazy, borne out of the shock and terror of my prognosis. But there's a bigger, far more powerful part of me that doesn't want to listen to any of that. All that matters is protecting my children in any way I still can, and I don't care how crazy or controlling that makes me seem.

# 10

## HOLLY

Lou and the kids will be here soon. My beautiful pristine kitchen will probably look like a bomb has hit it within minutes of their arrival and I cannot wait. The house is always tidy, aside from when Tigs decides to shed some of his marmalade orange fur on the sofa, or leaves scuff marks when he has a one-sided fight with the rug. It shouldn't be like this. There were going to be children, three ideally, who'd drive me mad by leaving their shoes and coats wherever they fell at the end of a long day. I'd roll my eyes and look at Jacob, the two of us exchanging a silent understanding that the children were hard work but worth every moment of it. Except, in the end, there hadn't even been one child.

Even before my breast cancer diagnosis, I'd started to try and come to terms with life as a family of two, in case the IVF didn't give us the results we so desperately wanted. I forced myself to think about all the things we could do that people with children couldn't, and by the time of the third failed IVF I was really getting there. I didn't want to put my body through any of that again. I wanted to let it rest and recuperate, and for me to get strong again – physically and emotionally – ready to embrace a life of travel and adventure, and long lie-ins on the weekend with the Sunday papers. Maybe there'd even be a chance to lose myself in painting or drawing again. It was something that had been important to me when I was growing up. Lou and I both had our own coping mechanisms, to help us deal with a chaotic and painful childhood. Writing was her escape, and that passion was something she turned into a career. I'd always retreated into my own, safe world – one that I could create and control – with the aid of a sketch book, or a blank canvas that I could transform. Our grandparents kept us supplied with the things we needed for what they called our 'hobbies', but Lou and I both knew they were far more than that, they were essential to our survival.

Like my sister, I dreamt of one day turning that passion into a job, but I sought security in a different way to Lou. She has always needed a Plan B, but I've always needed to be certain that I could provide for myself financially, having never had that kind of certainty as a child. That caution stood me in good stead when it turned out that my body had another surprise for me, and that Jacob had an even bigger shock in store.

He waited until just after I'd got the all-clear to finally leave me, even though he'd checked out emotionally long before then. So two became one, until I bought Tigs, a bundle of soft ginger fur that was wet with my tears for much of the first year of his life. He's ten now, getting on a bit and too set in his ways for me to get the dog I've been longing to get for the last couple of years. Flo will love that; she's desperate for a dog and I think Lou and Tom were getting close to giving in, but they've got too much on their plates right now. Even as I catch myself thinking that, I know it's a ridiculous way to put it. *Too much on their plates* makes it sound like they're busy with work, or in the midst of a house renovation.

What they're facing is a terrifying diagnosis of incurable and terminal cancer.

Being told I was dying was the thing I feared the most when I first got the news I had cancer and, after that, it was the thought of it coming back. For a few weeks after Jacob had left, a tiny part of me almost wished that I hadn't made it through the cancer, because I didn't want to be here any more. I shook it off quite quickly and I hate myself for thinking that way now, not least because it was Lou who got me through the darkest of those days. And looking back, wasting any time on missing Jacob feels like a joke, especially given his reaction when I first realised I had a lump. My almost non-existent boobs were something I've been teased about since secondary school, and my husband used to joke about not being able to find them in the dark, but it was probably because of their small size that my cancer was detected so early.

'Christ, what the hell is that?' Those were Jacob's exact words when he felt the pea-sized lump under his fingertips, with more repulsion than concern in his voice and I should have known then how useless he'd turn out to be in terms of offering any support. It was Lou who was there for me through every appointment, who ran around making sure I had everything I needed, and who let me cry and rage during the treatment and afterwards, when Jacob decided he didn't love me any more and I was left questioning whether he ever really had. So it isn't fair that Lou's the one facing a far more aggressive cancer, now.

I started volunteering for some charities after my first year in remission, and it's really helped with getting a wider perspective on things. I read a great blog post last night from a woman living with stage-four cancer who wrote something that really hit home. Being human in itself is a terminal condition, and just because someone has a grade-four diagnosis, it doesn't mean they have to think of themselves as waiting to die, any more than the rest of us do. So whatever the results of her PET scan, I don't want to think of Lou like that, because the thought of her not being around will do so much to take away from the time we've still got together. And, who knows, she might still outlive me. There are so many new breakthroughs all the time and I was on a different forum last night, reading posts from people undergoing successful immunotherapy treatments for grade-four cancers that are holding them at bay indefinitely. There's no reason why Lou shouldn't get on one of those trials, and with Tom's connections, he'd be in a great place to find out about them.

I'm determined to be hopeful and there's no reason not to be. I'm going to treat Lou the way I always have done and, whatever the results, I'll help her keep focusing on what matters the most. We're going to bake with kids when they come over, make the best chocolate chip cookies in the world, like our nan taught us to when we were around Flo's age, and I'm going to give it to her straight, if she starts getting fixated on the worst-case scenario. I'm more than happy to dish out a bit of tough love if that's what it takes, because she'd be the first person to do that for me if our roles were reversed. And the truth is, it'll be easier to try and manage Lou's fears than to face my own.

'Auntie Hols!' Small fists hammer on my front door, at the same time as my name is called out, and I can't help smiling as I open it, even before Stan hurls himself into my arms and gives me the sort of hug I firmly believe could solve any problem. I just hope I'm right.

* * *

The kitchen is every bit as wrecked as I thought it would be, but the kids have loved making cookies as much as Lou and I used to.

The biscuits are cooling on the racks now, and to distract Flo and Stan, I've given them Tigs' special brush and he's letting them pet him and brush him without too much complaint. Smiling as I watch them, I turn to Lou, expecting her to be smiling too, but her face looks like stone.

'Are you okay?'

'Will you show me how the rose bushes you planted for Nan and Gramps are getting on?' It's been more than ten years since I planted those bushes and I've got no idea why she's suddenly so interested in their progress, but Lou's eyes are pleading with me not to question her.

'Okay.' As I say the word, a shiver goes up my spine and I notice the pinched look on Louisa's face, and I know why she wants us to go into the garden. She's going to tell me about her results, and all the confidence I had that they'd be as good as possible has evaporated. I'm not sure how I'll even be able to follow her outside, but I know I have to.

'We'll be back in a minute, kids, Auntie Holly is just going to show me some of her flowers in the garden, but we'll be watching you through the window.' The children barely look up, and Lou knows as well as I do that the garden holds nowhere near as much appeal for them as Tigs does.

'What did the doctor say?' We're barely out of the door before I fire the question at her and I can tell by her face what the answer is going to be before she even opens her mouth, and I can't stop the tears that fill my eyes.

'It's spread much further than we hoped, which means there's no chance of a cure.' Lou somehow manages to get the whole sentence out and then her chin starts to wobble, just before she bursts into tears. We're both crying and I hold on to her, but the truth is she's holding me up too. This can't be happening. I can't lose Lou; she's everything to me.

I don't know how long we stay like that, but eventually Lou recovers enough to tell me more about what her doctors have said, including the potential prognosis and the treatment plan.

'What can I do?' It's a stupid question, because nothing I can do will make this go away and that's all either of us want.

'I don't know.' Lou glances towards the French windows, where Stan and Flo are visible on the other side, still lavishing attention on Tigs. 'I can't leave them Holly, they need me, they need their mum.'

'You're not going anywhere.' I'm saying it because I desperately want it to be true, but Louisa shakes her head and grabs hold of my arm.

'Don't Hols, please. I need your help.'

'How?' Something in her face has changed; there's a look of determination I've never seen before and, whatever it is, I know she won't take no for an answer.

'Tom isn't going to manage on his own.'

'You know I'll be there for him for anything he needs.' My throat is burning with the urge to cry again, but I'm no good to Lou if I'm constantly in tears, so I blink as hard as I can to try and keep them at bay.

'I know, but he won't want to be on his own forever. He's not cut out for it. He's gone from one relationship to another and there'll come a day when he'll want to meet someone else. I'm scared that when he does he'll make the wrong decision. I'll get no say in who's going to raise my children and the thought of who that might be terrifies me.'

'Lou, I know you must feel as if you can't think straight, but none of this is important right now. You're talking about what-ifs and maybes that might never happen. Tom couldn't even bear to contemplate life without you when we spoke about it before, so he's hardly likely to rush out and start a new relationship.' I want to promise her that even if he does, it will be years away, because the chemo she's about to start will work its magic and hold the cancer at bay for much longer than the average person gets. I can't accept a scenario where that isn't the case, but I know she doesn't want empty platitudes, and she squeezes my arm hard.

'Just because Tom said he wouldn't want anyone else, doesn't mean it's true. Look what happened when Jess died. No one thought that Jack would be living with someone else so quickly, but then he moved Megan in. She seems like a nice enough woman, but there's no knowing who Tom might pick. I can't risk that for Stan and Flo, I need to know that they're going to be okay.' Lou holds my gaze and I know nothing I do or say will stop her fixating on this.

Our cousin, Jess, was killed in a car accident when she had her two-year-old son strapped into the back seat. We were all so grateful he'd survived unscathed, but it was a shock to discover that within nine months her fiancé, Jack, had moved his new girlfriend into the family home. He'd seemed completely devoted to Jess, and I would have bet my house that he wouldn't move on for years, if at all. Yet less than a year after she'd died, he had a whole new life. So Louisa knows it can happen.

I know Lou needs me to promise I'll help, but how the hell am I supposed to help her plan for her husband moving on, while she's still around? Especially as I don't want to give her any scope to believe we'll be okay without her and to even think about giving up. She needs to have every reason to keep going no matter how tough the treatment gets. Even as the thought enters my head, I realise how selfish I'm being, but I can't help it.

'You don't need to worry about any of that, you just need to focus on the treatment so you can be here for as long as possible. Nothing else matters.'

'I can't focus on anything, not until I have a—'

'Plan B?' I ask and Lou nods. She mentioned having a Plan B for Tom meeting someone else when she first got diagnosed, but I thought focusing on that had been borne out of shock. I knew she'd want a Plan B for the children, but I can't help thinking she's fixating on the wrong things. I can see she's serious, though, and I doubt there's anything I can do or say to change her mind.

'See, you know me better than anyone, and if I'm not here to make sure Tom doesn't do anything stupid I need to be able to rely on you. I can't bear Stan and Flo going through what we did, especially as it could be even worse for them if the wrong person comes into their lives. Please, Hols. I need to know you'll make sure that never happens.'

I nod, understanding exactly what she means without the need for her to expand. However much our parents let us down, we knew that in their own twisted way they loved us, their addiction just had them in a stronger grip. We never had to live with a stand-in parent who resented our existence, the way we feared Dad's girlfriends would have done if any of them had stuck around for long enough. We also had grandparents we could rely on. Flo and Stan don't have that, but they do have a father who knows how to put them first, something we never had. I need to help Lou see that, but right now I know what she needs from me most of all is my support, and it's as unconditional as my love for her and the children. 'What do you want me to do?'

'I need you to make me another promise.' I hold my breath as I wait for her to continue, but whatever it is I'll find a way.

'I want you to make sure that when I'm gone, Tom picks the right kind of person, and I want you to help me to start laying the foundations for that while I'm still here.'

'How are we going to do that?' I want to tell her it's a crazy idea, but she needs me to be there for her and there was never any doubt that I would be, because I understand why she needs to believe she can influence Tom's future decisions. Her sole focus since the children arrived has been to protect them from getting hurt. She can't do anything about the fact that they're going to lose her, so in her mind the next best thing is having some kind of say into who takes her place. What she can't seem to understand is that those are impossible shoes to fill, and that Tom would never allow anyone into the children's lives if he thought it would be detrimental to them in any way. Her thoughts aren't rational and I'm probably the only person who'd understand why she feels she has to do this.

'I don't know yet, but when I work it out, just promise me you'll be on board.'

'I promise.' Lou hugs me tight and whispers a thank you into my ear, before turning to head back towards the house. I've still got no idea how she thinks this is going to work, but it doesn't matter, because it won't have to. The treatment will do what it's supposed to, and in the meantime, I'll go along with whatever she wants, because she's right, I do know her better than anyone else, and there's nothing in the world I wouldn't do if she asked me to. Nothing.

# 11

## LOUISA

*Do the things you want to now.* That was the advice Mr Whitelaw gave me, which feels impossible to follow, but I know I have to try to find a way to make the most of every day I have left with the people I love. So much of my time is taken up with thoughts of the future, and of trying to safeguard the children once I'm gone, but what Tom said yesterday made me realise I'm letting the here and now drift right past me as a result. Although it took another row about the future for us to finally make some plans for the present.

'I want to talk to you about what happens when I'm gone.' It was a subject I'd tried broaching before but Tom has always refused to acknowledge that I'm dying. As if saying it out loud is what makes it real, rather than the results of the tests and scans I've had, all that hard evidence that my impending death is now a certainty. I was more determined than ever not to let him shut me down, psyching myself up in an attempt to follow the advice I'd been given online to be open and honest with Tom about my concerns for the children.

'Lou, please, I don't want...' He stopped then, left unable to finish his sentence as he has so often been lately and that's when I lost it.

'Do you think I want to talk about this? Do you think I don't wish I could pretend it wasn't happening? But it is, Tom, and you need to fucking well get it into your head that I'm dying.' He flinched then, because I never swear like that. At least not since having the kids. They were out with Holly; she'd taken them down to the park for Flo to practise riding her bike, and for Stan to try out his new scooter. So I knew they wouldn't overhear anything, and if I wanted to use every swear word I could think of I would, because if what we're facing doesn't deserve every expletive under the sun, I don't know what does.

'You need to put your energy into the treatment.'

'The treatment is not going to work though, is it?' I said the words slowly and deliberately, as if I was speaking to someone with only a limited grasp of English, but there was a vicious edge to my tone too, because I was losing my patience. I was directing all of my anger at my husband, even though I knew that wasn't where it belonged. I was angry at the situation and frustrated as hell that I couldn't seem to make him understand how important planning for the future was to me, even though I wouldn't be here to see it. He knows me, and he should understand that, but all he wanted to do was keep grasping at the straws Mr Whitelaw had already set fire to. There is no cure, I'm not going to survive this, but for some reason Tom was still trying to pretend that I am. I wasn't going to give up on the conversation again, though. 'The treatment will buy me a few more months, a year or so at best. I haven't got time to waste, putting off conversations about the future. I need to have them now, no matter how difficult they might be.'

'But you are wasting time, because all you want to focus on is what happens afterwards. How many more days have you got with the kids? With me and Holly? Are you going to do something to make the most of that time, or do you want to spend all of it talking about what happens when it's too late for us all to be together?' There was a flash of anger in Tom's eyes too, but it wasn't the look he gave me that made me gasp, it was the fact he was finally acknowledging how quickly time is running out. And it was the first time I understood the danger of focusing too much on what happens after I die, instead of making the most of the time I have left. But I knew there had to be a compromise.

'You're right.' My words clearly took Tom by surprise, and his shoulders dropped in response. 'Time is running out, and I do need to make the most of it, but it also means we've got to have those difficult conversations while we still can. How about we talk while the kids aren't here, and then tomorrow we do something fun together and we don't have to talk about anything to do with me dying?'

'I can't bear it, Lou.' Tom bit his lip, but he didn't walk away, like he did the last time I raised the subject, when he ended up slamming out of the room.

'Neither can I, but we've got no choice.'

He nodded and straightened his shoulders, but I could tell he was trying not to cry, because I was too. 'What do you want to talk about?'

'I want to talk about everything, from where the kids will go to secondary school, to whether it might be a good time to finally consider getting them a dog to help them through their grief. I want to talk about my funeral too.' There was something else huge I wanted to talk about, but I knew I needed to bide my time to avoid Tom shutting down again. Now that he's finally started to open up, I've got to take this at a pace he can cope with, and that particular subject will have to wait.

Tom flinched for a second time in response to my mention of

the funeral, before he nodded. 'Okay, we can talk, but for every difficult conversation we have, I want us to plan at least one fun thing in return. They don't all need to happen straight away, we can spread them over weeks, months even.' He gave me a hopeful look then and I knew what he was doing, mapping out a future to give us both hope. If I had things planned with the children, it would give me all the more reason to strive to be here. I understood his logic, but I've known from the moment I was diagnosed that I'll do whatever it takes to be here for as long as possible for my children's sake, and for Tom and Holly too. The difference between us, is that I've already accepted I have no control over how long I'll get to stick around, but Tom isn't there yet and it wasn't a battle I needed to fight right at that moment. We'd made enough progress for one day and the energy I had to stand my ground was already flagging.

'You've got yourself a deal, Mr Forbes. We'd better shake on it.' I felt my shoulders relax just a tiny bit, as I held out my hand and Tom smiled, rolling his eyes at me. We might not be at a place of total honesty yet, but it was a step in the right direction, towards trying to have the most important conversations of all. I've just got to pick the right moment, but it wasn't yesterday, and it won't be today either. Today is all about the fun things we agreed to plan and they're starting right now.

'Are you ready?' Tom plants a kiss on the top of my head as he comes into the room and I nod. We're setting off on a mini adventure, just the four of us, and for once I'm determined to focus on the moment and not let the chance of making special memories pass any of us by.

\* \* \*

'Is it nearly midnight?' Stan widens his eyes as he asks the question, and I have to smile as Tom shoots me a look. These past couple of months we've had to do battle with Stan at bed time, when it's still light outside, and for a while he kept coming downstairs long after we'd said good night. One evening in late May, at about nine o'clock, when the sun was just setting, he came down and announced that he was 'not at all tired, not even a little bit'. Tom responded by telling him it was very late, and that the setting sun meant it was nearly midnight. He's clearly taken this as fact and I wonder how Tom is going to handle his question.

'Not quite, darling, but sometimes it's way past bedtime by the time the sun sets. In the summer the sun doesn't set until very late, but it will be autumn soon and by then the sun will almost be setting when you get home from school.' It's a simple explanation that Stan should be able to grasp, yet it hits me like a physical blow. *It will be autumn soon.* I've always loved the changing of the seasons, the shift from one to the next, but it suddenly terrifies me because there's a chance I won't be here by the time autumn comes. Forcing myself to push the thought away, I don't allow it to take up residence in my head. I promised myself and Tom that this day would be all about the present, not the future.

'Can I open the new paints?' Until a moment ago, Flo had her head leant against my shoulder, but she looks up at me now, her eyes shining with excitement.

'Of course you can, sweetheart, we need to start painting if we're going to capture the sunset.' I help her open the lids of the paints, tipping some into each of the four plastic paint trays Tom carried up the hill with the rest of the art supplies. There are four blank canvases too, which can be slotted together and displayed on the wall once the artwork is complete. The idea came courtesy of Holly, but when I asked her if she wanted to come with us, she insisted this should be a moment for just the four of us. When I tried to argue, she joked that she'd only show me up if our work was displayed side by side, and I stuck out my tongue in response, both of us laughing. It felt so good to be teasing one another the way we always used to, and I'm determined to cling on to those moments of normality whenever I can.

'The sky looks like fire.' Flo is smiling, the light creating a kind of orange glow around her. I love the way she looks at things, and I'm thrilled that the sunset is as spectacular as it is tonight. It's stunning, and the chances are that Flo will remember it, even without the aid of our artwork to give her a nudge. Tom is busy snapping photographs, capturing me and the children against the sunset, and the two of them sitting next to me as we start to paint.

'I think Stan could do with your help, Daddy,' I call over to him, spotting the signs of our son getting frustrated that the paint won't stay on his brush, which is hardly surprising given how much he's overloaded it.

'I'm coming.' Tom heads over and sits down, squeezing Stan between us, with Flo on my other side, and within minutes the three of them are concentrating on their paintings, but I don't start mine straight away. Instead, I watch them all, wanting to soak in the moment, as the glorious light of the sunset dances on their cheeks. These are my beloveds, the family I always wanted and I'm so grateful I got the chance to create it, even if the idea of leaving them is breaking my heart into a million pieces. Taking a deep breath, I finally take hold of my paintbrush and apply the first slick of paint to the canvas, because that's why we're here, to make memories they can all hold on to, when I'm finally forced to let them go.

\* \* \*

Watching the sunset with the children was even more wonderful than I'd hoped it would be, and for a precious few moments I was completely absorbed by the present, but I was jolted back to the horrors that are just around the corner when I checked my phone on the way home. There was confirmation of an appointment to choose a wig, for when the chemo makes me lose my hair, as it almost certainly will. I'm acutely aware of time running out again, but for a different reason this time. I need to tell the children and my parents what is going on, because there's no way I'll be able to hide it and I want the news to come from me. As soon as I get home and the children are in bed, I go back online, posting a message in The Grapevine forum asking for advice about how to break the news to loved ones.

> I haven't felt ready to tell my parents or my children yet that I have incurable cancer. I've been told I could have as little as a couple of months, depending on how I respond to treatment. I know I'm going to have to break the news to the people I love once I start the chemo, as I won't be able to hide it, so any advice you have on how you approached it would be very gratefully received.

I re-read my post, amazed at how normal I've made it sound, as if this is something everyone has to go through, when it's anything but. Scrolling back to my previous posts, I check whether there are any new responses, hoping that someone will have some incredible advice about how to ensure my children aren't ruined by my death, but all the new messages are variations on a theme, and the one from @melanomawarrior66 sums it up.

> The only answer to this is to talk to your husband and tell him how much it worries you. If you trust him, and he can make

you promises about what he'll do if and when he gets a new partner, it might help you to feel less panicked. You need your strength for the treatment and focusing on this might drain that. Speak to him and take care of yourself, it all sounds very tough xx

It's a lovely thoughtful comment; some of the others aren't nearly so gently worded, but they all have the same message. I need to talk to Tom, and for a moment, I'm tempted to do it now, despite the fact that it's only been a day since my last attempt to talk to him ended in an argument. But I know I need to pick my moment, so that he doesn't refuse to discuss even the possibility of him one day finding someone else. It was hard enough getting him to discuss anything to do with me no longer being around, and I don't want us to go straight back to square one by rushing it. I'll bide my time, but not for long, as I can't risk even the tiniest chance of leaving it too late to have the most important conversation we'll ever have to have.

**12**

## TOM

I've always loved watching Lou, from the day we met, when I
found my eyes drawn to her again and again. One of the first
things I noticed was the way she threw her head back when she
laughed, really committing to the feeling, instead of worrying
about how she might look. She never needed to worry about that,
because how she looked was beautiful, and not just on the
outside. When she laughed, I could see the joy in her eyes; it was
infectious and I struggled to look away.

Now, almost fifteen later, I still love watching her, but these
last few weeks have changed everything. When I watch her now, I
find myself looking for evidence that they've got her diagnosis
wrong. If she seems like she's glowing with health, that must
mean she can't have cancer, except I'd be lying if I tried to pretend
there's a glow. She looks exhausted, the dark circles under her
eyes spelling out how little she's sleeping right now. I'm not doing
much better, but when I do drift off, I often wake with a start. Lou
is hardly ever in bed beside me and, on the rare occasions that
she is, I can see the light from her phone reflected on her face.
She's spending hours online and I can't blame her, I am too. It's

easy to believe the internet has the answer to everything, and that all you have to do is google your question. Except it isn't true. There's no miraculous cure for pancreatic cancer and I don't think that's what Lou is searching for anyway. When I asked her, she gave a deliberately vague answer that makes me feel like she's hiding something. Only I can't imagine what secret she feels she needs to keep from me now.

'Why are you staring at me?' She narrows her eyes as she looks up from her phone and catches me watching her.

'I just like looking at you, I always have.' I smile, but the ache in my chest never seems to lift these days, and I don't want to admit that I'm terrified that a time might come soon when I won't have the chance to look at her any more.

'I'm a mess.' Lou tucks a strand of honey blonde hair behind her ear. 'But I've got a feeling it's about to get much worse.'

'It might not be as bad as you think.' Even as I'm saying the words I want to stuff them back down my throat. We're sitting in the waiting room and she's about to go in for her first chemo session, so why the hell am I trying to feed my wife that kind of bullshit? We both know the treatment is going to suck, we've been warned by Mira who came to see us at home yesterday. I freaked out when Lou told me that Mira had suggested coming to our house. I'd read through all the information she gave us when Lou was first diagnosed, and from what I could make out Macmillan nurses only did home visits as part of a patient's end of life care.

'Why's she coming here?' My tone was aggressive, like I was spoiling for a fight, and in that moment, I was prepared to have one. I wouldn't accept that's where we were, and if Mira even tried to suggest it, I'd happily slam the door in her face. I might finally have agreed to talk to Lou about some of the things she wants to ensure will happen once she's gone, but I'm not ready to accept that the treatment won't buy us a lot more time and that she's a long way off from needing palliative care. Thankfully Lou's response to my question was like a lead weight lifting off my chest.

'She doesn't usually do home visits, but she's going to see a friend in Little Halsham and, as it's only four miles away, she asked if she could pop in for a chat.' Lou had rolled her eyes. 'It's probably because I haven't made another appointment to see her. She's been lovely, but I've got enough appointments already, without adding optional ones.'

'Did she say what she wants to talk about?' The icy fear that never seems too far away these days gripped my spine again. I wasn't sure I could believe Mira's story about visiting a friend in a neighbouring village, but surely she wouldn't turn up on our doorstep to bring us more bad news. I couldn't imagine there was anything worse someone could say than what we'd already been told, but then again, a few weeks ago, I could never have imagined our lives would be devastated in this way. It's like a bomb has gone off.

As it turned out, the reason for Mira's visit seemed to be about helping Lou to prepare for what the chemo might bring, and so that I would know what to expect too. Given that we now know the harsh reality, all my talk about it not being as bad as Lou might expect is even more unforgiveable and I'm so sorry. I wish I could take this from her, and that it was me going through it instead. I'm not just saying that to try and be some kind of hero, because I know it's not a game of pass the parcel, I really mean it. A world without Lou will affect far more people than a world without me, and I can't imagine any version of me without her. So I'm not even going to try. I won't do it until I'm forced to.

'My hair is going to fall out and I'm going to be so sick. You know how much I hate being sick.' Lou takes a shuddering breath, and I'm tempted to grab her hand and make a run for the doors, away from this room where everyone around us is waiting for treatment. Some of them are clearly old hands, with coping mechanisms to get them through the torture that's to come. One woman next to us, who looks to be in her mid-fifties, is knitting, the click-clack of the needles relentless. She hasn't stopped once since we arrived, and I suspect it's because she doesn't want the time or space to think. Her head is covered by a bandana and her eyebrows and lashes are missing. She's like a mirror of all the fears Lou has for herself. Opposite her, a young lad who can't be much more than about twenty is watching his phone. Every so often he laughs at something on the screen, and I wonder if I could be anywhere near as stoic in his shoes. He is painfully thin and is seated in a wheelchair; a girl of about his age has her head pressed against his shoulder as they laugh together at whatever it is they're watching. I'm useless compared to this young couple, and it feels as though I forgot how to laugh or smile when Mr Whitelaw explained just how extensively Lou's cancer had spread. But I need to say something to try and reassure my wife, and this time I take her hand.

'I'll stay with you if you're sick, I promise I won't leave you alone.' She nods and I let out a long breath, grateful that I seem for once to have said the right thing. No one likes being sick, but I know why it scares Lou so much. When her father was in the heaviest phase of drinking he almost died choking on his own vomit. It was only because Lou and Holly came back early from their grandparents' house that they found him in time. They were able to clear his airways and raise the alarm, at just eleven years old. No child should ever have to see something like that, and it's no surprise she's carried a phobia of being sick for the last three decades as a result. She struggled with that more than anything else during her pregnancies, and she was scared of being alone until her morning sickness had passed.

'I need to talk to you about something.' Lou is holding my gaze, and I already know this is another conversation I don't want to have. Ever since the C word was mentioned, she's been pushing to talk about her death, and what comes after that. I know it's hurt her when I've refused to do it, but I've been terrified that if we even consider the possibility, we'll be creating some kind of self-fulfilling prophecy. I wanted to focus on a very different outcome, visualising the treatment doing what it's supposed to do and holding the cancer at bay for as long as possible. It was inevitable that Lou would lose patience with me trying to fob her off. I don't blame her for feeling frustrated, especially because however positively I try to think, even I've got to face the fact that we haven't got forever, or anything like it. Yet I still feel the fight or flight kicking in every time she wants to talk about the 'after', and that hasn't changed despite the conversations we've started to have.

'Aren't you going to ask what I want to talk about?'

'Maybe now's not the time; it's your first chemo treatment and that's enough for one day.'

'I think I should be the judge of that, don't you?' Lou's tone is tight, and the pitch of her voice is raised, making the woman next to us finally pause the click-clack rhythm of her knitting needles.

'Let's at least wait until we get home.' I don't care if the knitting lady wants to eavesdrop on our conversation, that's not what bothers me, and I don't care if I cry in front of strangers, because it's happened so many times already. Yesterday I even cried in the queue at Sainsbury's, buying the conditioner Lou always uses and wondering whether she's ever going to get through the bottle, let alone need me to buy her another one. What bothers me about having the conversation now is the chance of me upsetting Lou and making the experience of her first treatment even worse.

'I don't want to wait, I need to talk to you about what will happen when you meet someone else.'

'For Christ's sake Lou, how can you even think about that?' I feel like a total bastard for snapping at her when she's going through so much, but this is something she started mentioning a few days ago and she can't seem to understand that it's the last thing on my mind.

'There's no point pretending it's not going to happen because it will.' Lou's mouth is set in a grim line, but she can't stop her chin from wobbling, the way it always does when she's about to cry. It's hurting her so much to imagine this scenario, and she doesn't need to, because I don't want anyone else. I want Lou and if I can't have her, I'd rather be on my own forever. I've told her this already, but it's like I'm not even speaking. I try again anyway.

'I don't want anyone, if I can't have you.'

'That's because I'm still here. It will be different when I'm gone.' She swallows hard enough for me to hear it, and I just want to hold her and keep repeating what I've just said until she finally realises I mean it. But I don't think it will matter how many times I say it, so I try a different tack.

'What do you want me to say, Lou? That I'm going to replace you the moment you're gone? Is that what you really think of me? Of us?' I'm not angry at Lou, I'm broken-hearted that she feels so replaceable, but the rage I feel about the situation is threatening to erupt too.

'I'm not saying it's going to be the day after my funeral, but it will happen and that's okay, I want you to move on.' The catch in Lou's voice suggests otherwise, but she swallows hard again. 'What I don't want is for you to pick the wrong person. I won't be here to make sure of that, but if we talk about what will be important for the kids, in terms of anyone you do bring home, then maybe that will be the next best thing.'

'Lou please don't, this is not—' I'm desperately trying to find a way to end the conversation, but she cuts me off.

'Shall I start? The most important thing is that she's kind to Stan and Flo, and that—'

'Lou, no! I'm not going to talk about meeting someone else, because I don't want to, not now, *not ever*.' It's my turn to cut her off. I can't do this, I'm not ready and the truth is I don't think I ever will be. I'm a selfish coward, because I can see how much she needs this, but she has to believe the doctors can find a treatment that holds back the cancer for long enough to allow her to see the kids grow up. I need to believe it too, and that by then some genius in a lab somewhere will have found a way to get rid of it all together. We need to put all of our energy into holding on, not planning for a future I can't bear to contemplate, and so I take the most cowardly way out possible and remove myself from the situation.

'I'll go and get us both a coffee.' I don't wait for her to answer, and when she calls out to me as I walk away, I pretend not to hear, catching the eye of the woman who was knitting instead. She shakes her head, and I can't tell whether she feels sorry for me, or thinks I'm the biggest idiot alive, but I don't care either way. The only person whose opinion matters to me is Lou, and I suspect that right now she doesn't like me very much. I knew cancer was toxic, spreading with an indiscriminate cruelty and poisoning everything it comes into contact with. But I had no idea just how widespread that contamination could become, or that it would do its best to poison the relationship between me and my wife when we should be making the most of every second we have together. By the time I reach the coffee machine the rage that's been threatening to boil over suddenly explodes and I punch the wall next to it so hard, I can hear the crack as the bones of my hand make contact with the rock-hard surface. And the weird thing is that I'm grateful for the physical pain, because just for a moment it relieves the emotional torture, but I know it won't last. There's nothing I can do to stop it coming back and there's nothing I can do to stop my children from eventually losing their mum either, or to stop me from losing the only woman I've ever loved. And the thought makes me want to punch the wall again and again.

# 13

## LOUISA

Tom has broken the knuckles on his right hand. He came back from getting the coffee at my first chemo session and I could see how swollen his hand was straight away, coupled with the way he was wincing, but he tried to pass it off as nothing. It was only when one of the medical staff spotted it and insisted he get it checked out that he admitted he'd knocked it against something. I wish I could believe that was true, but I know it isn't. He's punched something. Not a person, but a wall or a door maybe. He has such an ingrained sense of justice, it's what driven him to do what he does and to expose the things he feels are unfair, even when it's put his own life at risk, and he just can't accept the injustice of my cancer diagnosis. I'm with him on that, but I haven't got time to be angry any more, there's too much that needs to be done, and sadness has been my overriding emotion ever since this started.

Tears come so easily now. Just brushing Flo's hair this morning made me cry, realising how long it has grown since the photograph taken at Christmas that faces me on the dresser. I couldn't help wondering, as I began to plait her hair ready for school, whether I'll be around by this December. Christmas always feels like a whirlwind of activity, where I barely have time to take it in. My phone has over thirty-five thousand photographs on it, because I snap every moment, and looking back at the Christmas photographs is my favourite part of January. It's what gets me through the grey days, and I can almost take in the joy of the celebration more after it's over and everything's gone quiet, than I can at the time. I've never minded the frenetic pace of December, because it's about fitting in everything that the kids love, but as I looked at that photograph this morning, I know things are going to be different this year, even if I do make it. The chances of me being able to keep up my usual pace are non-existent and, even if I could, I've realised I don't want to. I want to slow down time and take in every moment, because even if the chemo works, there's a very good chance this could be my last Christmas. When the thought struck me this morning, I couldn't blink back the tears and to my horror Flo noticed, as she turned to look at me when I'd fastened the bottom of her plait.

'Why are you crying, Mummy?' The straightforwardness of my daughter's question was such a contrast to the way adults talk to me now, skirting round the edge of what they want to ask. I've begun to drop my guard a bit about what's happening since I started the treatment last month, telling a few of my closest friends but only on the proviso that they kept it to themselves. I don't want people who have no usual investment in how my life is going, to suddenly feel the need to get involved, and the prospect of it somehow getting back to the children, or my parents, before I can talk to them myself is horrifying. I thought it might help to tell other people, so I could talk to my friends about my greatest fears, but it's like they've all been coached by Tom.

They're all focusing on 'the battle', telling me that I'm brave and strong and that if anyone can fight this thing and keep it at bay it's me. I want to tell them they're wrong on every single count and the idea of this being a fight is stupid. No one just allows cancer to take them, but it's not a fair fight and sometimes the victor is pre-determined before the start. So all their pep talks do is make me feel like a failure, because I haven't got what it takes to fight this thing and win. None of them will allow me to be honest about the fact that there'll only be one outcome to this, so when my daughter asked such a straightforward question, I very nearly blurted out the truth to her. Instead, I took a breath and shook my head.

'My eyes are just a bit sore, darling; I'm not really crying.' Flo pursed her lips and gave me an appraising look, clearly trying to decide whether to believe me, before hitting me with another killer question.

'Can I plait your hair?' That one was like a punch to the gut and my hand instinctively went to my head, touching the satin turban-style hat I was wearing to hide the already obvious hair loss from the first round of chemo. The turban is turquoise blue and covered with daisies, a cheerful pattern for a miserable purpose.

'Not today, darling, we've got to get going for school, but maybe we can do it at the weekend when we've got more time.' I managed a small smile, so tight it made my cheeks hurt. I've got my wig fitting appointment soon, and I've got no idea how secure those wigs are, but maybe there'll be a way to allow Flo to try and plait my hair without the risk of her pulling the wig off and discovering the truth in the most traumatic way possible. I know I can't delay telling my children for much longer, but I've still got no idea how to do it.

The Grapevine cancer forum is more or less my only reading source now. I've always loved losing myself in novels, or escaping into a world of celebrity gossip to de-stress, but I can't focus on even the most inane of articles these days. Instead I spend all my time on there, reading about other people's journeys and talking about mine. It's the only place where I'm able to be completely honest, and I've found lots of support there. I also seem to have got myself an enemy in @booblesswonder777 who has made sniping at me a hobby, ever since my post about wanting to influence Tom's choice of future partner. Her responses to me usually disappear quite quickly, apparently reported to the site administrators by other users. I wouldn't have believed it was possible for words from a stranger on the internet to hurt me, when I'm already facing a terminal diagnosis, but it turns out they can. Her response to my question about how to break the news to the children was particularly awful.

> Just tell them. It doesn't matter how you dress this up, losing their mother is going to hurt them and only an idiot would think there's some kind of magical way around that.

The viciousness of her response literally took my breath away, and I could feel the beginnings of another panic attack starting as the words on the screen swam in front of my eyes. I had to get away, to try and stop it escalating, but once it began to subside, anger took over and, for the first time, I decided I was going to report @booblesswonder777 myself. Except by the time I got back online, her barbed words had been replaced by something else.

> This user's comment has been removed for breaching the forum's rules.

And there were lots of comments from other users underneath, criticising what @booblesswonder777 had said, and accusing her of being a troll. There were also loads of other

messages with far kinder suggestions, including this one from
@itsnotalloveryet2.

> I'm so sorry you're going through this @worriedmum1982.
> There's no easy way to have this kind of conversation, but I
> think the best advice is to keep it simple. Tell them where the
> cancer is, what your treatment will be like and any side effects
> there might be, so those things don't scare them when they
> start to happen. Be as honest as you can and perhaps tell
> them that the doctors can't make you better, but the medicine
> will help to stop things getting any worse. I truly hope it will.
> That will leave you in a good position for if and when they
> need to know more, depending on their age. If they ask if
> you're going to die, only you can decide how to answer that,
> but whatever you say you'll need to reassure them that other
> people who love them will always be there to care for them, no
> matter what happens. Sending you strength and love xx

I cried again then, but for completely different reasons. The
kindness of strangers can be every bit as a breathtaking as their
cruelty, but it is @itsnotalloveryet2's advice that I'm determined to
draw upon when I speak to my precious children, and I know I
can't put it off for much longer.

* * *

St Martin's has increasingly become my sanctuary. It's the quiet of
the place that I love the most. Like many village churches, it's
more often empty than not and I know there's little risk of me
bumping into someone I don't want to see. Right now, I need
somewhere to sit and think after my latest chemo session. When
Mr Whitelaw told me my treatment was called GemCap, it didn't

sound too bad. After all, nothing with the word *gem* in it couldn't be too awful, could it? The treatment itself is bearable, and it comes in four-weekly cycles, with a combination of medications called gemcitabine and capecitabine. I go in once a week for the first three weeks so that they can administer a drip of gemcitabine, as well as taking tablets. Then I get the fourth week off treatment, but it's nowhere near as much of a holiday as it sounds because the side effects don't seem to realise they're supposed to be on a break. I won't make it to menopause, but I'm getting all the symptoms; hot flushes, skin rashes, headaches, and a pain in my bones that I can only describe as feeling like toothache.

Sometimes I can't face the thought of having anyone come with me to chemo and I know I'll be in trouble later, because I told Tom that Holly was coming with me today, but I told Holly that Tom was. They've always been quite close, but these days they're talking far more often, and I know my lie will be found out when one of them is the first to text the other to ask how it went. But I needed to go alone. It's bad enough that I have to go through the hell of treatment, without having to drag either of them through it every time too. They're not even allowed to sit with me to keep me company, while the 'good' poison is dripped into my veins, in an attempt to hold back the bad poison of the metastatic tumours. That means all they can do to while away the time is to sit in the waiting room and think or doom scroll on their phones. I'd much rather they were out there doing stuff to try and take their minds off things, even for a bit of the time.

Tom has been keeping up the pretence that he's in the research phase of his next big project, something that happens from time to time, but I've never known him to work from home as solidly as this. And Holly seems to have sidelined work too, claiming it's a quiet time of year and she's just taking some well overdue leave. But I know the truth, they don't want to leave me alone, and they don't want to miss time that we might not get the chance to make up. I love them both for it, I really do, but it's suffocating and I have to paint on a smile far too often when I'm at home, so that I can reassure the people who mean the most to me. All of which make my now regular visits to St Martin's essential to my ability to continue with a gruelling regime of treatment. It gives me time to process everything, and the space to actually feel the things I'm feeling, without having to put on an act for anyone else's benefit.

I don't know how long I've been here, with my eyes closed, but the cool of St Martin's is even more appealing today in the midst of a heatwave. I haven't heard a sound in what feels like hours, so when I open my eyes I'm stunned to realise that Kate is standing up by the altar, silently adjusting the position of a floral display. I noticed the flowers when I arrived, smelling their sweet aroma before I even saw them. There's a wedding tomorrow, I know that from the noticeboard in the church porch, where a message reminds the bell ringers to arrive promptly at 10.45 a.m. It's almost impossible to believe that other people are celebrating new beginnings like that, and I wish I could go back to my own wedding day and relive it, and the years that followed, over and over on a never-ending loop. Except I can't, and I pinch the fleshy part of my hand, between the index finger and the thumb, to stop myself from thinking about the next 'celebration' I'll be a part of in this church. I don't want my life to be celebrated after just four decades, it's far too short a time as far as I'm concerned.

'I didn't hear you.' I call out to Kate to let her know she doesn't have to try and move silently any more, and she smiles as she turns towards me.

'I didn't want to disturb you.'

'Thank you.' I nod to emphasise my gratitude. I desperately

needed the quiet time today, and I really am thankful for the effort Kate went to in order to give it to me.

'How are you?' Kate is closing the distance between us and I'm grateful again for how normal her question sounds. There's no saccharine sweetness in her voice, and no tell-tale tilt to her head to indicate just how hopeless she thinks my situation is.

'Sad, scared, scarred, sick. There's another S word I could give you, but I'm trying to respect where we are.'

'I'm praying for you.' Kate's words could easily annoy me, but I know the intention comes from a good place and so I nod again. 'I know that's not a lot of practical use to you, but if there's ever anything I can do. Drive you to appointments, help out with Stan and Flo, school pickups. Anything, just name it.'

'That's really kind of you.' I smile again, knowing Kate's offer is genuine. It's funny the people who have stepped up to offer help and support since I've been more honest about my diagnosis, because they haven't always been the ones I'd have expected. It's only been three weeks since I've let anyone other than Tom, Holly and Kate know, but some of the people who promised to be there for anything I needed have already stopped even checking in on me. Giving them the benefit of the doubt, I might put that down to them not wanting to overwhelm me with 'how are you?' texts, but the reality is that their own lives are taking priority and I understand that too. It's just a bit humbling to realise how little you matter to almost everyone when it comes down to it. My cancer is not at the forefront of their minds, I get that. I just wish to God that it wasn't at the forefront of mine.

'I was hoping I might see you, because I've got something for you.' Kate heads to the back of the church and pulls something out of her bag, before coming back and handing me a book. Turning it over, I read the title: *The Cancer That Wouldn't Go Away*.

'I couldn't stop thinking about what you said that first day about breaking the news to the children.' Kate shook her head. 'I can't even imagine what that feels like, but I did a bit of research and I found this book. A lot of people said it helped their children understand and find a way to make the most of every day, without having to avoid the truth about what was going to happen.'

I reach out and squeeze Kate's hands, touched that someone I barely know has gone to this much trouble for me. 'Thank you.' I breathe the words out and she nods, but doesn't respond, instead giving me the space to talk about how I'm feeling and it's something else I'm incredibly grateful for.

'I just wish that Stan and Flo could take having me around for granted, but they'll never be able to do that again once I've told them.' I run a hand over the cover of the book, shutting my eyes for a moment, before opening them again. 'But I'm going to read this to them tonight. I can't keep pretending everything's okay, especially when Flo is starting to pick up on the fact that something is wrong. Telling them is going to be so hard.'

'You can do it.' Kate fixes me with a look of such certainty that I find myself nodding. I've still got no idea where I'll find the strength, but the only thing that's certain is that I don't have a choice.

# 14

## LOUISA

Stan is nestled into the crook of my arm on one side of my body, and Flo is lying pressed up against my other side, her head resting on my rib cage, probably just inches away from the site of the original tumour that is going to take me from them. When that thought entered my head, I almost pushed her away, scared that the evil inside me might somehow reach her, even though I know it's a completely irrational thought. Cancer isn't catching, but the evil will still get to her when I break the news to them. I've already read three books; usually after one they start wheedling for more and I always give in. I normally draw the line at two, but not today. Tom is sitting in a chair beside the bed and every time I look at him, he gives me an encouraging smile. We've discussed the need for us to tell the children and have both agreed that reading the book Kate gave me will be the best way to introduce the subject, but I still feel paralysed. That's why I'm about to reach for a fourth book, which has nothing to do with cancer, but then Tom intervenes, picking up the book that is lying on the table next to me.

'Why don't I read this one next?' He gives me a level look and

I raise my eyebrows in surprise. It's been so hard for Tom to accept my prognosis, and I didn't think he'd have the strength to be the one to tell the children, but then I'm not sure I do either.

'Okay.' It's all I can manage, and my stomach is already churning because of what's about to happen. In the next few moments my children's lives will be changed forever.

'What's can-ker?' Flo's reading is coming on leaps and bounds, and her teachers have told us she's reading at a level way above expectations for her age, but she still sounds out the second C in the word I hate more than any other, as a hard sound. I don't want her to be able to pronounce the word properly, or to have any idea what it means. I want to protect her innocence for as long as possible. My mind seems to work overtime constantly, and another unwanted thought hits me. I won't be around to give Flo 'the talk' when the time comes. Someone else will have to tell her about periods, how to stay safe and say no, and to be there to listen if she gets her heart broken by unrequited love, the way I so often did as a teenager. But those are heartbreaks for another day. Today Tom and I have to make our children understand the meaning of the word cancer, and how drastically it's about to change all of our lives.

'It's called cancer, and Daddy's going to read you a story about it, so you'll know what it means.' As I speak, Tom slides on to the bed next to Flo, so that she's suddenly like the sandwich filling between us.

'Why?' Flo wrinkles her nose and looks from me to Tom and back again. She really is far too bright for her own good some-times, and she's clearly picking up on this story having far more significance than *Sir Charlie Stinky Socks* did.

'Because Mummy is poorly and the thing making her poorly is called cancer.' I can hear the wobble in Tom's voice and I reach across and squeeze his hand.

'It is like a cold?'

'I wish it was.' The blistering rawness of Tom's pain is spelled out in those words and I feel it right down to my soul. Almost any other illness would be preferable to this, but it turns out you don't get to choose the form of torture that's inflicted on you.

'Mummy?' Flo's lips start to quiver and there's no doubt now she knows something is wrong, but this isn't the way it's supposed to go. So instead of giving in to the tears that are already burning my eyes, I paint on the biggest smile I can manage.

'It's okay, darling, everything's okay and you don't need to worry about anything, because you're always going to be looked after and loved to the moon and back again.'

'Me too! Me too!' It's what I say to the children every night and Stan's demand to be included makes my smile genuine. I let go of Tom's hand, so that I can hug them both close to me, squeezing so tight that Stan is already trying to wriggle free. I can see Tom furiously wiping his eyes, and I focus on my son in an attempt to stave off my own tears for long enough to get through this.

'Of course it means you too, baby.'

'I'm not a baby, I'm a big boy.' Stan gives me such a serious look that I can't help laughing. I love these two little people so much it hurts, but if the pain of leaving them is the price I have to pay for the privilege of having shared their lives, even if it wasn't for nearly long enough, then I'd willingly pay it again and again.

'Right then, shall we read this story?' Swallowing hard, I ease the book out of Tom's hands, knowing that he won't be able to get through it, because he's still wiping the tears from his eyes and turning away in a desperate attempt not to let the children see just how upset he's become. Opening the book, I begin to read, offering up a silent prayer at the same time. I still don't really believe in all of that, but seeing as Kate gave me the book, if there is a merciful God up there somewhere, listening to what I have to say, I hope she'll have put a good word in for me. I'm not even asking for miracles that I know won't be bestowed, I'm just asking for the strength to get through reading this story, and that what it reveals to my children won't ruin their lives in the way I'm terrified it might. Either way, as I start to read, there's no turning back.

'So the doctors can't make you better?' Flo's eyes are wide. It's the fourth question she's asked since I started reading and I can almost see her brain ticking over as she tries to process the implications of what she's just said. Stan, on the other hand, seems completely unfazed, but his understanding at only just four is a world away from his sister's.

'No darling, but they're giving me some medicine that will hopefully stop the cancer getting any worse for a long time.' I'm using the words from one of the responses on The Grapevine forum and they seem to be reassuring Flo.

'I think we should make a list.' Tom finally seems to have regained control of his emotions, and he sits up as he makes the suggestion, grabbing the notebook he always keeps on his bedside table, in case he comes up with an idea for a story, or an investigation in the middle of the night and doesn't want to risk having forgotten it by the following morning.

'A Christmas list?' Stan understands the concept of that, and he grins at the idea.

'Kind of, but not quite. It's more of an all-year-round list, but of things we really want to do, rather than presents we want to get.' Tom does his best to make it sound exciting, but Stan's face falls at the idea of presents being removed from the equation. So Tom is forced to try and rescue things. 'It could be anything... like maybe a trip to Disney.'

'Yes, yes, yes!' Flo leaps up from the bed and throws her arm around his neck. 'And I want to see some baby seals, and a penguin.' Before *Sir Charlie Stinky Socks*, we were reading a book about the Antarctic, which is why those things are at the forefront of her mind.

'I want to go to the toy shop!' Stan chimes in and I have to laugh again. My children are truly brilliant, and within less than a minute he's worked out a loophole in the rules of the not-a-Christmas-list list.

'Okay, Stanny.' Tom ruffles his hair. 'And what about Mummy, what do you want to put on the list?'

'Just to spend as much time as possible with you guys.' It's a cliché, but it doesn't make the words any less true. I suspect they're probably the truest thing I've ever said, because it's the only way I want to spend my time now.

Thinking about the future has been unbearable ever since my diagnosis, but nothing has been more difficult than trying to imagine Stan and Flo's future without me. I just have to hope that all the things I've read about the ability of children to live in the moment, when someone they love is dying, turn out to be true. And, if they do, that my babies can teach me how to make the most of the days we have left too, because I don't want to miss a single one of them.

* * *

Holly texted half an hour ago to let me know that she'd got to our parents' flat and that they'd be leaving there in about twenty minutes. I waited until I got her text to start dinner, because we both know from experience that plans made with Mum and Dad don't always come to fruition. There was every chance she'd get to the flat and discover that they weren't there, because a better offer had come up, or because they'd gone on a bender and forgotten about the arrangement altogether. I'd half-hoped that would be the case on this occasion, because then I wouldn't have to tell them about the cancer.

Tom, Holly and I discussed the possibility of keeping the news from them altogether, until after it was over. It isn't like they just drop in for visits, or even check how we're doing all that often. Occasionally I get a text, but it's more likely to be asking to borrow money than enquiring about my wellbeing. In the end we decided they needed to know, despite their lack of interest in what's going on in the lives of their children and grandchildren. They'd be hurt if we didn't tell them and they found out from someone else, and deep down I think it would crush them if they didn't get the chance to say goodbye. No matter how poor their parenting has been, I don't deliberately want to hurt them.

We arranged a dinner, without telling them why, just that it was a long overdue catch up. Even that has taken some lengthy negotiation, and Mum told me how difficult it is for them to get to the village since Dad lost his licence again, after a second charge of drink driving. It was only when Holly offered to pick them up that we finally settled on a date. They only live about ten minutes from here, and they could easily get a taxi, but any obstacle can seem insurmountable to my mother, and I suspect it's her inability to cope with everyday stresses that feeds her addiction. I have no idea whether news as big as the sort I'm about to deliver will overwhelm her in the same way small problems can, or whether she'll surprise us all and be the epitome of calm in a crisis. Either way, we're about to find out.

There's pasta sauce bubbling on the side and the smell of garlic lingering in the air is almost making me feel hungry. Except I'm never hungry these days and, even if I suddenly was to rediscover my appetite, the nerves fluttering in my stomach about what's to come would soon take the edge off that. I'm still wondering if I should let them eat first and enjoy one final meal before they discover their daughter is dying, or do I get it over and done with and blurt it out the moment they walk through the door?

It might seem like a ridiculous idea to come straight out with it, maybe even cruel, but I don't think there's any way I can keep up the act that everything is okay for an hour or so after they arrive, even if they don't ask about the bandana I'm wearing. Mum won't be able to resist commenting, because she'll probably be delighted I'm embracing a more bohemian style, as she'll no doubt put it. That's how she describes the life she and Dad lead now too, which in their case equates to not having a job, or making any attempt to find one. They haven't worked since they gave up running the pub. Before he lost his licence, they were fully intending to buy an old ambulance and do it up to live in, travelling around and being 'free', as Mum describes it. Maybe she'd hoped that unburdening themselves from all responsibility would finally allow them to stop self-medicating with alcohol, but their addiction had scuppered yet another dream and now they're stuck in the flat, in a grotty part of the town they live in, above a kebab shop.

Tom has taken Flo and Stan to the cinema, because I don't want them to be here when I give my parents the news. It's always a tense time when the children have contact with my parents; I never know if Mum is going to be in one of her maudlin moods, where she'll start crying about how she wishes things could be different and how she'd love to spend more time with them. Those are the occasions when she promises to change and do whatever it takes to become the kind of grandparent my children deserve, but the commitment to change never lasts and I stopped hoping a long time ago that it would.

I can't trust my parents to contain their reactions either, or to think about what they're saying in front of the children. We can't take the risk and all the careful talking we've done to the children about the cancer will be for nothing, if they have to witness full blown hysterics from my mum. Something I think is highly likely. But when my parents arrive and discover the children aren't here, they'll immediately demand to know why, and Mum will become upset anyway, thinking that I'm keeping the children from her. Which is why I need to tell them what's wrong straight away.

The sound of Holly's car pulling on to the gravel of the driveway makes me shoot up from my seat, the nerves in my stomach fluttering up to my chest and prickling my scalp where my hair used to be. Now there are intermittent patches, which I'd need to knit together like the strands of shredded wheat in order to try and hide the baldness. Instead, I have about twenty different turban-style hats, headscarves and bandanas that I'm wearing on rotation. I've had my wig fitting now, and I'm due to collect it this week. It's really good quality, but somehow it still doesn't feel like me. My eyebrows have been micro-bladed, and I've got only got eyelashes because a lovely nineteen-year-old girl who lives in the village comes round and glues them on for me. I wanted to get all of those things in place before I looked so different to the children that they found it scary.

'Lou, it's us,' Holly calls out. She always lets herself into the house and I know there are probably some people who think that's weird, but our house has always been as open to Holly as if she lives here too. Luckily Tom has never had an issue with it, and these days I think he's just happy to know that she can pop in and check on me, if I don't answer the phone or respond to their messages.

'Oh hello, how was the drive?' I hug my parents in turn as they come into the sitting room, but Mum is already craning her neck to try and look past me. She and Dad both speak at the same time.

'Where are the children?'

'I never I thought I'd see you in a bandana, Lou. Finally loosening up, I see.'

'Can we sit down?' I gesture towards the sofa, but Mum gives me the same kind of look that Flo did when we broke the news to the children, and she knows something bad is coming.

'What's wrong?' She narrows her eyes, but the words I want to say seem to have slipped away, and all I can do is shake my head. She turns to my father instead. 'I told you, Stuart. I said there was a reason the girls were so insistent we came.'

'If this is about the drink.' My father's tone is tight. 'We've told you a hundred times, it's not a problem as far as we're concerned.'

I can smell alcohol on his breath even now and I want to shake him and tell him that it is a problem, whatever they might claim, one that Holly and I have had to suffer the fallout from our whole lives. But I still can't seem to make the words in my head come out of my mouth and it's left to Holly to respond.

'Lou has cancer, and it's incurable.'

'No!' My mother's response is an echo of Tom's reaction on the day I was first diagnosed and I know, despite everything, that her distress is genuine. She wanted to be a good mum, and she tried to get sober more times than I can count, but her addiction was always just that bit stronger than her love for us. Now it's too late; there'll never be the chance for her to try and make up for all the times she wasn't there when I needed her to be, and it's almost as if I can see the recognition of that in her tortured expression. There's nothing I can say to take the edge off this. At least when Tom reacted with the same utter denial that this was happening, when I was first diagnosed, we still had hope to cling to. I can't even offer her that. I'm going to have to tell her that there's very little the doctors can do. The treatment they can offer is already ravaging my body, and that's not something I can hide any more either. One thing I haven't shared with anyone, even the people I love the most, is my fear that the brutal chemotherapy I'm putting myself through isn't working. There's no way of knowing until I have another scan, yet somehow I can feel it. I'm desperately hoping it's just my mind playing tricks on me but I can't seem to shake the feeling that the cancer is spreading with every passing day.

'But you can't have cancer. You do everything right: you don't smoke, you eat healthily, you...' My father's sentence drifts away and his mouth falls open. All I can do is shrug in response. It feels strange to be sharing such devastating news with them, when I gave up looking to them for any kind of support decades ago. I had no idea how my parents were going to react, but it's obvious how shocked and upset they are. Mum is trying and failing to sniff back tears, and there's a muscle going in Dad's cheek, the way it always used to when he and Mum had one of their terrible rows. He's mad as hell.

'This isn't fair.' Mum is shaking her head, as if her continued refusal of what's been said can make it all go away; I only wish it were true. Then she turns to look at Dad again. 'This should be one of us, Stuart, not Lou. Both of the girls have had cancer, but we're the ones who've treated our bodies like shit for decades. It should be one of us!'

I can tell she's getting angry now too, even before she hammers her fists against Dad's chest, and for once he doesn't argue back.

'You're right, it should, but it isn't and there's nothing we can do to change that.' He holds Mum tight against him, and looks towards me. 'What we need to know is what we can do, and I promise we won't let you down this time. We'll try a different doctor, there must be something they can do and whatever it is, we'll help you find it.'

'Thank you.' I finally manage to speak, but my words are barely more than a whisper. Right now, in this moment, I know Dad means what he's saying with all of his heart, but I already know they won't be able to keep the promise he's just made. They'll turn to the same source of comfort they've always sought refuge in, choosing oblivion over the pain my news is causing them. Even if, against all odds, they manage to break the habit of both their lifetimes and stay off the drink, they'll still break the promise, because there's no doctor who can change my prognosis, and no miracle cure just waiting to be found. All I can do is hope that I'm wrong about the chemo, because if it isn't working, I'm already living on borrowed time.

## 15

## HOLLY

I wasn't sure whether Lou would come today, and despite organising this event, I wasn't sure I would either. Holding a fundraising afternoon tea and silent auction in the village hall and gardens of St Martin's church has become an annual event since I was given the all-clear from breast cancer. I put it on the first year because I wanted to raise funds as a way of showing my gratitude for making it through to the other side and it's been a great success from the start, with support from Kate and some of the others who are involved with the church. I've always donated the funds raised to cancer charities, and the Castlebourne village trust, which helps maintain services for the local community, including the village hall and the church itself. It only seemed fair, given that I couldn't host the event without accessing the venue, but lately I've been questioning more and more what the word 'fair' even means. None of what is happening right now is fair. Lou has been such a great supporter of the event ever since it started, and I don't think it would have happened without her. We've raised more than fifteen thousand pounds for cancer charities over the years, but none of that has done anything to help

Lou. That can't be fair, and it's why I've been struggling to find the will to go ahead with it, but that's not why I thought Lou might give it a miss this year.

She's been doing her best to keep the cancer quiet, and I assumed she wouldn't come. It's only in the last two days that she's broken the news to the children and our parents. So far, the kids seem okay, but I don't think they're anywhere near realising the implications of it yet. It was a different story for our parents. Taking them to Lou's house felt like I was walking prisoners from death row to the execution chamber, without them having any idea of what was to come.

They'd both been drinking before I picked them up, I could see it in the high colour on their cheeks and their attempts to hide it by crunching on extra strong mints only made it all the more obvious. They weren't drunk, though. I suspect it takes a lot to do that these days, and they were chatting happily, Mum talking about how glad she was that she was finally getting a chance to see the kids, and how it had been far too long since she'd seen any of us. On a different day I might have responded that it was a two-way street, and she could make more of an effort to visit, but I probably wouldn't have, even if I hadn't been trying to keep things light. Lou and I both gave up the battle to try and make our parents see sense years ago. It suits Mum to pretend she can't understand why we're not closer than we are, but she knows why, and me reminding her of that just before she got the news about Lou would have been unnecessarily cruel.

I tried to say as little as possible on the journey, worried that I'd blurt it out before we got there, thinking that would make the situation worse, but that wouldn't have been possible. I knew they'd be upset, because they were when I got my diagnosis, and it was during my treatment that Mum made her last attempt to get sober. She'd wanted to take me to Florence, promised me that she was going to do it when my treatment was over. I'd always wanted to go, ever since an art teacher had told my class about the opportunity to go on a trip to the Galleria dell'Accademia, to see the works of Michelangelo. I'd never been the sort of child to beg my parents for stuff, mostly because I'd known it was futile, but this time I couldn't help myself.

I tried everything to make it happen, even getting myself a part-time job in the local fish and chip shop, at the grand old age of thirteen, when I'm not sure it was even legal for me to work there. I managed to put a deposit down for the trip, but despite getting covered in burns from splashes of hot oil, I just couldn't earn enough to cover the whole thing. My teacher approached me, when I said I wouldn't be going after all, and said, very gently, that there was a hardship fund the school could tap into for pupils whose families couldn't afford to send them on trips. I should have said yes and begged her to see if I qualified for help, but I couldn't bear the thought of the school staff talking about why we needed to access a fund like that, when my parents ran a busy pub. They must have known Mum and Dad were drinkers, the whole town did, but they always did a just good enough job of holding it together to avoid the involvement of social services. At least that's probably how it looked from the outside, but the truth is that Lou and I were the ones who held it together for ourselves and, if we hadn't had each other, things would have been very different.

Lou always says I'm the one who mothered her, and I tried my best to fill that gap, but she was always there for me too. I cried every day of the week that I should have been in Florence, and Lou would come and sit on my bed and talk about all the trips we were going to take together, when we had wonderful jobs and enough money to go wherever we wanted. We were going to go to Florence, of course, and to Paris, Barcelona, Amsterdam and

Rome. After that we'd travel beyond Europe to South America, to trek through the jungle, and up to Alaska and Canada, before heading to Africa on a safari. We were going to go everywhere, and I often wonder if those conversations are what gave Lou the wanderlust that led to her job. Even then, she could paint crystal clear pictures of any location with just her words, and she ended up visiting all of those places and many more. I still haven't even been to Florence yet.

Predictably, Mum fell off the wagon even before I got the all-clear, according to her because it was just too stressful to attempt to quit while I was ill. Once I got the news that I was cancer free, there were lots of reasons for Mum to celebrate and of course she couldn't do that without a drink. I should have taken myself off to Florence then, but I didn't, because I didn't want to go alone. If I'd asked Lou, she'd have gone with me in a heartbeat and paid for the whole thing knowing her, but I didn't do that either. I didn't want to admit to anyone, not even my sister, that my marriage to Jacob was falling apart and that I didn't think there was any way of saving it.

I should have swallowed my pride and taken the chance to spend that time with Lou. Even without knowing what I do now, I was aware back then that my own cancer might one day come back, and I was terrified that the tests would reveal some kind of gene mutation that would put Lou at risk too. There were plenty of warnings to seize the day, but I didn't, and the fear that might have driven me to do so was eased with each check-up, which moved further and further apart until I only got seen once a year. The lack of any kind of genetic mutation, and the clear mammogram for Lou, was all the reassurance any of us needed that she was going to escape this dreaded disease, and any thoughts of seizing the day drifted away. Except she didn't escape it, and now it's too late for us to have all of those epic adventures we promised we'd have together one day.

I don't care about the big things, though, it's all the small, shared moments I'm going to miss, and my heart contracts at the thought of not being able to phone my sister for a chat or send her a silly video I've found online. Our lives are so enmeshed. After Jacob left, all I had was a steady, well-paid job that I didn't really enjoy, and a broken heart. The volunteering helped, and it still does, but it was Lou who mended my heart. She included me in her family as it continued to grow, and if I had to swap being Stan and Flo's auntie for the chance to have had my own children, I wouldn't even consider it for a second. I adore them, and being a part of the family Lou has created has brought me so much joy. I don't want to think about myself in all of this, because it's Lou who's losing everything, but I can't help wondering how things are going to change when she's not here. She's the glue that binds me to Tom and the children, and I've got no idea how the dynamic will change without her. Will he still want me around to play such a big part in the children's lives? And what if Lou's right, and he does meet someone else? Someone who doesn't want his dead wife's sister hanging around on the edge of their shiny new life together. A lump lodges in my throat and I hate myself for even thinking about that, when Lou is going through utter hell, but I'd be lying if I said I wasn't terrified of having nothing left to live for when she's gone.

'Do you think people will be able to tell?' Lou's voice jolts me out of my reverie as she looks at me, smoothing her hand over the wig she's wearing. She's had it a week, but it's the first time she's worn it, because she's terrified something might happen to suddenly whip it off her head. We're squashed into the disabled toilet of the village hall together, neither of us actually needing the loo, but neither of us in any hurry to head out to see anyone else either. We left Tom watching Flo and Stan on the inflatable bouncy castle.

'No, it looks amazing.' It really does, and when I study the parting it's hard to believe that it isn't Lou's own skin. 'But does it matter if people do know? Now that Mum and Dad and the kids have been told?'

'I don't want to be what everyone is talking about. I've told the people I really care about it, and it'll just be entertainment for people like Billie.' Lou raises her eyebrows, daring me to say otherwise, but I can't. It might sound harsh, but it's true. Billie will be full of sympathy, at least on the surface, but I'm almost certain she'll get a buzz from gossiping about just how long Lou might have left, once she hears that the cancer is incurable.

'Okay, you don't have to tell anyone unless you want to.' I squeeze Lou's hand. But now that the children know I suspect it won't be too long before even that decision is taken away from her. 'Right, shall we go out and do this?'

'Uh huh.' Lou puts a hand on top of her wig one more time, as if giving it a final push to keep it firmly in place. As we face our reflections in the mirror, we paste on matching smiles, and we've never looked more identical than we do in that moment, but I've never felt more terrified about the prospect of losing my other half either.

# 16

## LOUISA

I was warned that the effects of the chemotherapy would probably worsen with each infusion, and they have. My hair started falling out in the week after the second treatment. I'm still not completely bald, but I reckon I could earn a living as a Homer Simpson impersonator. I've got the sparse strands of hair and yellowing skin off to a tee. I expected the chemo to make me sick, but it's always been worse a couple of days after treatment, going hand to hand with the exhaustion that built up to a point where for the last two treatments I couldn't drag myself out of bed for about forty-eight hours. I know from posting on The Grapevine that everyone's experiences with chemo are different, but almost every response to my latest message, which I posted last night, said the side effects got more intense with every infusion.

> Is it normal to feel like every part of you is damaged forever as you approach the end of the first cycle of chemo? I can't imagine my body being able to take much more.

One of the handful of messages that weren't incredibly kind

and sympathetic came from my old nemesis @boobless-wonder777.

> Chemo is shit, cancer is shit and there's nothing anyone can say to you to make that any better.

I still have no real idea what I did to offend this stranger so much, other than airing my desire to have some say on who gets to raise my children in the future, but within minutes of her comment, I had loads of other messages of support saying that she's out of order, that the message had been reported to the site admins again, and that it was about time @booblesswonder777 got banned.

Some of the other posters asked me to remind them of the type of cancer I had, and whether I had any specific symptoms, so that they could offer me more constructive help. So I followed up my original post with the one below, maintaining the original white lie I'd told about the cause of my cancer. I was in too deep already with that and the last thing I needed was to give @booblesswonder777 any more reason to come at me.

> I've got stage four breast cancer and to be honest everything hurts, but right now it feels like I'm peeing broken glass.

There were a host of messages after that urging me to get it checked out because I probably had a water infection that could become a lot more serious if I didn't get it treated. I assured the concerned forum users that I would see my doctor as soon as possible, not adding that Flo's seventh birthday was going to take priority first. What I hadn't expected was a private message from one of the forum administrators @itsnotalloveryet2.

Hi @worriedmum1982. I just wanted to get in touch to apologise for the way you've been treated by another member of The Grapevine community. We take breaches of our site rules very seriously and @booblesswonder777 has already had several warnings. Given the nature of our community and the need for our members to have support, we try to give posters a chance to redeem their behaviour before banning them. Unfortunately, the member concerned appears unable to moderate their behaviour and you are not the only person to have been targeted by unhelpful or unkind posts from @booblesswonder777. As such, we have now banned the user from the site. There is always a chance they may re-join with another username, but if you experience any other unpleasant or concerning comments from another forum user, please do not hesitate to get in touch and I will personally look into it for you.

I also wanted to send a private message to respond to your latest post. You have had some great advice already and as others have said, the risk of infection is increased by chemotherapy treatment, due to the suppression of your immune system. I am sure your doctors have been completing regular blood counts to check your neutrophils, but if you are not due one soon you may want to request this. I would also urge you to get a urine test as soon as possible, as a UTI can develop into something far more serious, including sepsis, if your immune system is suppressed. I don't want to scare you, but this really is urgent, and having liaised with members of the medical team at The Grapevine, that's also the advice they give, which you can read more about at the link below. Take care of yourself and please do not allow the unkindness of one person to stop you from continuing to reach out for support from the other wonderful members of the forum.

It was such a kind and comprehensive message, and I didn't for one moment doubt the validity of what had been said. I fired off an immediate thank you, and I am going to act on what @itsnotalloveryet2 said. As soon as Flo's birthday party is over. I can't do it before then because I've got to do whatever it takes to make my daughter's birthday the best it can possibly be, in case I'm not here for the next one.

* * *

Flo seems to be having the time of her life and thankfully the weather decided to behave itself. Holly has been a Godsend, helping Tom to organise all the games. When Flo said she wanted an Olympic-themed birthday party for her next birthday, after becoming obsessed by the games last year, I thought she'd forget by the time her birthday came around again, but she didn't. Almost everyone has been completely on board with my need to go all out for this, and I try not to think about why none of them have questioned it. It doesn't take a genius to work out it's because they know as well as I do that it might be my last chance. I can't overthink these things, so I'm focusing on today, even though the burning in my bladder won't seem to ease up even for a second, and it feels as if my knickers are made out of Deep Heat.

Tom made Flo a podium with bronze, silver and gold levels, and Holly has managed to source medals to match, as well as having bought enough sporting equipment to start up her own athletics club. Mini cones have been set out to create racing lanes, and much to her delight Flo is already sporting two medals. One gold, for the bean bag race, and one bronze for the hopping race. They might not quite be Olympic events, but it's only two weeks since the school sports' day and the kids seem determined to give it their all. Holly came up with the list of races and other events, and I can see what she's done, in trying to make sure there's a chance for everyone to win something. There are even prizes for the best cheerleaders, and I know she'll make sure they go to anyone who isn't wearing a medal for another reason by the end of the day. A few of Flo's classmates have got younger siblings, and we told the parents to bring them along too, so that Stan can have the chance to race with children his own age, and he's already bouncing up and down with excitement at the prospect.

'Mummy, is it my turn to run?' He tugs on my sleeve, asking the question he's asked at least six times already.

'Soon, darling, it's the last race before we eat.' I glance towards where Tom is getting the BBQ going on the other side of the garden. Usually, I'd do a big spread with lots of choices, but Tom insisted we keep the food element simple this time. He's not the sort to put his foot down about much, he's always left any decisions about the running of the house and the family to me, seeming grateful that he doesn't have to give up the head space to think about it. This time was different.

'Maybe we should just have the party at the soft play centre and let them do the food and everything. I don't want you overdoing it.' Tom had held my gaze, as I shook my head. 'Lou, you need to take care of yourself.'

'No, I've got to do this for Flo, I might not...' I hadn't been able to bring myself to finish the sentence, because I knew we'd both end up in tears. 'We don't know what will be happening this time next year, and she's been talking about having an Olympics' party for months.'

'If we do it, you've got to leave organising the food up to me.'

I'd laughed then. Tom had never really got to grips with anything much more challenging than a cheese toastie. 'Oh right, what are we having, a Domino's delivery?'

'Maybe, or I can order some party food in. If the weather looks good, I might just do a barbecue.'

'As long as there's no chicken.' I pulled a face, and it was Tom's turn to laugh. Neither of us could forget the time he'd attempted to cook chicken drumsticks on a portable barbecue while we were on a camping trip and nearly poisoned us all. The sausages and burgers were okay, as long as you didn't mind a bit of charring, and he could probably pull that off. In the end, I decided that fighting with him over catering a kids' party wasn't a hill I was prepared to die on. We ended up ordering in some party platters from a local supermarket, so between that and Tom's attempts at barbecuing, no one should go hungry. I just wish I wanted to eat. There's an almost constant feeling of nausea nagging inside me now and bone-aching fatigue. Neither of which are helped by the effects of the medication I'm taking for the pain that seems to radiate around my back and abdomen, like I'm wearing some kind of medieval torture device. I'm doing everything I can to fight through the physical symptoms and letting go of the small things that really don't matter, like catering for the party, is helping me to keep going.

'I'm going to win, aren't I, Mummy?' Stan's question breaks into my thoughts, and I look down at him.

'As long as you give it your best try, sweetheart, that's all that matters.'

'Look how fast I can go!' Stan charges off in Tom's direction and I follow him, wanting to make sure he doesn't get too close to the barbecue, or make it even more likely that Tom will incinerate the food.

'Is Stan okay here with you?' When I reach Tom, the harsh sunlight reveals how much the last couple of months has aged him. I heard him crying in the en suite in the early hours of this morning, when he thought I was still asleep. He does a great job of remaining upbeat a lot of the time, still trying to convince us both that he's certain the treatment will keep the cancer contained, but the terror and sadness he's feeling comes straight to the surface when he thinks I'm not looking.

'He's fine, I'm teaching him the secrets of barbecuing the way Forbes men have done for generations.' Tom grins for a moment, instantly knocking ten years off his age, but then he gives me an appraising look. 'Why don't you stay and hang out here with us for a bit, sit down and have a rest. You look tired.'

'I'm fine.' We both know that's a lie, but I do feel as okay as it's possible to right now and I flash him a smile. 'I should go and chat to some of the other parents. Anyway, I wouldn't want to accidentally overhear the secret of how the Forbes men can burn sausages and undercook chicken, all at the same time.'

'It's an art form.' Tom mirrors my smile, but then he turns serious for a second time. 'Just promise me you won't overdo it, running around after everyone.'

'I promise. I don't think Holly will let me lift a finger anyway.' Tom looks in my sister's direction and his shoulders relax a little. Holly has been rushing around for days to get this party organised, and she is circulating now, making sure all the parents have drinks and setting down bowls of snacks until the food is served. She was here to take delivery of the order from the supermarket, plating it all up ready to set up the buffet when Tom gives her the nod that his charred offerings are done. He was up early too, getting the garden ready and setting out the lanes for the Olympics. Making sure the ice machine was on, and that there were enough different drinks to cater for everyone's taste. I'm largely out of action, but the two of them without me still make quite the team, and I'm so grateful to have them both.

I just wish it was me rushing around, feeling frazzled and a tiny bit irritated by the hassle of it all, as I have at almost every party we've ever thrown. It's always been worth it, but that doesn't stop it from being stressful too, and more than once I've uttered the phrase 'never again'. Except now that's probably true. Shaking off the thought so that I don't cry for the millionth time since my diagnosis, I lay my head against Tom's shoulder.

'Holly's got it all under control.' Lifting my head up, my hand instinctively moves to check that the wig hasn't slipped, despite the aid of double-sided tape, and Tom pulls me towards him again.

'You've got no idea how much I love you, Lou. You look beautiful, and the wig... no one would ever know.'

'I love you too.' I squeeze him tightly for a moment, and then let go. I need to walk away now before our emotions start to get the better of us. The last thing I want is for Flo's memory of her seventh birthday to be of her parents standing by the barbecue sobbing. I just hope Tom is right about the wig. I know it won't be long before everyone in the village knows what's going on, now that Stan and Flo have been told about the cancer. It's only been a few days, and Flo's been too excited about her party to give anything else much thought. But eventually she'll tell her friends, and it will get back to the parents, including the ones I only tolerate because their children are a part of my daughter's life. Billie tops that list of people, but she'd be in my life even if her daughter wasn't one of Flo's classmates, because she's married to Tom's best friend. I can't help wishing she wasn't a part of our lives at all, and that his best friend, Jonathan, had married someone else. But he didn't, he chose Billie, and so I have no choice but to grin and bear it, when I have to include her on special occasions, like today.

'Well hello, Louisa, I wondered where you'd been hiding!' Billie looks at me over the top of her expensive-looking sunglasses as soon as she spots me, my attempt to sneak past where she's sitting to get to Holly a total failure. I give her a tight smile, which I hope conveys the message that I haven't got time to stop. Just in case it doesn't, I spell it out for her.

'So glad you could make it, Billie, I'd love to chat, but I've got to go and start getting the food out.'

'Really? I thought you had Holly doing all the donkey work today, so you can take it easy. She's been rushing about ever since we arrived, bless her.'

'That's what sisters do for one another.' My smile is saccharine sweet now. I know Billie hasn't spoken to her own sister in about five years. Their relationship started to sour when Beth had the audacity to fall pregnant in the run up to Billie and Jonathan's wedding. According to Billie, her sister ruined the photographs by having an obvious bump at the wedding, and failed in her duties as chief bridesmaid by not even being able to attend the hen do, let alone organise it. Poor Beth had hyperemesis gravidarum for the first six months of her pregnancy, suffering from sickness morning, noon and night. I went to the hen do, because back then, before I'd witnessed Billie as a mother, I was still trying to give her the benefit of the doubt for Jonathan's sake. He's a lovely guy and he and Tom have been best friends since primary school. I feel guilty that I've made things even harder on Tom by asking him not to talk to Jonathan about my diagnosis. It means he hasn't been able to lean on his oldest friend for support, but I couldn't bear the thought of Billie being one of the first people to find out. It would have taken away all my choices about when to tell the children, or anyone else who's important to me.

'Not everyone is fortunate enough to have a sister who puts themselves out for you quite the way Holly does. You're so *lucky*.' I could mistake it for genuine sentiment, if I didn't know Billie and if she hadn't just dragged out the last word for so long. I might also have felt sorry for her about the breakdown of her relationship with her sister, if I hadn't witnessed so much of Billie's behaviour for myself.

'I am very lucky to have her.' For the first time my smile is genuine as my sister walks towards me, and I put an arm around her waist. 'The luckiest, in fact, and Holly knows how grateful I am for all her help. Not just today.'

'It's teamwork and I've lost count of the number of times Lou has been there for me, so it's the least I can do to help out when…' Holly catches herself just in time, stops talking and takes a long, slow breath. '…when she's got a house full of children and their parents, and all hands are needed on deck.'

'I thought you were about to say while Louisa is out of action. We've been wondering, haven't we?' Billie leans conspiratorially towards Natalie and Keely, all three of them nodding in unison. 'It's just that we haven't seen a lot of you and there are rumours going around.'

'Oh really, about what?' I fight to keep my expression neutral, but it feels as if my right eye is twitching like a dying fish.

'That you've had skin removal surgery.' Billie's eyes are twinkling and I'm tempted to tell her that she's a genius for working it out and leave it at that. After all, the more they come up with their own conclusions, the longer it will be before they know the truth and I have to face Billie's attempts at sympathy. Even if she tries her best to be genuine, I'm not quite sure she's got it in her to pull it off.

When neither Holly nor I respond, Billie decides to keep pushing. 'I mean I don't blame you. No one can fail to see how much weight you've lost lately. Personally, I don't think drastic diets are a good idea in your forties. They can be so ageing, can't they?'

'I'm not on a diet, Billie, and you've really got no idea what you're talking about.' My tone is so tight it feels like the tendons in my neck might snap. I don't need to justify myself to this woman, but the ridiculousness of what she's just said is making the white-hot anger that I've been fighting so hard to control bubble up inside me again.

'There's no need to get defensive, I'm just saying you can take things too far.'

'Yes, you bloody well can and you just have, you stupid cow.' Holly fires her words like bullets and Billie begins to reel, even before she gets to the final two words.

'Hey, there's no need for that, Billie was just—' Natalie, another of the mums, tries to interject, but Holly's having none of it.

'Billie was just being the same sort of bitch she always is.' My sister speaks with the assurance of someone who knows the evidence is on her side. Holly knows her well enough to know this isn't a one-off error of judgement.

I'm vaguely aware of other people beginning to look in our direction and I want to stop this, to tell Holly not to say anything else, but it's too late to put the genie back in the bottle and the best way of protecting my children from the hurt these rumours might cause, is probably to put the truth out there.

'Billie, you and I are not friends, we don't like each other and I don't think we should try to pretend any more.' She starts to splutter a protest, but I hold up my hand. 'I haven't got time to keep pretending, or to spend energy pursuing things I don't need or don't want. I haven't been on some kind of drastic diet. I've been having chemo, to try and hold back a cancer they can't cure. That's why Holly's been doing everything, and my appearance has changed so much.'

'Oh Lou, I'm so sorry, I—' She uses the derivative of my name that always grates when it comes from her, and I hold up my hand again to stop her. I really don't have time for this.

'Thank you for your sympathy, but what I really need from you is peace. No more rumours, no more attempts to pretend we enjoy spending time together when it's not the way either of us should be using our precious time. Cancer is a powerful tool when it comes to taking stock and from now on, I'm going to prioritise the things that really matter to me, and you're not one of those things.' As I turn away from her, I'm not even tempted to look back to see how she has reacted, because I meant what I said, it really doesn't matter to me any more. I've wasted far too much time already worrying about things that don't even warrant a footnote in my story. If I haven't got long left, I need to make every moment count and there's still one priority that outweighs everything else.

* * *

Stan's race is the last one before we serve the food, and I watch him bouncing up and down with excitement on the start line.

'Ready, steady, go!' Holly calls out the instruction and all the younger siblings of Flo's friends charge towards the finish line, stopping en route to navigate three hula hoops they have to pass over their heads and down their bodies.

'Come on Stanny, you can do it!' I shout out encouragement and Tom calls out to our son too, from where he's still busy trying to produce something edible on the barbecue, not far from the finish line.

'He's going to do it, he's going to win.' I sound like a mother in awe of their child performing at some high-level athletics event, rather than watching a four-year-old in his own back garden, but I know how important this is to him.

'Go on Stan, go on!' Holly is shouting now too, moving alongside the track to keep pace with him. Stan's so close to the line it's almost a certainty he'll win, but then he seems to stumble, as his foot catches on a tuft of grass and he's flying through the air, landing in an undignified heap as the rest of the competitors charge past him. Through the noise of the cheers for the winners, one sound is drowning out all of the others: the sound of my son sobbing. I try to get to Stan first to hold him in my arms and tell him everything is going to be okay, but my legs feel like they're made of lead, and there are others who are faster than me.

I'm still about ten feet away when Tom and Holly reach him at the same time, wrapping him in an embrace and whispering words of comfort that make his tears subside as if like magic. I stop dead and watch them. I don't know exactly what they're saying, but whatever it is it's working. Stan doesn't need me to make things better, and my absence in this moment isn't an aching void that nothing can fill. It's an agonising realisation, but at the same time it's like the missing piece of the puzzle has fallen into place, and the solution I've been searching for has been right here in front of me all along. It's Holly. My sister and Tom have become a team of two more and more lately, the best possible team my children could have if I'm no longer here. I can't believe I haven't seen it before. It's perfect and all I need now is a way to make them realise it too.

'Poor old Stan, he was so close to winning I think he could taste it and then one trip and it was all over.' Holly gives me a wry smile as she comes to join me, Stan now having been taken off by Tom to get a cupcake by way of consolation.

'It was lucky you and Tom were there, and the two of you have done a great job with organising the party exactly the way Flo wanted.' I put my arm around my sister's waist and squeeze. 'You make quite the pair when it comes to ensuring the kids get what they need.'

'It was a group effort and none of this would have happened without you.' Holly leans her head against mine and then pulls away slightly to look at me. 'Are you okay?'

'I'm good, I just feel so lucky to have you around and I know Tom does too. He's going to need you even more... after, and so are the kids.' I almost blurt out then that it would be okay with me if that became a permanent thing, but I've got to at least try not to freak everyone out.

'You know I'll always be here in whatever way I'm needed, but you're going to be around for a long while.' I nod in response, letting Holly have her fantasy and, for a moment, allowing myself to have it too.

'I wish you could have found someone like Tom, instead of Jacob, and I hope one day Tom finds someone like you. You're the kind of person the kids need.' It's not exactly subtle, but I can't afford to be. The way things are going, I'm scared I just won't wake up one day, and I need Holly to remember what I'm saying. 'Just make sure Tom finds someone like you, promise me.'

'I think he can do better than that.' Holly laughs in that self-depreciating way she so often does, but then she looks at me again, her eyes suddenly glassy. 'What he'll never find is someone who's anywhere near as good as you.'

'As long as you're on his team, he'll be okay.' Clutching her hand, I hope she knows what I'm saying and that my words come back to her when the time comes. I don't want Tom to have another partner, any more than I want the children to have another mother, but if I had to choose someone for that role, then I really couldn't think of anyone better than Holly.

\* \* \*

It's been a long day and I'm exhausted, yet I still can't sleep. Tom is snoring softly beside me and I know I should try to get some rest, but my mind is racing and I reach for my phone, needing to get my thoughts in order, in the only way I seem able to right now. Opening The Grapevine app, I click on the link to the forum and start a new thread.

If you've read my posts before you'll know I've got a terminal diagnosis. They might not call it that any more, but I know what incurable means for me, with my type of cancer. The end is coming, sooner or later. I hope it's the latter, but I need to be prepared if it's not. You might have seen that I posted about having young children and struggling with the idea of who my husband might eventually bring into their lives, and the role this person would then have in raising them. Some of you told me that trying to have any influence over that was controlling, maybe even crazy, but doesn't being a mother bring out the crazy in us all? I wanted to post again, because I think I might have found a solution. There's someone in our lives already who'd be perfect to step into my shoes. She's been in my children's lives from the day they were born, and she and my husband already love one another, just not romantically. The question is, would I be completely insane to try and sow the seeds for it to become something more while I still can? And, if it's not crazy, how the hell do I do it?

I shut the app immediately, not wanting to read the replies tonight. I'm not sure I can cope with being ripped to shreds, as some users of the forum will no doubt do, and maybe they're right. I deliberately don't say that this woman is my sister, because I think for most people that would definitely be a step too far. But unless they're in my shoes and facing the prospect of leaving their babies behind, they've got no right to comment. And if just one person, who really understands my situation, not only agrees that this could work but also has an idea about making it a reality, then perhaps it's worth a try. After all, what's the worst that could happen?

# 17

---

## TOM

When Jonathan texted me this morning, asking if we could meet for lunch, I wasn't sure whether to agree. After what happened at Flo's birthday party yesterday, he might have things to say that I don't want to hear. He wasn't at the party, he was flying back from a business trip to Italy, so he didn't witness things finally coming to a head between our wives. I suspect he'll feel the need to defend Billie, and tell me that Lou shouldn't have been as blunt with her as she was. But Jonathan and I know better than anyone that sometimes the only way to get through to Billie is to be blunt and, in the circumstances, I think Lou had every right to say what she did. If I'm totally honest, right now I couldn't give a damn about any kind of hurt feelings Billie might have. All that matters is our family, but sometimes it feels like I'm suffocating. I'm not working, at least not properly, and in the past, I've always used work as a temporary distraction when I've been going through a difficult time, like losing my parents. Lou's cancer feels relentless in a way that nothing ever quite has before, so even if Jonathan is planning to call me out about the row between Lou and Billie, at least it's a reason to get out of the house that doesn't involve going taking Lou to yet another hospital appointment, knowing she's going to be pumped full of poison again.

I've been pinning all my hopes on the chemo working, but it's making her so ill. Holly ended up having to take her to an out-of-hours clinic last night when we realised how much pain she was in from a UTI she'd been trying to hide until Flo's party was over. I'd had a few beers, just to get through putting a brave face on things, which meant I couldn't drive. I hated myself for that. I should be ready to drop whatever I'm doing if Lou needs something right now, but I wasn't. Thank God for Holly. I seem to be saying that so often lately. She was ready, of course she was, and so it was her who got Lou in to see a doctor and made sure she was given the meds she needed, while I stayed at home with the children. The doctors have told Lou not to delay getting help for any sign of infection again, because with the chemo suppressing her immune system, a simple infection risks turning into something life threatening. When Holly told me they'd mentioned the possibility of sepsis, I felt even worse about the fact that I'd prioritised a few beers over her. It won't happen again, that's for sure. I'm going to make certain I'm ready for whatever Lou needs from me from now on.

The doctors are running some tests to see just how compromised her immune system is, and the results will determine whether she's well enough to continue with the chemo. I don't even want to think about what the implications of that might be. It was Holly who relayed all of this to me last night when they got home, and all Lou was able to do was to crawl into bed. Holly and I stayed up talking after that, trying to make sense of everything and find solutions for the unsolvable. We couldn't of course, but it was good to talk and be able to be completely honest about how we felt. Shit mostly, is the way I'd sum it up, and angry as hell that this is happening to our beautiful Lou, the glue that binds this whole family together.

It was cathartic to get it out, to rage against the injustice, and use every kind of swear word we could come up with to describe just how shit this whole situation is. None of them capture it adequately, so we started trying to come up with one of our own, one that can really do the situation justice. Although I'm not sure a word bad enough truly exists. Perhaps I should ask Jonathan. We've had our fair share of boozy, sweary nights out in the past, particularly when we were both playing for the village rugby team in our early twenties.

Lou's oldest friend, Joanna, one of the first she confided in about her diagnosis, is at home with Lou and the children, effectively babysitting them all, because Lou is so poorly at the moment that I didn't want to leave her. It was Holly who intervened again, lecturing me that I needed a break in order to be the best support I can for Lou. When I challenged her to take her own advice, she promised she would, if I did, and arranged for Joanna to cover for us both. Holly has gone to the cinema with a friend from one of the places where she volunteers, Dan, I think she said his name was, and I found myself wanting to ask about this 'friend'. Holly has always been like the little sister I've never had, and I feel protective of her, especially since her own cancer diagnosis and then Jacob walking out. She means a lot to me, there's no denying that, but there was something else niggling at me, making me want to ask more about this person she's out with.

It crossed my mind, just for a moment, that if this 'friend' is more than that, Holly might start a relationship with him that could lead who knows where. I should be happy for her if that's the case, I know that, but my feelings are confused. It's been such a long time since she was in a relationship, and it's been easy to take it for granted that she'll always be around and available to slot into mine and Lou's life. I've never needed her more than I do now, and the thought of losing even a part of that support scares me. Although it doesn't even compare to the thought of losing Lou, which is so terrifying I can't really let my mind go there. But Holly having a relationship of her own – something she deserves more than anyone else I know – is all too easy to imagine and, as selfish as it is to even think it, I can't help hoping that now won't be the time.

Shaking off the thought, I focus on what I want to say to Jonathan. Now that Lou has spoken openly about her cancer, there's nothing to stop me talking about it and if I start to lean on my friends, perhaps I won't feel quite so reliant on Holly.

We're meeting in the village pub, The Happy Farmer, a place where we spent many nights after the age of about sixteen trying to persuade the barmaid to serve us a pint despite not having any ID, and still looking easily young enough to get a half price kid's ticket on the bus that was our only independent route to freedom and life beyond the confines of the village where we grew up. That was until Jonathan turned seventeen and passed his test almost straight away, having learnt to drive on his parents' land. He had the keys to a silver Ford Focus within a month of turning seventeen and as far as I was concerned that made him the king of the road. It was the start of us both discovering how much more there was to life than what Castlebourne could offer. Funny really that we've both ended up back here, but it's only as an adult that you realise what a charmed childhood you had. Or didn't, in Lou and Holly's case. I wanted the same for my kids when I eventually had them, which is why I bought my first house in Castlebourne and why these days I can't imagine ever really wanting to live anywhere else. I try not to think about what life will be like here without Lou, or how our house won't feel like a home without her. I need to talk to someone about everything that's happening, and I feel sorry for Jonathan that he's the one I'm going to confide in, because I know this isn't going to be easy to hear.

When I walk through the doors to the pub, I spot him straight away. He's nursing two pints and what looks like two whisky chasers. He clearly means business and I'm glad. Suddenly the idea of numbing some of my emotions with alcohol is incredibly appealing. I know it's not the answer, and that it'll probably just make my anxiety worse tomorrow. But nothing can alleviate that anyway, so I might as well enjoy tonight.

'I got the first round in, mate. I thought you could probably use it.' Jonathan gets to his feet and gives me a hug, thumping me on the back before he pulls away again, like he's a cornerman trying to pump up his fighter ready to win the next round, and that's probably his intention. Sadly I've got no chance in the match I find myself in; the doctors have already pre-determined the winner.

'Thanks, I definitely need this.' Lifting the pint, I drain half of it before I even sit down. When I do, I wonder if I should broach what went on between Lou and Billie at the party, but he doesn't look like he wants to confront me about anything. If anything, he looks like he wants to cry.

'I'm so sorry, mate. Not Lou, not Lou.' Jonathan shakes his head. 'This is so fucked up.'

'Yeah.' It's all I can manage, and I take another huge slug of my beer to try and stop myself from crying. It's not as if we haven't cried in front of each other before, but I don't want to start today in case I can't stop. We cried together when my parents died, and when all of our kids were born. Christ, even on my wedding day when Jonathan was best man, and I was completely over-whelmed by the sight of Lou walking towards me, unable to believe my luck. There were no tears when Jonathan married

Billie, and the poor sod got into trouble for that, because it didn't follow her script.

'I'm sorry if Billie made things any harder, and I know she feels terrible about it.'

'Nothing can really make this worse.' I drain the last of my beer, but the numbing effect isn't coming nearly quickly enough.

'I don't suppose anything can make it better either.'

'No.' I swallow so hard it feels like my Adam's apple might tear through the skin on my neck. 'I can't lose her, I just can't, but there's not a single fucking thing I can do to stop it.'

I shoot the whisky back and it burns my throat, but the physical pain is a relief, and Jonathan pushes his whisky chaser towards me, nodding in understanding.

'I'll get another round in.' Jonathan gets to his feet and I nod, before draining the second whisky. I want this all to go away, but there's absolutely nothing I can do, which means right now oblivion feels like the only option.

* * *

Three rounds in I decided enough was enough. Jonathan was doing his best to try and comfort me, but having to relive the diagnosis, and the prognosis that followed, seemed to neutralise the effects of the alcohol, and I felt every stab of pain again as if it was freshly inflicted. He said all the right things, sympathising with what we're going through, and I know there was genuine sadness there too, because he likes Lou. A lot. But he doesn't love her, and I realised as soon as the third round of drinks was set on the table that what I really needed tonight was to be with someone who loves Lou and who really understands what the prospect of losing her feels like. Which is why I'm standing outside the cinema, eight miles from Castlebourne, desperately hoping that Holly is about to emerge, as other people begin to drift out from the seven thirty showing of a rom com.

'Holly!' I call her name as soon as I spot her. She's walking side by side with a man, their hands close enough to be touching without actually doing so. A pang of guilt that I might be ruining her night hits me, but I can't stop myself from calling out again and moving closer towards her. 'Holly!'

'Tom, what on earth are you doing here? It's not Lou, is it?' Panic is written all over her face, and I shake my head.

'Oh God, Hols, I'm sorry, it's okay, it's not Lou. I texted Joanna from the pub, before I got a taxi over here, and she said Lou went to bed early, but she's fine. Except she's not fine, is she? And she's never going to be fine again. I tried to have a night off and not think about it, I really did, but I just can't stop.' I'm vaguely aware of the uncomfortable look on the face of Holly's companion, but I don't care. I feel as if I'm going to explode if I don't find a way of getting all of these feelings out, and the only person I can share them with is Holly, because she's the only one who truly under-stands. We're both going to lose our other half, and neither of us will ever be the same because of it. If that makes some random bloke a bit embarrassed, I can live with that, but I've got no idea how I'm supposed to live without Lou.

'I can't stop thinking about it either.' Holly's eyes fill with tears, mirroring my own, and when she steps forward I wrap my arms around her. For the first time all evening, I don't feel like I'm in danger of floating away and never finding my way home again, the way I've felt so often since we were given Lou's prognosis, because this is what home feels like and as long as I've got Holly, I'll always have a piece of Lou too.

# 18

## HOLLY

Hearing the results from Lou's latest tests were like someone slamming a baseball bat into my abdomen, and I was every bit as winded by them. The chemotherapy is poisoning her. Her immune system is shot to pieces, and her kidneys are on the brink of failing altogether. Even worse than that, it doesn't seem to be doing anything to shrink the tumours. Tom and I were both there with her when we got the news, and he gripped my hand as Mr Whitelaw outlined the options, Lou's consultant taking her hand before either of us could. The fact that even he seemed to be feeling the emotion of the moment, and the implications of what that meant, made me shiver, and I could feel Tom shaking too. Mr Whitelaw might have been outlining Lou's choices, but it feels like they're running out far more quickly than we ever feared they would. There was talk of targeted treatments, and the possibility of radiotherapy, but then Mr Whitelaw had closed his eyes for a second, before opening them again.

'Of course, there is another option, which is to stop treatment altogether. Sometimes patients decide that quality is better than quantity, and it might be something you want to think about.'

'No way.' Tom hadn't even given Lou the chance to respond, and he said exactly what I wanted to say, but my eyes slid towards my sister, who was biting her lip. We can't bear to let her go, and I know that's the last thing she wants to do, but I'm scared that we're putting pressure on her to go through hell when all the torture of the treatment won't change anything. I need to talk to Tom about it, but I've got to wait for the right time, when Lou has had a long enough break from the chemo to hopefully start to feel a bit better. She's so weak right now that we had to take her to the appointment in a wheelchair, and I've taken indefinite leave from work to help out. I need to be here for Lou and the kids, and for Tom, because he's in danger of falling apart. It's only two days until the end of term, and it's about to get even harder to hide the progress of Lou's illness from the children, so Tom can't afford to collapse, and neither can I. We've got to keep trying to prop one another up, because although I might not be able to predict which way Lou will go with deciding whether to continue treatment, one thing I know for certain is that she'll want us to prioritise the kids over everything else.

'Auntie Holly, look at my hat!' Flo suddenly appears in front of me, twirling around and risking dislodging the straw boater perched on top of her head. I remember that hat, Lou wore it when we went to Bruges last summer, on a glorious day when the prospect of anything like this happening would have been laughable. We took a boat trip down the river, and then a horse and cart ride around the cobbled streets, before lunching in a restaurant in the square. The whole trip consisted of people watching, eating delicious food and drinking good wine that almost cost less than the water. Every so often we'd plan that kind of day together, just the two of us, and I was always grateful that Lou made time for me, despite how much else she had going on in her life. She told me recently that she feels she never did that enough, and I did my best to reassure her that she's wrong, because I never once felt sidelined in her life. I just wish we could have a thousand more of those days. Although right now even one would do.

'That looks great, sweetheart.' I smile for the first time in what feels like forever, as I look at Flo's hat. The children in her class have all been asked to decorate a hat for the end of year school assembly, and with everything that's been going on she's been left to her own devices a bit. There's a tiny teddy bear tied by a ribbon around its neck safety pinned to the band around the hat, and coloured splodges of paint all around the brim. Flo has taken some of the dried lavender from the vase in Lou's hallway and attempted to stuff it into the crown of the hat, in the gaps where the strands of straw are woven in and out of each other. Unfortunately, most of the lavender seems to have been lost in the process, and what is left is a series of greyish, brown stalks.

'It needs some glitter.' Flo makes the assertion with confidence, like a fashion designer who knows just what final touch will complete the outfit and I smile again.

'I think we can arrange that.' Ten minutes, some craft glue and a pot of rainbow glitter later, and Flo is satisfied with the finished product. I know there's been drama at her school in the past where parents have been accused of getting too involved in 'helping' in the children's competitions, but I don't think anyone looking at Flo's hat, which is now drying on the table, would suspect even a moment of parental involvement. And I figure aunties don't count anyway.

'I wish Mummy was coming.' Flo's happiness at adding glitter to the hat has completely evaporated and, as she looks at me, the sadness in her eyes is so agonising it's as if I can actually feel something inside me breaking.

'Me too, sweetheart.'

'You'll be there, won't you, and Daddy?' Flo's eyes are round with concern, and I nod, pulling my niece towards me and holding her as tightly as I can, for my sake as much as hers. 'Stan will be there too.'

'Who's going to look after Mummy?' Flo's words are muffled against my chest, and I wonder if she can hear how fast my heart is thudding, as I try to think of a way to respond that won't make her worry about Lou even more than she is already. I thought I'd come to terms with my parents' shortcomings a long time ago, but over the past few weeks the anger I was convinced I'd buried has come bubbling back to the surface. They should be the ones we're leaning on, but they're far too flaky to trust with Lou's safety. Instead, we're having to call on friends to bridge the gap and, just as we'd suspected they would, my parents have turned to an old friend of their own: alcohol.

'Mummy's friend, Joanna, is going to stay here to keep her company, because she's going to be feeling a bit sad about missing your assembly, but I'm going to record you so Mummy can watch it. We might even be able to FaceTime her so that she can see it straight away.'

'Cool.' Flo suddenly sounds seven going on seventeen, and I'm glad her disappointment seems to have been so easily alleviated, for now at least. There's going to be so much more disappointment and sadness, but if we focus on what's coming, we'll miss the chance to snatch whatever good moments we have left with Lou. Tom and I have been hatching some plans to make the most of that time. When he came to find me, the night I went to the cinema, we spoke about everything. He told me how sad he felt that the only reason he and Lou seemed to have to go out these days was appointments at the hospital. Lou had already confided in me how sad she was that she's going to miss so many milestone moments, so I came up with an idea about how to give her at least one of those back.

Something else Tom told me was that when they broke the news of Lou's cancer to the children, they made a list together of fun things they wanted to do, and so far the only one they've crossed off is a visit to the toy shop. Lou had started off fired up with enthusiasm about taking them on a trip of a lifetime to Disney, and visiting a country where Flo could see penguins in the wild, but as her illness has progressed she just hasn't had the energy. Lou's doctors have already said they won't sign her off as fit to fly, but there must be a way around that, so we can still make some of those things happen, and we're both working on it. The reality might not be as perfect as Lou wanted it to be, but we've got to face the fact that's where we are now. The chances of any day being perfect are almost certainly gone forever, but I have to believe there will still be good moments for Lou and for the people who love her the most. I'm going to do whatever I can to make every single one of them count, because once she's gone, I've got no idea if there'll be any good moments left for those of us she leaves behind.

\* \* \*

Mira from the Macmillan nursing team is everything a nurse should be. She breezed in today, bringing a wave of optimism with her that I don't think any of us have felt since Lou got her last results. She talked about things getting better again for a while, as though that was a real possibility, and she explained how the chemotherapy can sometimes be worse than the disease. But she also sensed that Lou needed to talk about what the end result of stopping chemo will be, and that Tom and I might not make it easy for her to do that. It's why she sent us both off ten minutes ago to make tea, as if that's a two-person job. I thought for a moment that Tom was going to argue and insist on staying, but I shot him a look I hoped he would understand – that Lou needs the space to be honest with someone who's ready to hear what she has to say – and thankfully he seemed to get the message. Lately, we often don't need words to communicate; we're on the same wavelength because the shared pain of losing Lou makes it feel like we understand one another in a way no one else does. When Tom turned up at the cinema, I felt bad for my friend, Dan, because it was as if he wasn't there. Luckily he seemed to understand that I needed to cancel our plans to go for dinner and drinks after the cinema. Dan knows only too well the hell cancer can wreak and, even though I still felt bad about it, there was no way I was going to do anything other than be there for Tom. I didn't tell Dan quite how bleak Lou's prognosis is, because every time I talk about that, it becomes a little bit more real. So he's probably wondering why I broke the promise I made to call and rearrange for another time. He doesn't know that that the progress of Lou's illness has taken over all our lives, and that making plans to do anything other than be there for her is on indefinite hold.

Joanna has taken the children to the park, and Tom is currently searching around in the back of the cupboard for biscuits, while I set up the tea on a tray as if we always put milk in a jug, and use the Wedgewood tea set that I think someone bought Lou and Tom when they got married, and which is usually for display purposes only. The truth is, it's usually mugs all round, but what's the point of saving things for best and never enjoying using them, especially at a time like this?

'Do you think she's going to stop the treatment?' Tom pulls himself upright, clutching a packet of chocolate HobNobs that have somehow evaded the children.

'I don't know.'

'But you're okay if she does?' It almost sounds like an accusation, and I understand why. Until the last couple of days, I'd have felt much the same way as he does, insisting that she keeps trying every treatment available. But now I'm not so sure, and I need to try and make Tom understand why I've changed my mind.

'Of course it's not okay, none of this is okay. It's the worst thing that's ever happened to me, way worse than my own cancer. I've only ever lived twenty-three minutes of my life without Lou, and I don't remember that, so I've got no idea how to navigate the rest of my life without her. But what's even worse than that, is the thought that, because of me, or you, or Stan and Flo, she'll keep putting herself through treatment that we know isn't going to work, and that it will rob her of the time she's got left.' My emotions feel as if they're battering up against one another, like waves in a storm. I'm filled with rage that this is happening to my lovely sister, and at how much she's suffering, but I'm terrified that she might want to stop treatment, and desperately sad that whatever decision she makes, we're still going to lose her. I can't think straight, so I can't even imagine how Lou feels right now.

'What if the treatment gives her a lot longer than she would have had without it?'

'Do you really think that's going to happen?' It's my turn to ask the difficult question, and Tom holds my gaze, unblinking, until his shoulders finally drop.

'No and I'm so fucking angry that not one single thing has gone the way it's supposed to. Even in the midst of this shitstorm, things just keep getting worse. This isn't the way our lives were supposed to be, and it's so far from being what Lou deserves that it fills me with rage. It's our tenth anniversary next month, and I should be taking her to Paris to eat amazing food in a beautiful restaurant, but instead...'

'You're left with a horse shit sandwich at the Fucksuckery Inn.' For a moment Tom just stares at me, and then he starts to laugh and so do I. Of all the words we've tried out lately to sum up the situation, this one feels the closest to summing it up for me and he clearly thinks so too.

'You finally nailed it. That's it, fucksuckery, that's the word we've been looking for.' Tom's laugh dies in his throat, as a strangled sob takes its place. 'I'm just so scared that's what the kids' lives are going to be like once she's gone.'

'We won't let that happen.' I'm crying too, but there's something else surging inside me, a determination not to allow losing Lou to be her legacy, and I put my arms around him.

'Look who's come down for some tea and biscuits.' The sound of Mira's voice makes us pull apart, and I spin around to see my sister standing next to her, leaning on her arm and looking exhausted, just from getting down the stairs. There's no sign of anything else on her face, no confusion at seeing Tom and I embrace, but my scalp prickles anyway, because it feels like boundaries are being crossed and I don't know how to redraw them with the situation we're in.

'Turns out even with cancer I'm scarily motivated by the promise of a chocolate biscuit.' Lou smiles, but I barely recognise her as the person who's not just my sister, but the love of my life. And another little piece inside me breaks forever.

# 19

## LOUISA

I knew Holly and Tom were up to something when I kept catching them having whispered conversations, and clamming up immediately when I came into the room. I thought they were conspiring about my treatment, trying to work out ways to encourage me to keep going, but I was wrong. I'm so grateful for everything we've done together over the past two days, even if I'm not sure whether the exhaustion I'm experiencing right now can ever be alleviated, because it was worth every bit of it.

'I hope you're feeling a bit better, we've got a busy weekend planned.' Tom planted a kiss on my forehead yesterday morning, when he came in to bring me a cup of coffee. I used to love tea first thing, but ever since the chemo my taste buds have changed, and I can no longer stand the taste of my beloved morning cuppa.

'Have we got people coming?' I tried to keep my tone neutral, but I could hear the desperation in my own voice, willing him to say no. Friends have rallied round since I shared my prognosis, and Joanna has been particularly kind, stepping in to help out whenever Tom and Holly are stretched too thin. But I didn't want more visitors, I just wanted time with my family, which meant I slumped against the pillows with relief when Tom shook his head.

'No. We're going out. Me, you, the kids and Holly.' He'd smiled then, and there was a twinkle in his eye that I hadn't seen for a very long time.

'Where are we going?'

'Never you mind.' He tapped the side of his nose, still smiling. 'Just wear something casual and comfortable this morning, and Holly will take care of the rest. Although you might want to bring a coat.'

I peered towards the window as Tom drew the curtains back. 'It looks lovely outside and it's the height of summer.'

'Not where we're going, it's not.' He dropped a wink then, and despite all my attempts over the time it took before we were finally ready to leave home, neither Tom nor Holly would tell me where we were going. The children didn't know either, or they wouldn't have been able to keep the secret. Stan was already hinting at something that was coming later, something he had a special outfit for, and Flo kept furiously shushing him.

The children got even more excited when we pulled up outside a wildlife park about half an hour's drive from home. Tom took the wheelchair I'm now reliant on a lot of the time out of the boot, and we were ushered into the park like VIPs by a member of staff who came out to greet us when we gave our names at the gate.

'This is a lovely idea.' I smiled up at Tom as we headed along the path through the park, soaking in the children's excitement and their squeals of joy as they spotted different animals along the way.

'You haven't seen the half of it yet, but this is down to Holly, not me.' I reached out and squeezed my sister's hand, hoping she knew how grateful I was for organising everything. It sounds stupid, but just lately I've found making plans for a simple day out overwhelming. I keep telling myself that I should be making more memories, ever since the success of painting the sunset, but I'm just too exhausted to make things happen. This was different, and somehow, I could feel it reenergising me.

I still had no idea what was coming, but the smell hit me before I saw the sign. The last time we'd come to this wildlife park, the enclosure that was up ahead hadn't been there. Flo's feet left the floor as she began jumping up and down with excitement, when she realised where we were.

'Penguins! Mummy, look, penguins, hurry up!' She pulled at my hand with excitement, and I turned my head to look up at Tom.

'How fast can this wheelchair go? I think our daughter is getting more than a little bit impatient, so don't spare the horses.'

'Your wish is my command.' He broke into a jog, both of us laughing as he pushed me up the ramp and into the enclosure itself, where the zookeeper welcomed us all by name, explaining that we'd be feeding the penguins.

The smell of fish was powerful and far from pleasant, but it didn't do anything to detract from the unadulterated joy of the moment. Seeing the expressions on the children's faces was magical, and I couldn't fail to smile as I watched them tentatively picking up silvery fish from a bucket, the same sort that Flo had seen recently lying on a supermarket fish counter, which she'd declared disgusting. All of that previous distaste was forgotten, and feeding the penguins was half an hour of pure happiness. None of us could stop ourselves from laughing at the way the penguins waddled, but not half as much as we laughed at Tom and Stan's attempts to imitate them.

'This is the best day ever!' Flo declared when we finally left the enclosure.

'It is!' Stan agreed, as he skipped along the path ahead of my wheelchair.

'Well it's nowhere near over yet. Any guesses as to where we're going next, Lou?' Holly raised her eyebrows as she looked at me and I shook my head.

'All I know is that it better be somewhere they won't mind if the smell of fish is lingering on my clothes a bit.'

'Don't worry about that, I've got a whole different outfit planned for you!' My sister tapped her nose then, in exactly the same way as my husband had done hours before, and it crossed my mind again just how in tune they were.

* * *

If someone had given me a million guesses about where we were going next, I still don't think I'd have got it right. When we pulled up outside St Martin's church, I kept asking what was going on, but there was a conspiracy of silence. Well almost. Both the children were twittering with excitement, and Stan was clamping his hands over his mouth by the time Tom got my wheelchair out of the boot again.

Holly whisked me inside, through the main body of the church and into another room at the back of the building. Hanging up inside was a beautiful green dress and a matching fascinator, along with another dress and fascinator in shocking pink.

'Which one do you want?' My sister gestured towards the dresses.

'The green, of course. You know it's my favourite.' I still had no idea what we were doing there, or why we needed such dressy outfits, but I realised I didn't care. Whatever it was that Tom and Holly had planned was fine by me. My sister had picked out a dress I fell in love with immediately, because she knew me better than anyone else ever could.

'Well thank God for that, because it would never fit me, and I've always looked better in pink anyway.' She laughed then, and stuck out her tongue, sharing a joke only the two of us would understand. We hardly ever rowed growing up, but we'd had what was quite possibly our worst row ever, about who looked best in a pale pink top Holly had bought from a charity shop, when we'd been about fourteen. The truth was she had looked far better in it, but I just hadn't been willing to admit it back then, and it had been a running joke ever since.

It took a while to get into our glad rags, because everything I do seems to take forever now, but when we eventually re-emerged into the main body of the church, there were lots of people there, all of them smartly dressed too.

'Is someone getting married?' I whispered to my sister, and she shook her head, as I leant heavily on her arm, having decided I could make it into the church without the aid of the wheelchair.

'No, but it is a very important event.'

When Tom got up from the front pew, he was wearing a navy suit and crisp white shirt, and he kissed me gently, before he helped me into a seat.

'Welcome, welcome everyone.' Kate suddenly appeared at the front of the church, beaming out at the congregation and catching my eye for a moment, before refocusing on the crowd in front of her. 'It's so wonderful to see so many proud parents here to witness this year's graduates from Little Acorns nursery, and from Castlebourne Infants School, as they receive their diplomas.'

I barely had time to react, as Kate began reading out the names of the children, who each came up in turn to collect a scroll of paper, tied with a scarlet ribbon, and shake Kate's hand.

They were wearing silky black capes, and matching mortar boards, the type you can buy from an online fancy dress store, rather than an academic outfitters. The sight of them brought a lump to my throat, even before Stan appeared, beaming broadly, every inch as proud of himself as I was of him. Flo's class were the last to be called up, and she looked just as excited as her brother to be collecting her certificate.

I was crying long before the service came to an end, and even though the moment was tinged with sadness, my overriding emotion – just like at the zoo – was one of happiness. I've been so scared that the children won't remember me, especially Stan, but the impact of a day like that has to last, I'm sure of it, and I love my sister and Tom more than ever for making it happen.

'Can I bring Dad and Irene to see you next week?' Kate asked later, after I'd thanked her profusely for her part in making the graduation happen.

'I'd like that,' I said. I might have had enough of visitors, but I haven't forgotten the conversation I had with Kate in the church when I was told that the cancer was incurable, and I want to speak to Kate's parents more than ever, to find out whatever I can that might help Tom navigate a new relationship after I'm gone.

\* \* \*

I think I was more exhausted than I've been in my entire life by the time I got to bed last night, but I was still shocked when I woke up this morning to discover it wasn't morning at all. It was already twenty past twelve.

'Hello sleepy head.' Tom was sitting in the corner of the room, and he smiled when I finally opened my eyes.

'You know I find that creepy, you watching me.' I pulled a face, but he was still smiling.

'And you know I can't help it. I can't take my eyes off you when you're in the room. I haven't been able to since day one, not even when you're asleep and slobbering into your pillow.' He laughed then and I stuck out my tongue, not sure I was strong enough to hurl a pillow in his direction.

'I was not slobbering!' When we first got together, I might have worried that he was serious, but he's always teased me about stuff like that and, anyway, in the time we've been together, he's seen me in just about every undignified situation possible. Giving birth takes away all your dignity and, since my diagnosis, any shred of mystique I might have had left has well and truly disappeared. Amongst other things, he's held my hair back while I've vomited, seen me wigless and bald, and had to unblock the shower when what used to be my hair formed a makeshift plug on more than one occasion. So even if he had sat watching me dribbling into my pillow, it wouldn't have been the least attractive side of me he'd ever seen.

'All right, you weren't slobbering, but you did look peaceful, and I didn't want to wake you before I absolutely had to. I was going to give you another half an hour, then I'd have had to give you a gentle shake.'

'Have we got plans again today?' I pulled myself more upright against the back of the bed, testing to see how badly I ached. We'd only been at the wildlife park for an hour, and spent another one at the church, but there'd been travelling in between and the night before it had felt like I'd run a marathon in lead-lined boots. Thankfully I didn't feel too bad, but then I had been asleep for eighteen hours, so perhaps that explained it.

'I told you, it's a busy weekend. Holly and I wanted to fit in all the things the kids mentioned wanting to do, into an action-packed couple of days, and she also had the idea of squeezing the graduation in because...' He hesitated for a moment and we both knew what should have come next, but it was obvious he still couldn't bring himself to say the words out loud: *because you won't be here when they eventually do graduate.* 'Because it's a big moment, both of the kids moving up to the next stage of their education, and what could be cuter than Stan in that little cap and gown?'

'Nothing,' I agreed, the memory making me smile, despite the fact that Tom's hesitation had brought reality right back to the fore. It was why I couldn't stop myself from asking a question I already knew the answer to. 'It's been brilliant, but why did you decide to do so much in one weekend?'

'Because I wanted it to be the best, most memorable weekend any of us have ever had.' His response was so quick it was almost like it was rehearsed, and I suspect it was. I wasn't going to push him, though. I didn't really want a truthful answer and we both knew the real reason: time was running out fast.

'It's been the best weekend already.' I reached out a hand towards him. 'I can't even imagine what today has in store.'

'A Disney marathon, all the popcorn we can eat, and a cuddle on the sofa.' That twinkle in his eyes was back and I gave him a suspicious look.

'Sounds perfect, but is it really as simple as that?'

'You'll just have to wait and see! Everything that happened yesterday was down to Holly, but today was all planned by me.'

* * *

Most of Flo's birthday presents, and everything she's spent her birthday money on since, have been *Lilo and Stitch* themed. Her love of the films and the TV series is one of the main reasons she's been desperate to visit Disney. Stan loves the films too, so I understand why Tom thought the next best thing was a marathon binge-watch of all things *Lilo and Stitch*. Just as he'd promised, the five of us had been squashed up together on the huge corner sofa that dominates our lounge. The children were wedged between me and Tom, with Holly on my other side.

'This is my favourite bit, Mummy, watch!' Flo nudged me as Stitch started to get up to some particularly naughty escapades and I played along about how exciting it was, as if I hadn't already seen it at least ten times before.

'I might order some pizza.' Tom stood up as he spoke, and Holly followed suit.

'And I need to empty the dishwasher,' she said by way of explanation. I should probably have twigged then that something else was going on, but I didn't. I just mumbled an okay and snuggled back down with the kids.

It must have been less than ten minutes later when the door suddenly burst open and in walked Lilo and Stitch. The costumes were incredible, no online fancy dress store this time around. They were the quality of costumes I'd have expected to see the characters wearing if we were in Disney itself, and the shrieks of delight let out by the children could probably have been heard in Paris.

'Mummy, it's Stitch! And Lilo!' Flo was up on her feet in an instant, her brother right behind her, and within moments they were hugging the characters, before dancing on the spot in excitement. Their enthusiasm for our 'guests' reached fever pitch by the time Lilo and Stitch performed the 'He Mele No Lilo' dance from the movie, complete with grass skirts. I have no idea when Tom and Holly learnt to do all of that, or where they got the costumes from. What I do know is that every moment was magical for Flo and Stan, and that they had no clue their aunt and father were the ones wearing the costumes.

When Lilo announced that she and Stitch had to leave, the

children's pleas for one more dance were accommodated, and
then there was a prolonged round of hugs, before they finally
accepted that Lilo and Stitch had to go.

'Do you still think yesterday was the best day ever?' I asked
Flo when her excitement levels had finally dampened down
enough for her to form a coherent sentence.

'I don't know, I did love the penguins and getting my special
certificate.' She wrinkled her nose, trying to solve what was
clearly a dilemma. 'But Lilo and Stitch are my favourite. Can they
both be the best days?'

'Absolutely, sweetheart,' I nodded, pulling her and Stan closer
towards me, just as their father came back into the room.

'The pizza's on its way.' Tom's eyes met mine and I mouthed
the words *I love you*, before he mouthed *I love you too* in response.

'Daddy, Daddy! Lilo and Stitch were here! They came in and
they were dancing and everything. Just like on the videos we
watched on YouTube from Disneyland.'

'Are you sure?' Tom furrowed his brow, doing his best
doubtful dad impression.

'They were, Daddy.' Stan jumped up in support of his sister.

'What's this I'm hearing about a visit from Lilo and Stitch?'
Holly came into the room and I blew her a kiss. My husband and
my sister had worked a small miracle, somehow cramming so
much into a weekend that it felt as though we'd made years'
worth of memories.

'The kids reckon Lilo and Stich came to visit while I was
ordering the pizza, and you were emptying the dishwasher, but I
can't believe it, can you?' Tom looked at Holly, who shrugged in
response.

'We can always check the nanny cam.' She gestured towards
the camera that was set up when I first got ill, so that she or Tom
can keep an eye on me even when they aren't in the room. I

resented it at first as another sign of my fading health, but I'd been grateful for the peace of mind it's given us all as things continue to progress. 'It will have recorded everything that went on while we weren't here.'

It was Holly who blew me a kiss this time, and I knew exactly why she wanted the footage. It's another thing they'll be able to show Flo and Stan later, to remind them of a perfect weekend and to bring back precious memories of them with their mum, when I'm no longer here. I blew her another kiss in response to her suggestion, not sure if she had any idea just what she'd done. But I'll make sure I'll tell her and Tom just how grateful I am, as soon as the kids aren't around to eavesdrop. They pulled off the perfect weekend, which will be etched on Stan and Flo's memories for the rest of their lives. Even if there's a chance of them forgetting, because they're so young, the videos and photos will prompt them to remember a magical time, when I was still right here at the centre of their lives, loving every moment of being their mum.

The last thirty-six hours have taken it out of me, and I've had to leave Tom and Holly to put the children to bed, while I crash out on the sofa, until I can summon the energy to get upstairs too. Despite the exhaustion, I wouldn't have swapped it for the world. Even though I know the end is coming fast, I feel incredibly grateful to have experienced true love, and to have shared my life with the four most amazing people I've ever known.

## 20

### LOUISA

I assumed that the nagging nausea would stop once the chemo did, but it hasn't fully lifted and I'm still finding it hard to face food. Since the weekend of all the excitement, I've barely had any energy and I don't suppose that's helped by the fact that I'm barely eating. All the positivity I had about making memories with the children seems to have ebbed away too, I feel like I'm existing rather than living, but I can't seem to summon up the strength to do anything about it. I suspect I'm depressed and that the sickness in the pit of my stomach is dread as much as anything else and I'm not sure what can lift that. Ever since my diagnosis I've told myself that if I can't be cured, I only want one thing, to know that my children won't suffer from missing having a mother around in the way Holly and I did. When I posted on The Grapevine forum that I might have found a solution to ensuring the children don't end up with a replacement mother who's nowhere near up to the job, once I'm gone, the responses were mixed to say the least.

I got comments from some people telling me that they understood and asking me more about who this woman was. I didn't want to give too much away, because telling them that it was my sister would make most people feel uncomfortable. I'd have felt the same way myself until very recently. So I told them that she was someone I loved, and who the children and Tom already knew and loved too, and that she was single and already involved in all of our lives. A few of them suggested I talk to this 'friend' about my idea, to see if she might be on board, but a lot more of them told me this was a step too far and that I just needed to ask this friend to make sure she remains a part of my family's life, come what may. One post from @itsnotalloveryet2 really hit home:

> Oh @worrriedmum1982, I'm so sorry that you are facing this and I understand why you want to feel that you aren't leaving any 'loose ends' behind, but there are some things you just can't fix. Even if this woman really is the best person you know, as you've said in your post, she won't be able to take your place, because she's not you. She can be part of the support network that helps your children to eventually move forward without you, though. There's a saying, isn't there, about it taking a village to raise a child? I think that's even more likely to be the case with a child who has lost a parent. Talk to this friend, and to your husband, and tell them that you want her to be a part of that village, and to make sure that there are other good people who become a part of it too. That's all you can do, because there's only one you and you're irreplaceable to those who love you xx

It was such a kind message and it really made me think. Most of the other posters were kind too, although they didn't shy away from being honest, and a few of them suggested I was focusing on trying to find my children a new mother rather than facing the fact I was dying. I tried to dismiss it, but it's true. I'm starting to realise that no matter how hard I try to line things up for the children, in an attempt to make sure the gap is filled for them, I'll still be gone.

I want to pause every moment and make it last a hundred times longer than it does, because they're all passing far too quickly, and yet at the same time it's getting harder to be present. I feel too ill to build on the momentum of the weekend that Holly and Tom pulled off so brilliantly. All I can do is keep showing up while I can and simply try to be a part of the minutiae of the children's lives. That's why I'm in the kitchen attempting to make them breakfast. It's just the usual mum stuff I've done hundreds of times before, but suddenly even that feels precious and fragile, every small action magnified in significance because I might be doing it for the final time.

'What do you want for breakfast?' I ruffle Stan's hair as I speak, and he looks up from the iPad he's been glued to for the past ten minutes. There was a time when I'd have been really strict about screen use, especially around the table, but I don't have the same kind of energy these days and I have to pick my battles.

'Pancakes!' Stan puts down the iPad, such is his excitement, and Flo is nodding with enthusiasm too.

'Can we have syrup please? Lots of it.' She adds the last part of the instruction with a heavy emphasis on the word *lots*. She always wants a little bit of pancake with her maple syrup, rather than the other way around, and it's something else I would have stood firm on in the past, but not now that everything feels like it could be the last chance to make a lasting memory. I want to be remembered as the mum who made the best-tasting pancakes, so that every time they have them in the future they remember me. That's the thing, you see, ever since I realised that some of the posters on the forum were right, and that I was focusing on finding my children a replacement mother, so I didn't have to face the fact I wouldn't be here, I can't get the idea out of my head that they might not remember me at all. Despite everything Tom and Holly have done to help capture lasting memories, I still haven't been able to stop the fear from creeping back in that it won't actually be *me* they miss, but a second-hand recollection, from videos and photos, and the testimony of others, an abstract idea of who I was, not the mother who loved them with the whole of her heart. It kills me that they might not know just how much I love them, or ever understand how devastating it's been to know I'm going to be ripped from their sides, when I would have given anything to stay and continue being their mum.

'I want bananas too!' Stan claps his little hands together, drawing me back to the moment, and I smile broadly, despite another wave of nausea surging up inside me as I pick up a banana from the fruit bowl. I can smell its aroma even through the skin and it turns my stomach, but I'm determined to deliver on my promise.

'Coming right up, my darlings.'

I used to be able to do this kind of thing with my eyes closed. It was a breeze, knocking up a batch of home-made scotch pancakes, or drop scones as my nan always called them when she taught me to make them. She insisted they tasted better than the shop bought ones, and she was right. Except not this time, because the mixture won't seem to go right and they keep sticking to the pan. I've already binned two batches, and the third lot don't look great either. I'm just hoping if I smother them in enough syrup that the children might not notice.

'This tastes yucky.' Stan wrinkles his nose almost before the first bite touches his tongue.

'My pancakes are burnt.' Flo lifts up the edge of hers with a fork, then pushes the plate away. As desperate as I am not to cry, I burst into noisy tears.

'I'm sorry, I tried, I really did.' I can barely get the words out between the sobs, and Flo gets to her feet and wraps her arms around my waist.

'Mummy, don't cry, it's okay.' Her words just make the tears come all the faster, and both she and Stan are crying now too.

'Hey, what's going on in here?' Holly comes through the door carrying a box, and Tom is right behind her carrying more stuff. I asked them to give me some time on my own with the kids and Tom said that they'd only be gone for half an hour or so, and they were. I desperately wanted that time with my children without feeling like I had to be babysat, but I couldn't even manage that, and I can't answer Holly's question because I'm crying so hard.

'Mummy burnt the pancakes.' Flo's chin is wobbling and she starts crying again as Holly folds her into her arms.

'Don't get upset, darling, we can easily make some more.' When Holly says *we*, I know she means her. She knows they're the children's favourite thing to eat, and she knows how to make them just the way they like them, because our grandmother taught her to do it the same way she taught me. An irrational stab of anger hits me at the thought and I realise how envious I am that she might step into my place when I'm gone. I've spent so much energy trying to control who will be there for my children, but deep down all I want is for that person to be me, and it breaks my heart that I won't get the chance.

'I said mine was yucky and it made Mummy cry.' Stan hurls himself towards Tom and I feel like a spare part in my own family. Holly and Tom are comforting my children, the children who I upset because I'm useless. I can't do anything for them any more, not even make their favourite breakfast. I feel left out and jealous – horribly jealous – that Stan and Flo are seeking comfort elsewhere. Anyone looking at the scene would think they were the children's parents, and it hurts so much, but I wanted this. Or at least I thought I did, until I saw for myself what my family will look like without me in it. But I don't want it, I don't want any of this. Holly taking my place won't make things any better, because the truth is I'm desperate to stay and I'd do anything – anything – to make that happen. Now I'm terrified that my fear about the children not missing me is already coming true and I'm crying even harder, because I know how selfish that is, but I still can't bear the thought that I might be right. If there is anything after this life, I'm going to miss them so much, but it feels like I'm already being forgotten by the people I love most.

* * *

It took a good ten minutes for everyone to gather themselves together after my meltdown and for Holly to begin remaking the children's breakfasts. Despite Tom and Holly urging me to stay, I made my excuses to leave, saying that I needed to lie down, but the truth is I couldn't bear to watch them all playing happy families for another moment. As Holly started to prepare the pancakes, she and Tom began listing all the things they'd bought for the children to play with. Stan and Flo were getting more and more excited, their tears already forgotten while mine still burned in my eyes. I slipped away and the children didn't even notice. I tried to lie down, so that my excuse to leave didn't become yet another twisting of the truth, but about fifteen minutes later I heard the sound of laughter start to drift up from the garden.

I'm standing at the window now, looking out as Flo and Stan gleefully run through the new garden sprinkler that criss-crosses through an inflatable rainbow arch. They're urging their father and aunt to join in, but no one is asking for me. There isn't even a glance up to the window where I'm standing, and I know now what I need to do.

As I make my way back down the stairs, I struggle to catch my breath. This is hard going, but it's got to be done. As I reach the final step, I haul my suitcase off it and on to the hallway floor, just as Tom comes through the kitchen door, his hair dripping wet and a look of joy on his face that slides off when he spots my suitcase.

'Oh my God, Lou, what's wrong? Do you need to go to the hospital?' It's the only reason he can think of for me leaving and even that makes me sad. I'm such a shell of a person, that in his mind the only place I can possibly be going to is the hospital. Except this time I'm not.

'I'm leaving.'

'What do you mean you're leaving?'

'I don't want to be here any more; you and Holly have got it all covered and the children prefer being with her than with me. I'm just in the way.' Somehow, I get the words out without crying again. Tom isn't nearly so successful, but I can't tell whether his tears are driven by anger or sadness.

'Of course you're not in the way, we all love you and Holly has just been doing what you asked her to do.'

'Of course she has, because she's just fucking perfect, isn't she?' I can't stop the bitterness from exploding out of me and it's so ugly, but everything about this is ugly.

'Don't be ridiculous, we're all just trying to make the best of a terrible situation.'

'Well, it's my terrible situation and I get to call the shots.' The sound of a car pulling on to the gravel outside makes Tom's head jolt back. 'That'll be my ride.'

'Where are you going?'

'To my parents' flat.' Part of me hadn't wanted to tell him, but that really wouldn't be fair on anyone. I'm sad, angry and hurt, but I'm putting everyone through enough worry already, they don't deserve me to pile on more.

'Why the hell would you want to go there?' Tom looks incredulous. 'They can't even look after themselves, let alone you.'

'I think they need this chance to put things right.' It's a blatant lie, but I don't care if Tom can see right through it. I've got to get out of here and I can't think of anywhere else to go.

'Lou, it's a crazy idea, you can't really think that's the place to—'

I raise my voice, cutting him off. 'Stop trying to control every fucking thing I do! It's my life and I've got the right to do what I want with the time I've got left!'

I never swear this much and I loathe myself for the things I'm saying, but anger and jealousy are swirling inside me. I hate the situation too, I hate everything, but it's Tom who's taking the brunt of my rage and I can't seem to stop myself from lashing out. Just days ago, I was thanking him from the bottom of my heart for such a special weekend with the children, but it's like bitterness has poisoned the memory of that and I can't seem to find my way back to the place where I finally felt as though I'd found a bit of peace.

'If that's what you want.' Tom sounds exhausted, but he doesn't argue back, his tone still reasonable. He's accepted my decision far more easily than I expected him to and I don't know how to feel. 'At least let me drive you.'

'The taxi's already here. You get back to Holly and the children.' I do my best to mirror his even tone, but I have to turn away before he sees me cry. If he reaches out to me again, I don't know if I'll be able to go and I need to leave because it's killing me staying and feeling like the third wheel in my own life. The worst thing is the only person to blame is me, because I put all my energy into replacing myself before I was even gone and now it feels like there's no going back.

# 21

## HOLLY

I could tell something was wrong as soon as Tom came back into the garden. He kept saying it was nothing and when I still pushed, he shot me a look that could have frozen water. I knew then not to say anything else in front of the children, but an hour later, when we'd finally tempted them out of the garden, with the lure of ice cream and yet another viewing of *Lilo and Stitch*, he fell to pieces. When he told me what Lou had said, how upset she'd been, and that she'd insisted on getting a taxi to our parents' flat, of all places, I felt that baseball-bat-to-the-stomach sensation again, and Tom must have seen how hard it hit me.

'I shouldn't have told you everything she said. She doesn't mean it; she's just lashing out because she's scared and in pain.'

Mum said a version of the same thing when I called to check how Lou was. I'd tried phoning Lou directly, but she didn't pick up my calls and my messages have gone unread too.

'She'll be home again soon, I'm sure of it. She's just really sad and she needs a bit of space; it's nothing you've done, sweetheart.' Mum hasn't used a term of endearment like that in years, and the only comfort I took from the call was that she sounded stone-cold sober, seeming to understand at last how important it is that she keeps a proper eye on Lou. But I couldn't take comfort from her attempts to reassure me that I've done nothing wrong, because she doesn't know the full story. This whole time I've been telling myself that I was doing what Lou wanted and stepping in to fill her shoes, so that the children don't feel like they're missing out. I painted myself – if only in my own mind – as some kind of self-less, paragon of virtue, doing all of this to help my poor sister out. Except that isn't true. Of course I want to help out and to be there for Lou, Tom and the children, but I've been doing it for me too. This is the first time I've felt truly needed for a long time. Tom and Lou have always made me feel wanted, but this is different, I felt their desperation to have me there and a part of me liked the fact that I was suddenly an integral part of a family, rather than an add-on who was happily accommodated. Don't get me wrong, I'd have traded my new role for Lou to get her health back in a heartbeat. I'd give anything to go back to how things were if it meant she was well again. And if it was possible, I'd even give up having any role in her family's life at all, if it meant she wouldn't die. Except that's not a trade-off anyone can make. But somehow I might still have blown it, and lost my place in Lou's life. I hope to God that this is something we can get over, but the limits on the time she has left make the separation even more painful.

She's been at our parents' place for less than forty-eight hours, but I've been terrified the whole time she's been there that she isn't being properly looked after. The palliative care team have already been in touch, and a first meeting has been sched-uled to coincide with Mira's next visit. Suddenly this doesn't just feel like the beginning of the end any more, it feels as if we're racing at breakneck speed towards the end of the end, and my sister still won't speak to me.

From day one, I thought her plan to try and line someone else up for Tom was crazy; I only played along with it in an attempt to help her find some peace, but I'm scared now that I somehow crossed a line without even realising it. I told myself that going along with the idea was for her benefit, but I should have been able to reassure her that she didn't need to worry and that she can trust Tom to pick the right person, if and when the time eventually comes. But the truth is that I'm almost as scared as she is of the decision he might make. I can't lose Tom or the children, and I'm terrified that one day someone will come along who doesn't just step into Lou's shoes, but takes my place too. In reality, I know that my sister is irreplaceable, but I don't think the same can be said for me. My life has been lived in parallel with hers, but I can see now that it's left me very little that's really my own.

Right now, I feel closer to Tom than I do to anyone else. He's the only person I want to talk to, and I'm confused about what that means. I'm not in love with my brother-in-law, but what I feel for him has changed and maybe Lou has picked up on my confusion. Even if she hasn't, I can see why she might feel as if I'm pushing her out. I've been trying to help out and anticipate what might be needed, but I've got a horrible feeling that means I've overstepped the mark, and taken away the bits of parenting from her that she could still have done. I don't know what to do with myself, or how to make it better, and I've barely slept since Lou walked out, but I still can't rest.

Ever since Lou's diagnosis, I've found myself wishing my grandmother was still around. She always knew the right thing to say, or do, to make things a little bit better, even in the worst of situations. Although she never had to face anything as horrific as this, and I suppose it's a small mercy she isn't here having to witness what's happening to Lou. Yet I wish she was. I need to ask her how I can put things right with my sister, and still be there for Tom and the kids as well. I've spent so much time working with cancer charities, that until this happened, I would have sworn I'd know exactly how to react if someone close to me was diagnosed. The reality is there's no magic formula for this, and nothing can make what Lou is going through okay, but my brain can't seem to stop searching for a solution, so I keep walking, with no more idea of where I'm going than I have of what to do.

St Martin's. I didn't expect to end up here and I certainly didn't plan to, but perhaps the draw to the church has something to do with me missing my grandmother so much right now. Nan was always a confidante to me and Lou, someone we could talk to about anything. She was also the one person who really understood how much our parents' addiction, their on-again off-again relationship, and our mother's absence, really affected us. Her ashes are buried in the churchyard and we shared so many landmark family days here. So it's where I feel closest to her.

'Nan.' I murmur the word as I take a seat on the bench outside the church, close to the spot where both my grandparents' ashes are buried. There's a whisper on the wind through the trees in front of me, almost like she's responding, and I close my eyes, trying to imagine what she would say if she was here, but I can't.

'Please help me.' I don't even realise I've said the words out loud until there's a response.

'What do you need help with?' My eyes shoot open and Kate is standing there. Heat rises up my face at the realisation that she's caught me talking to myself, but I quickly shake off the embarrassment. Kate is a lay minister, she must have seen and heard it all, and I need to speak to someone.

'I've messed up. I've hurt my sister, at a time when she needed me most and I don't know what to do to put it right.'

'Do you want to talk about it?' Kate has such a gentle tone and I nod in response. I can't imagine there's any way she can help, but perhaps just laying it all out there will help me make sense of it.

'Shall I sit down?' I nod again and she takes a seat beside me, not pushing me to start talking. We sit like that in silence for a few seconds, while I try to work out where to begin so that she doesn't think I'm an awful person. But this is not about trying to come out in a good light to Kate, it's about being able to reconnect with Lou. That's all that matters.

'I think I've done something to make things worse. I mean, I didn't think that was even possible in a situation like this, but it turns out it is. I've driven Lou out of her own home, by taking over and making her feel as if she's not needed.'

'I think it's only natural to want to do as much as you can to help, but maybe you just need to talk to Louisa about what she wants support with, and what she'd rather be left to deal with herself. Serious illness takes away a lot of autonomy for people, and it can challenge their perception of themselves. If Louisa thinks you see her differently too, as someone who can't do anything much without help, she's quite likely to lash out. She's got every right to be angry about what she's going through, but it's not directed at you, not really.'

'I think it is. She won't take my calls or answer my texts. I can't remember a day when we didn't exchange at least one message, and it feels like there's a gaping hole where those conversations should be.' I promised myself I wouldn't cry, but it turns out to be just one more promise I haven't been able to keep. 'And the worst part is that even if we sort things out, I know an even bigger hole is going to open up when she's gone and we're wasting precious time not talking, when we've got so little of it left.'

'Oh Holly, I'm so sorry.' Kate hugs me for a moment, but I pull away, suddenly feeling as if I'm suffocating, rising panic washing over me.

'I've got to get this sorted.' I move to get up, but Kate puts a hand out to restrain me.

'I know, but this needs to be on Louisa's terms and, if she thinks you've taken over, you demanding that this all gets sorted out here and now might not be the best course of action. I know you want to fix things, Holly, and anyone can see how much you and Louisa love one another, but perhaps you need to let her come to you.'

'What if she doesn't come to me?'

'She will.'

'I don't know, what she said to Tom made it sound like she hates me. She thinks I'm trying to take her place with her husband and her children, and I'm worried that I am.' I can't look at Kate as I speak, scared that I'll see the judgement in her eyes. 'I love them all so much, and from the moment Lou was diagnosed she said her biggest fear was leaving a gap in the kids' lives, because of what happened to us as children. She started talking about what a great team Tom and I were, and how she hopes that one day he finds someone like me to bring into the children's lives. I've never thought of Tom that way, he's been like a brother to me, but I played along with the idea for Lou's sake. Except now I've realised it might not just have been for Lou's sake. I liked the feeling of being needed, and of having the children want to come to me. I've got closer to Tom than I've ever been. I love him.'

Kate's intake of breath is audible, but I'm already shaking my head. She doesn't understand and I'm not sure I did really, until now. 'I'm not in love with him, but I do love him on a level I didn't before. He's the one person who really understands how this feels for me, and we've been spending a lot of time together, even when Lou isn't around, because we can be truly honest with one another. There's nothing inappropriate about it. I could never... I *would* never, but maybe that's not how it looked to Lou. Maybe she thinks I took the things she said about us being the perfect team seriously, but no one can take her place, least of all me.'

'The idea of someone taking her place – even you – was abstract when it first came into her head. She spoke to me about it not long after her diagnosis and it felt to me like a distraction from facing reality. It was a fixation on something she believed she could control, when everything else felt so out of her control. But seeing you with the children and Tom has forced her to confront the reality of what her family might look like without her. She doesn't want to imagine that, and she doesn't want to let them go. That's why she's angry, not because of you.'

'I get it, I really do, and I want to give her the time she needs to process everything and let me in again, but like I said before, I'm terrified of how much time we're losing, when there's so little of it left.'

'I don't think it will be long, but if she hasn't come home by tomorrow, I'll talk to her.'

'She'll hate me even more if she thinks I've talked to you about it.'

'I won't tell her that, but she might open up to me again and hopefully I can help her realise sooner rather than later that the anger she's feeling is completely justified, but that the only place it should be directed is at the cancer.'

Kate makes it all sound so easy, but I think she's wrong. Lou has a right to be angry with me too, because it felt as if a place inside of me – a void that's been empty for so long – was filled up when I stepped into her shoes, with Tom and the children. Whatever Kate says I still hate myself for that, and I can't blame Lou if she does too.

## 22

### LOUISA

Waking up in my parents' flat is so strange, that for a moment or two I wonder where I am and, when I remember, I'm filled with an aching void of loneliness. It's the same feeling I had when I missed my mum as a kid, but if we were back at the pub on those dark days and not with our grandparents, Holly would always be there. She'd sense when I was having a tough time, and she'd wrap her arms around me, holding me tight.

I'd never heard of a weighted blanket being used to calm anxiety back then, but she was the human equivalent of that. She weighted me down with her embrace, until I felt grounded and safe again. She was my rock, she still is, and yet I've pushed her away at a time when I need her more than ever. But I don't want to need her the way I do right now, and I don't want my husband and children to need her either, even though I know she's the one keeping us all going. She's the person I've been able to talk to about everything my whole life and yet I can't talk to her about this. I can't talk to anyone who'll understand, because how could they if they haven't been in my position? Instead, I do what I seem to be doing so often these days and reach for my phone, posting a message on The Grapevine forum.

> If you've seen my posts before. You'll know I thought I could make myself feel better about leaving my children behind by lining them up a 'new mother' for when I was gone. Some of you told me I was being ridiculous and it turns out you were right. I can't find the perfect person to take my place, because I don't want anyone to do it. I want to be there for them, for my husband, my twin sister, my parents, and everyone else who really matters to me. There's less and less I've got the energy to do now, and I'm watching the people I love carrying on with life from the sidelines. That makes it all too easy to imagine their lives without me in them and now, when I think about someone taking my place in any of those situations, the jealousy I feel is unbearable. Those people are my loved ones and I don't want someone else to have them. I know that sounds just as crazy as my other posts, and I know some of you will come back and tell me so, but it doesn't change how I feel. My children are so young and I'm scared they'll forget about me altogether. If they do, it won't be a case of this other person filling a gap I've left behind, because there won't be a gap. For them, it'll be like I never even existed at all.

My eyes are so swollen and sore from all the crying I've done lately, that I would have sworn there were no tears left. Turns out I was wrong about that too. I know I'll get some replies saying that it doesn't matter if my children don't remember me, because I won't be around to experience the pain that brings, and it's probably better that way because then at least they won't experience the pain of missing me, but right now it feels like it's the only thing that matters. My children are the best thing I've ever done and I want to believe I'll mean something to them when I'm gone. I don't buy into that crap about not missing what you've never had either. Holly and I never had a happy family set-up, but we both still missed it like hell.

It's only a matter of minutes before the responses start to ping in. To my surprise, they're all empathetic, and no one is accusing me of being selfish or self-indulgent. Most of them tell me that the people who love me won't allow me to be forgotten, and that they'll tell the children what I was like and how much I loved them. I know that's true, but apart from a handful of memories that we've made lately, which I hope will stay with them, most of those stories will still come through the filter of someone else's memories of me. When a response comes up from @itsnotalloveryet2, it's the first that contains some practical advice.

I don't know you, but having read your posts you don't sound like someone people could forget. It's different with your children being so young, I understand that, and I've worked with lots of people who are facing a similar situation to yours. My advice would be to video everything you possibly can, to focus on making and recording as many memories as possible that your children can watch back later.

They might be too young to recall everything, but those videos should help fill in the blanks and maybe even trigger their own memories. For me, my earliest memories are a mixture of vague recollections of the every day, and special occasions, although those might be a mixture of what I remember and what I've seen in photographs. If there's a special event you can organise, or a place they've always wanted to go to, it might be significant enough for them to remember it and your part in it, especially if there are a lot of photos and videos taken too.

If there is advice you want your children to remember you giving them, or things you want to be able to tell them later on that they're not old enough yet, you could write letters. Or if that feels too much right now, you could record messages. That way your children won't ever be left wondering what Mum would have said, or what advice you would have given at key moments in their lives, and you can still be a part of their memories of those special times, even when you can't physically be there xx

We've already done things to help embed lasting memories for Flo and Stan, so it's the last part of the post that makes my breath catch in my throat. It isn't that I haven't thought about writing letters before, but I never thought of it the way she's put it. The idea that those letters wouldn't just be words on a page at my children's weddings, or the birth of their children, but could somehow instead become an integral part of their memories of those days, fills me with hope. Something I was beginning to think I might never feel again.

'Mum!' Just seconds after opening the bedroom door and calling out I hear her rushing along the hallway.

'Are you okay?' Panic is written over her face and I feel a rush of affection for her. As far as I can tell, she hasn't touched a drink since I came to stay, and I know how hard she's trying to be what I need right now.

'I'm fine. I mean not fine, but you know.' I manage a half-smile and she looks shocked; it's the first time I haven't cried as soon as she's spoken to me since I arrived on her doorstep. 'I just need one of you to get some writing paper and envelopes if you don't mind going to the shop, and then I'm going to call a taxi to take me back home.'

'You're going back?' I can't read Mum's expression, at least not until I nod and then she smiles, the relief obvious. I don't know if it's because she's pleased I feel ready to go back to my family, or whether it's because she won't have the responsibility for me any more. Either way she looks happy and, for the first time since the children were dancing with Lilo and Stitch, I feel something close to that too. It might not be happiness in the way I used to know it, but I feel like there's a point to me still being here. I'm not just waiting to die, there are meaningful things I can still get to do, and that's more than enough for now.

* * *

Just as I'm about to phone for a taxi, a call comes through to my mobile from Kate, and a jolt of fear shoots through me in case she's calling to say something has happened to one of the children, my sister, or Tom. I know it's crazy, because it wouldn't be Kate calling if that was the case, but I can't stop my mind from going there. I seem to be catastrophising more and more lately, and I'm suddenly terrified that it might be too late for me to tell the people I love just how much they mean to me. Snatching up the phone, I can hear my own breathing, heavy and urgent, my voice high as I say her name.

'Kate.'

'Hi Lou, is it a good time? You sound a bit...' She catches herself, not wanting to say that I sound odd, or breathless, or whatever it is she was about to say, in case this is my new norm. People do that now, tiptoe around me for fear of saying the wrong thing, and quite a few of them have started to avoid me altogether. My illness makes them uncomfortable, forcing them to confront the idea of their own mortality. I get that, I really do, because every time I look in the mirror, or attempt a day-to-day task that used to be easy, I'm forced to confront mine too. 'I just wanted to check that I'm not interrupting anything.'

'Not at all. I've been staying with my parents for a bit, but I'm just about to get a taxi home.'

'Oh.' Kate sounds taken aback and I'm not surprised. It would shock anyone who knows about my life that I've chosen to stay with my parents at a time like this. Her family lived next door to my grandparents and I'm sure she knows more than I've told her about just how difficult my childhood was. 'Where are they living now? Still at the pub?'

'No, they've got a flat in Chetsford.' My parents' town is less than ten miles from Castlebourne, but it's about as different from our pretty village as anywhere could possibly be, at least at the grotty end, where my parents' even grottier flat sits above a kebab shop. Holly and I have both offered to help them move somewhere nicer in the past, but they always insisted they love it here. It's opposite their favourite pub, and there's a handy twenty-four-hour minimarket three doors down, which has a whole wall of alcohol on display, available any time they want it.

'Why don't I come and get you?' Kate's offer takes me by surprise and my immediate thought is that she's saying it out of pity. I can't help wondering why she hasn't asked about Tom or Holly either, and why I'm not getting either of them to pick me up. Maybe one of them has told her how irrational I've been, pushing them together one moment, and then screaming at them for leaving me out the next.

'It's fine. I got a taxi over here and you must have loads to be getting on with.'

'Not today. In fact I was going to ask if you were free to meet up with me, Dad and Irene for a coffee this morning? Brenda Lamb, who's in the choir at the church, is having a charity coffee morning in her garden, and we're all going to be there. I'm sure we can find a quiet corner to have a chat.' Kate pauses and when I don't answer immediately, she starts to apologise. 'Sorry, you probably don't want to do that. All those people, and if you're not feeling great...'

'It's not that at all.' I wonder if she knows I'm lying, because she's hit the nail on the head. The idea of being in Brenda's garden and everyone looking at me – poor Lou, the woman with not long to go – is almost unbearable. But what's even more unbearable is the thought of continuing to hide myself away, and missing out on the last good days that could have been mine. I can't pretend I'm not terminally ill, and hiding myself away won't change that. This new version of life is the only one I've got left and I need to try and wring every drop I can out of it. 'I can't stay too long, because there's a project I need to start at home, and I get tired so easily now. But if you wouldn't mind picking me up, I'd love to pop in and have a chat for half an hour or so.'

'Perfect. Text me your parents' address and I'll leave now. Dad and Irene are so looking forward to seeing you, and I really think it might help.' Kate's tone is warm, and it makes it easier to believe what she's saying. I really hope she's right, because then I might finally be able to stop trying to control the lives of the people I love, even when I'm not here, once and for all.

* * *

The journey back to Castlebourne was passed in conversation about the children. Kate's daughter is in the same class as Flo, and it was lovely to talk about ordinary things, like just how much paint they manage to get on their hands by the end of the school day, and the horrors of combing medicated shampoo through long hair, when there's been yet another letter about an outbreak of headlice. I even managed a joke about not needing to treat my hair any more, grinning at Kate and telling her that I'll just need to pop it in a boil wash next time there's an outbreak. She'd hesitated for a moment, not sure whether to laugh, but when I did, she joined in too, and it felt so good to be normal. Well, maybe not quite normal, given the subject matter of my joke, but it was wonderful to realise that my sense of humour isn't completely dead, even if it is much blacker than it used to me.

I'm sitting in Brenda Lamb's garden now, trying not to notice the furtive glances in my direction from some of the other people. It's late morning and there are eight trestle tables and a mismatch of chairs, all borrowed from the church hall, dotted around the sunny garden. Most of the tables are close to the house, where French doors open in to the kitchen. There's a tea urn on the counter and an array of cakes set out on the island, offered up in exchange for a small donation. Our table, which Kate's parents were already sitting at when we arrived, is away from the others, next to a beautiful weeping willow at the far end of the garden, much further away from the kitchen. I suspect it might have been moved to this position for my benefit, but I'm not going to ask.

The conversation so far has been pleasant but mundane, and I'm still working my way up to asking the meaningful questions that I came here to ask when Irene suddenly cuts to the chase.

'Kate told us you wanted to ask about our experiences of being a step-family?'

'Yes, please.' My response is even more straightforward than her question, but it really is as simple as that.

'I've loved it.' Irene smiles, putting a hand over Kate's. 'That's not to say it's always been easy, especially at first, but having Kate in my life has been one of the best things to ever happen.'

'That's lovely.' I wrap my hands around my teacup, gripping it tightly, because it's the tough bits I need to know about and I'm going to have to ask. 'What was difficult about the early days?'

'It was...' Irene pauses for a moment and turns towards her stepdaughter. 'Correct me if I'm wrong, but I think you resented me at first. It felt as if you didn't want someone else coming into your life, and that you thought I was trying to take your mum's place. It was almost three years after Sally died that Steve and I got together, but it still felt far too soon to Kate, I'm sure.'

'I don't think it would have mattered when it was. I probably would still have thought it was too soon.' Kate sighs and looks at me. 'I was pretty horrible at first, but Reenie was so patient with me, and it didn't take me long to realise that my life was better with her in it. Not to mention Dad's, of course.'

The two women exchange an affectionate look, and the nickname Kate has for her stepmother is another obvious term of endearment between them.

'It definitely made my life better, but it wasn't something I rushed in to by any means.' A look of sadness suddenly clouds Steve's face as he speaks. 'For the first two years I was too deep in grief to even contemplate the idea of meeting someone else. But when the worst of that fog finally started to lift, I realised just how lonely I was. Kate was beginning to get more independent by then. She was fifteen, and she had her own life. She didn't want to spend every waking minute of it with her dad. When I met Reenie at work, the attraction was instant, but it was the idea of what Kate might think that held me back for so long. I didn't want to do anything that would hurt her, when she'd already been hurt so much.'

'I don't think Steve would ever have made a move, so in the end I was the one who asked him out for a drink. See it's not just you youngsters who can be strong, independent women.' Irene laughs. 'I wasn't sure how I felt about getting involved with a man who had a teenage daughter at first, having never had a child of my own. I thought it might bother me, having my needs come second to Kate's. But the more Steve spoke about her, and the more he made it clear that she was his priority, the more I fell in love with him. I could see what a wonderful father he was, and just how much he cared for the people he loved. I wanted to be one of the people who he cared about that way. We both knew from the start that all the time Kate was living at home, she would always be his priority, and he was clear with me that I needed to accept that before we went any further.'

'And you never resented that?' I can't help wondering whether it would really be possible for anyone not to feel at least a shred of resentment that they weren't their partner's priority. I know people in biological families, who've found it difficult to cope when children became the centre of their partner's world, and they've felt sidelined as a result.

'No, because I knew what I was getting into. Honesty was the key for us. And once I lived with Steve, Kate became my priority too. I could see how much Sally's death had affected her, and it was easier not to take her difficult behaviour personally when I realised it wasn't about me, it was about her grief. This young girl had been through so much and it made me want to make her my priority too. It would have been easy to rush in and try to smother her with love, but I realised I had to hang back. The last thing she wanted was me trying to step into Sally's shoes, so instead I tried to prove that I was someone she could rely on, someone she could trust, and we built it up from there. Over time things changed, she softened towards me, and we became closer, realising we had things in common.'

'Yeah, like the desire to gang up on me!' It's Steve who laughs this time.

'We did usually get what we wanted when we worked together.' Kate nudged her dad gently, and grinned at Irene. 'But I think Reenie's right. It was honesty I needed, and they were upfront with me from the start. Dad also checked in with me regularly, about how I was coping with all the changes, making sure we had some quiet time on our own, where I could be really honest about how I was feeling. Things changed quickly in that respect, and the resentment I felt towards Reenie changed into gratitude that Dad had found someone like her. She was kind and loving, and most of all she made him happy. I didn't have to worry about him being lonely any more, especially when I went off to university a couple of years after Reenie moved in.'

'Things changed for us then too and I was shocked at how much I grieved the empty nest.' Irene shakes her head, looking surprised even now. 'It was a bit odd, suddenly being able to prioritise one another, but that's been lovely too.'

'I would have hated it if Dad had never met anyone else, because I'd have been so worried about him.' Kate briefly leant her head on her father's shoulder. 'It wasn't easy at first and there have been some bumps along the way, like there are in any family, but I'm so glad he met Reenie.'

'It sounds like she was just the right person to come into your family.' I smile at Kate, before turning towards her father. I don't know if there's a question I can ask him that will give me the answers I want, but I need to explain why I'm really here. 'I've been so worried about Tom finding the right person after I die, and it sounds crazy now, but I've even wondered if there's a way I can engineer who that might be. I know I can't, but I'm still scared of leaving it to chance. I just want to know that he'll make the right decision, but every time I try talking to him, he just closes down and tells me he doesn't want to meet anyone else.'

'Do you think Tom will prioritise your children?' Steve raises his eyebrows as he speaks.

'Yes, I do.'

'And do you think he'd want to be with someone who wouldn't allow him to do that?'

'Of course not, but what if she—'

Steve cuts me off. 'I think you can trust him, Louisa. This woman, whoever she is, won't be able to take your place, because she's not you. She won't be all the things you are to your children, there'll always be a space where you should be, and that's a good thing. But if you trust that Tom would only want to be with someone who adds to the children's lives, rather than takes away from them, then I think that's all you can ask for.'

'Thank you.' There are tears in my eyes as I reach out and squeeze Steve's hand. There's so much comfort in what he's said. I can't be replaced seamlessly, as if I was never even here, and he's right when he says that's a good thing, because I don't want to believe I'll be so easily replaced. But he's right about the most important thing too, that I can trust Tom to be the kind of father who'll put the children first. I might have doubted that at first, but I've seen it in action from the moment I got my diagnosis. Tom understands that this has all had to be about the children, even though I know how much the prospect of losing me is hurting him too. I might not be around to control what happens when I'm gone, but I'm leaving my family's future in the hands of the best possible person. Suddenly I know I can trust Tom to do the right thing, and the peace that's been evading me finally feels like it might be within reach.

Having Lou home again is amazing, because I was worried she might not come back. I've joined a support group for the partners of people with terminal illnesses, and it's not uncommon for those people to want to return to their parents' care in the last weeks of their lives. Their parents were the people who nurtured them and cared for them the last time they were vulnerable and reliant on others – as children – so it's probably no surprise that the same environment feels like the best and safest place to be in the final stage of their lives. Except none of that was the case for Lou. There are other reasons people choose to spend their final days elsewhere, though, not least because they don't want their partners and children to have to live in the house where they died. I wonder if that's been on Lou's mind, but I can't ask her, because even after the conversations we've been forced to have, I still can't bear to talk about her death as if it's just around the corner. Even though we both know it is.

For now I'm just relieved she didn't make the choice to stay with them until the end, and not just because I was worried that she wouldn't be safe there. Our house without her didn't feel like our home and the truth is it wasn't, because it's Lou that makes somewhere home for me. I'm trying not to think too much about what that might mean for the future, so that I don't spend the rest of the time we have together focusing on that.

She's been different since she came home, in a good way. She's trying to find ways of doing things with Flo and Stan that might not look like they used to, but which still involve her as much as possible. She hasn't felt able to go swimming with them for weeks and, because she couldn't go in, she didn't want to go at all. It was like she was punishing herself for not being the person she was before, but Lou has always been an all-or-nothing kind of person when it comes to parenting. When we talked about having children, she said she only wanted them if she could be around for them all the time, she didn't want to have to juggle a career with motherhood, and rely on other people to take her place when she couldn't make it back in time to pick them up, or take care of them when they were sick. It's not that Lou would judge anyone else for choosing that kind of juggling act, and we know we're lucky to even have the option, it's just that her own childhood meant that was a non-negotiable for her.

So I shouldn't have been surprised that she couldn't bear to do half a job since becoming so poorly, and that she was starting to withdraw and let more and more of it fall to me and Holly. Except now she's back from her parents' flat she seems transformed, as back to her old self as her physical limitations allow her to be.

It's been a huge relief, because I'd been convinced we'd have to continue walking on eggshells when she came home, and I wasn't the only one who was nervous about her return. When Lou texted to say she was coming back, I called Holly and asked if she'd be able to take the children out to give Lou and me the chance to talk.

'You can pick the children up from me later if that's easier.' Holly had looked almost furtive as she closed the door of the car after strapping the children in, as though she was looking over her shoulder for Lou to arrive, and didn't want to be caught standing on the driveway when she did. After what I'd told Holly I'm not surprised she felt that way. I should have kept my big mouth shut and if I could have taken back the words as soon as I said them, I would have. Hurting Holly didn't achieve anything, and a problem shared wasn't a problem halved. It just made us both unhappy.

'No, I think you should bring them here. Lou will want to see you.'

'How do you know that?'

'Because she told me she wants to go home to her family, and you're as big a part of that as me or the kids.'

'No, I'm not. I know you probably both feel sorry for me, and I've loved sharing in your family, but it's time I gave you some space. Lou needs to be able to focus on the three of you; she hasn't got forever any more. I've just latched on to her family because I didn't have one of my own, and I can't keep doing that.'

'You didn't latch on to Lou's family, you are our family. She told me on our first date that the two of you came as a package deal. You were engaged to Jacob then and planning a family of your own, so she didn't say it because she felt sorry for you, she said it because she loves you and not seeing you all the time would have made her sad. If you'd stayed with Jacob and had children of your own, then all of us would have been just as entwined as we are now. So when she says she's coming home to her family, I know she means you too.'

'Talk to her about what she wants. What she *really* wants, and whatever that is, it's okay with me.' Holly had got into the car then and driven the children to a trampoline park. I knew Lou would probably be desperate to see Stan and Flo, but there were things we needed to discuss that couldn't be said in front of the children.

'I'm sorry.' They were the first words Lou said after Kate dropped her off. 'I just started to feel like a spare part in my own life and that no one would even miss me if I was gone.'

'Oh darling, you know that's not true. I miss you already.' I'd rehearsed what I was going to say when she came back and that wasn't it. I definitely wasn't supposed to make any of it about me, but then I'd never expected her to say what she did either.

'I miss you too. I miss everything about my life before the diagnosis and it feels like I've been letting the time I've got left just slip away. I need to hold on to whatever bits I'm able to, while I still can, and find a way for the old me to come out, even if that looks different, but I'm going to need your help.'

'I'll do anything, you know that.'

'I want to plan a big party, another thing the kids might remember when I'm gone, and I want to celebrate what an amazing life I've had. I've been so scared that the kids will forget me, even with all the memories we've tried to make lately. This will be an opportunity for them to have photographs and videos of me, with all the people who were an important part of my life, so they'll understand who I was. A party will give me a chance to say goodbye to everyone too.' She'd held my gaze then, and I'd been so tempted to deny we needed to plan anything like that, but if Lou is going to make the most of the time she's got left, I needed to be honest.

'Okay, and what about Holly?'

'I don't need to say goodbye to her at a party, because I'm going to want her around right to the end. I came into the world with her by my side, and I want her to be by my side when I leave it.'

'Lou, please, I can't—' I came so close in that moment to saying that I couldn't bear to live without her, but I know I've got to, for the children and because she would have made damn sure she was there for them if things were the other way around. So I nodded, and as soon as I could I rang Holly to tell her what Lou had said. Within half an hour of my call she was back with the children. Stan and Flo had thrown themselves into Lou's arms, as if they hadn't seen her in weeks, and she'd hugged them tightly to her chest. When she'd asked what they wanted for dinner, and they'd said they wanted her to make pizzas, the way she always used to, she hadn't got upset that she didn't have the strength any more. Instead, she'd shown them the menu from a local pizza restaurant on her phone, and got them all fired and excited about ordering one that looked almost as big as the kitchen island. She was doing exactly what she'd said she would, making the best she could of a situation that had no chance of a happy ending.

It wasn't until later, after I'd helped Lou up the stairs to put the children to bed, and she'd been resting in our room, that she and Holly really had a chance to talk. I was sitting on a chair by the window and Lou was lying down, close to the point of exhaustion.

'I've put the plates in the dishwasher, hope that's okay.' Holly was so desperate not to make Lou feel like she was taking over that even the simplest of things clearly felt as though they might be off limits. 'I'll head off now and give you some peace.'

'No.' Lou patted the space beside her on the bed. 'Come and lie next to me for a minute, please.'

Holly climbed on the bed, lying down next to her sister as instructed, and Lou reached out and took her hand.

'Do you ever wonder if we used to lie side by side like this before we were born?' Lou turned her head to look at Holly, who nodded in response.

'I think we did.'

'Me too. I'm so sorry I pushed you away. I don't know why I did it, maybe some twisted way of trying to protect myself from losing the people I love, and controlling the situation by pushing you out of my life before cancer pushes me out of yours. I don't know, but whatever it is I'm sorry, and I want you here, right to the end.'

I saw all the same emotions cross Holly's face that I'd felt when Lou had forced me to face her death head on, but it was almost as if she and I had discussed it and agreed it's time to stop denying that Lou is going to die. She needs us to accept it, so that we can make the most of whatever time she has left.

'I love you so much and I promise I'll be here whenever you want me to be, but if there's ever a time when you don't, I'll understand that too.'

Lou nodded in response. There were tears in all of our eyes, but a look of peace had lifted the pinched expression she'd been wearing since we'd been given the diagnosis. I don't know if it was acceptance, but whatever it was it seemed to help.

I still don't know what I'd do without Holly. Knowing that she's taking care of Lou and the kids allows me to get on with other stuff. I'm on an indefinite sabbatical from work, but I've picked up a few freelance bits of writing to help cover some of the bills, and right now the plan is to get on with a bit of work before everyone comes home.

When I go to the laptop, there are ten tabs open across the top of it. I close down Lou's internet searches without looking at them. Last time I looked, and realised she'd been searching for wicker coffins, it physically winded me, but if making plans and lists of what she wants is helping her to cope, then that can only be a good thing. When I switch to Word there are files open too, and I don't want to close them without saving them, in case it's something she needs. The first one is a list of things she wants to have at the party; it already has a file name, so I just make sure I've saved the latest version, then I turn to the second file and start to read.

My darling Flo

You've got no idea how much I wish I was there with you today. Of course, you might not have wanted me in the delivery room with you, but trust me when I say I would have been pacing up and down the corridor waiting for news, no matter how long it took!

I know you are going to be a wonderful mother. You were so gentle and helpful when Stan came along, and you never once got jealous of your little brother. I hope the two of you are as close as you were when you were little, but if anything has come between you, now is the perfect time to build bridges. There's nothing as important as family, as you're about to find out.

There will be times that are tough, when you think you can't keep going, and you'll wonder every day if you're doing a good enough job at being a mother. Guilt and fear come with the territory, but it's the best job imaginable and one I'm so grateful I had the chance to do, especially as fate gave me the most wonderful children in the world. I wasn't able to be your mum for nearly as long as I wanted to be, but I wouldn't have swapped a handful of years with you and Stan for a whole life-time with anyone else.

Try not to worry about all the little things because, although it might be cliché, whoever said all children really need is love, had it spot on. I hope you can still feel the love I have for you, but if that's dimmed by the passing of so many years, I want you to remember just how fierce that love was. You and Stan brought me so much joy, and leaving you behind was the hardest thing I ever had to do. Soak in every moment of this new life you're starting my beautiful girl, forgive yourself for any mistakes you might make, and remember that all parents make them.

I would have given anything to be around long enough to share this with you, but even though I can't physically be there when you hold your baby in your arms, know that I'm there somewhere too, even if it's just in the stories Dad and Auntie Holly can tell you about how much I loved being your mum. I know they'll support you every step of the way, and I hope you've got a great partner too. But, whatever the situation, you'll rise to the occasion and there's nothing you can't do, my brilliant, brilliant girl.

All my love, Mum xxxx

I can barely breathe by the time I finish reading and now I know why I often wake up and discover her tapping away on the keyboard. I had no idea this is what she was doing, and I feel like I've betrayed her and stolen a moment from Flo by reading such an intimate exchange. It means I'm not even tempted to go searching for more letters. These are Lou's legacy and her gift to the children after she's gone. I've always known she was amazing, and so much stronger than me, but I've never admired her more than I do right now. I'm going to do whatever it takes to help her fulfil the rest of her plans, no matter how ambitious they might be, and I know Holly will too.

# 24

## LOUISA

I had a bit of a wobble when I turned forty. I could no longer deny I was anything other than a grown-up, entering middle age. Holly had wanted us to have a joint 'life begins' party, but I was too desperate to hang on to being thirty-something to embrace the idea of shouting from the rooftops that I was now in my forties. It seems so ridiculous now, and I wish to God I'd given Holly that party. She had far more reason to feel the sting of starting her fifth decade than I did. The pending fade of fertility scared me merely because it signified the passing of time and an ageing process I couldn't deny, but for Holly it must have brought a sharp sting of regret about the children she'd so desperately longed for. I was selfish and stupid, worrying about ageing, when now I know only too well it's a gift and a privilege that's going to be taken away from me.

I'm not going to see fifty, and there won't be a chance to make things up to Holly and give her the huge celebration she deserves for her next milestone birthday. Now that life has taught me the most unbelievably hard lesson, I'd happily wear a '50 Today!' badge as big as my head, an 'Older and Bolder' sash, and deely-boppers adorned with a five and a zero too. But I won't be here. That's still hard to get my head around, and my heart aches for all the things I won't get to do. I've known from the start that my regrets aren't about bucket-list moments, I don't care about the fact that I've never made it to New Zealand, Hawaii or Indonesia, even though those were top of my must-visit list of places before my diagnosis. I don't give a damn that I never got to do a parachute jump, or write a book, or climb Kilimanjaro. All the things I wish I'd had the chance to do are about sharing life-defining moments with the people I love most. I won't be around to celebrate ten years of marriage to Tom in November, unless something amazing happens with the alternative chemo the oncology team are talking about, but my kidneys aren't recovering enough for them to even try. I won't get to be there when the kids receive their exam results and head off to university, I won't even live long enough to see them go to secondary school. Right now, I'm scared I won't make it until Stan has his first day at our little village school. I need to hold on for that and it's so close I can almost touch it.

For all those other big moments, from end of school exams, to buying their first houses, getting married and having children of their own, all I can do is be there in the words I'm leaving behind. I hope the letters will help them, and I know writing them is helping me, because I can visualise those landmark days when I'm writing to my babies, and it's the next best thing to being there. Maybe that's an exaggeration, because it still hurts like hell and I cry every time I write one, but I can picture it so clearly, see Stan and Flo's faces in those moments, and I know I'm there somehow. Who knows, it might just be the cocktail of medication I'm on, but I feel a tiny bit of weight lift from my chest with every letter I write and I'm so grateful to the stranger on the internet who helped me see what those letters could do.

I thought about Christmas today. It's not even September yet, but someone on Facebook was ranting about having seen Christmas chocolates in the supermarket. Christmas has always been something Holly and I have gone all out for, especially since the children arrived. I think it's because our Christmases as young children were so far removed from the images we saw on TV, or even the things we heard our friends talking about. The pub was always open and busy, with both Mum and Dad downstairs drinking with the regulars while we waited upstairs in the flat above, listening to the sound of raucous laughter and watching TV, while we worked our way through our selection boxes.

My grandparents would have loved to have us, but Mum always insisted we had to stay together as a family at Christmas, which meant us being at the pub and snatching a quick meal together in the small window of closure the day afforded us. That was why, when Flo came along, even though she was only four months old on her first Christmas, Holly booked the Santa Train, and arranged for us to go to the reindeer sanctuary, the first of a series of Christmas traditions that have grown with every passing year. Mum and Dad still prefer going to the pub, and that's fine by us, because it's almost certainly better for the children that way. But Holly always spends Christmas with us, and sometimes friends will join us too. It might still not be the stuff of TV movies – it's too messy, noisy and chaotic for that – but it's perfect in every way. I'm so glad I've cherished every one of those Christmases and never taken them for granted, because I had no way of knowing that last year was almost certainly my final one, and the realisation of that when I saw the Facebook post was like another stab to the heart.

I want to celebrate my tenth wedding anniversary, to have another Christmas, and to share a milestone birthday with my sister, but the chances are I won't get to do any of those things and there's not a damn thing I can do about it... Except maybe there is, maybe there's a way of me being at all of those things, even if it means I have to play around with the space-time continuum in my own small way.

* * *

'Lou, I don't know what all of this is about, but it feels like an intervention. If it is, there's no need, because I can give up the peanut butter cups, I promise.' Holly laughs nervously as she looks from me, to Tom, then Kate and back again. I know she doesn't really think the lay minister is here because of her addiction to Reese's. She's worried that there's someone from the church here because I want to talk about my funeral and she's not ready for that. But it's okay, because I'm not either. So I lead with my own little joke to try and make that clear.

'I called you all here today because someone in this room is the murderer.' Shaking my head at the expression on their faces, I smile. 'It's all right, I haven't completely lost the plot, but I always wanted to be like Miss Marple when I got old, cycling around the village and sticking my nose in where it wasn't wanted, and maybe solving the odd mystery along the way. Except I'm not going to get the chance.'

'Lou—' Holly looks like she's about to protest, but I hold up my hand. We're past the denial stage now, it's time for action.

'It's what this is about, doing some of the things I really want to do now, because I won't get the chance to do them later, and I need all of you to help me with that.'

'What do you want to do? Whatever it is, we can make it happen.' Tom takes my hand and I almost forget why I'm here and start telling him how lucky I feel – despite the fact I'm dying

– that I got to share my life and my family with him. All of that can wait for another day, though, a special day, and that's exactly why I need their help.

'I want to celebrate our tenth wedding anniversary by renewing our vows, to have a Christmas with all our family and friends, and to throw the all-out milestone birthday party for mine and Holly's fiftieth that we should have had for our fortieth, if I hadn't been so pathetic about it.'

'Lou, it's great that you want to make so many plans...' Tom can't even finish the sentence, his eyes filling with tears, because he knows I probably won't get to do any of those things, but he doesn't understand.

'It's okay, I know I'm not going to make it to fifty, we all know that and there's no point pretending that I am. But I think I might be able to hobble across the line of forty-three, and what's more of a milestone birthday than your final one?' I try to smile, but it goes a bit wobbly, and Tom squeezes my hand while I try to regain my composure. 'Loads of people celebrate Christmas in July, so why not September? And it's the year of our tenth wedding anniversary, so that's got to count. It doesn't have to be the same day; it falls on a Monday this year anyway, and who wants to have a party on a Monday?'

'We can do them all, we can make them all happen.' Holly is already on her feet, as if she wants to start straight away, but Kate sounds a note of caution.

'I think they're all wonderful ideas, but it'll be a lot for you; have you thought about the order that might be the most important to you? In case you find you can't do them all?' Kate bites her lip. That must have been hard for her – to say out loud that I might not make it through three separate celebrations – but I'm grateful to her for her honesty and she's right.

'I want to do them all together, I want to have a Christmas-themed milestone birthday party, with a wedding renewal anniversary celebration thrown in for good measure. I thought maybe we could use the church and have a marquee in the grounds next door, and I wondered if you might be able to speak to someone about whether that's possible.'

'You can definitely use the church. I'll see what dates are available and the rest will be easy. At least when it comes to the venue. Depending on how soon you want to do it, we might just need to rope lots of people in to help.' Kate looks towards Tom, and I follow her gaze, wondering if I'm asking too much, but he's nodding and so is Holly.

'People keep asking me what they can do to help.' Tom strokes a thumb across the back of my hand. 'This is their chance.'

Holly pulls her phone from her pocket. 'I'll make some calls, while you two work out a date.'

'We need to make sure the date works for you too.' I lock eyes with my sister, and she pulls the same expression I saw a thousand times when we were teenagers and she thought I was saying something ridiculous.

'As if there's any date in existence that I wouldn't be free to do this.' Crossing the room, she hugs me close for a moment, then steps back, putting her other arm around Tom. Our team of three are back in business for one magnificent last hurrah. I'm not going to let cancer beat me, even if it is going to kill me. I'm going to be at all the events it's trying to steal from me, one way or another, and there's not a damn thing that bastard disease can do to stop me.

\* \* \*

I was on a high after outlining my plans to Tom, Holly and Kate, but that was six hours ago and now I just feel exhausted. Maybe I have bitten off more than any of us can chew; there's so much to organise in such a short time, and I still have Stan's first day of school to prepare for and more letters to write. It just feels like there aren't enough hours in the day, but the truth is there aren't enough hours left full stop.

I had a video call from my oncologist saying he wants me to go in for some more tests and a discussion about what happens if we can't start another kind of chemo without it presenting more risk of harm than helping. He talked about the chemo we tried being the gold star treatment for my kind of cancer and how frustrating it had been that it hadn't worked. I can think of another word beginning with F that I would have used instead, but I just nodded along like he was talking about not being able to fix a problem with the engine of my car, rather than not being able to prolong my life. I'm getting quite good at disassociation some of the time, and it's much easier when I'm not talking to people I love. That's when the tears come all too readily, but with the medical staff, I pretend they're talking about someone else as a way of coping with it. And, whoever the consultant was talking about this afternoon, they clearly haven't got long, poor thing. He might not have spelt it out exactly, but the cancer hasn't been contained by anything they've tried so far, and whatever else they have in their arsenal has almost no chance of doing anything other than killing me with friendly fire. Every hour that ticks by feels so much more significant now, but I just don't have the energy to make the most of them the way I want to. Instead, I waste far too much time scrolling on my phone. At least when I go on The Grapevine site I might see something useful, or read the posts from people who I feel genuinely understand.

Clicking on the forum's app, I spot some notifications of

further replies to my posts. There's also a notification of some private messages from other forum users. The idea of those weirded me out a bit at first. It felt like I might lose my anonymity and in turn the space I'd found for myself, where I can be completely honest about how shit all of this is. But it's actually given me a space where I can be even more honest. I've had messages from people with similar concerns about what might happen to their children when they're gone. One lovely lady, @ameliasmummy, has already lost her husband to another form of cancer, and now she's been given an incurable diagnosis too. She's got a daughter of five and no other close family. She'd probably give the world to be in my shoes, and it's funny how something like that can still make me feel lucky when I'm facing my own death head on.

Scrolling through the messages, I decide to read them all through before choosing which to reply to straight away. Even typing out responses uses energy that's in limited supply these days, especially the emotional kind, and some will warrant a longer response than others. Those that are just a quick, 'Checking in that you're okay?', or 'Wondered how you were doing?' can wait a while, but if there's something from @ameliasmummy I'll respond straight away. She doesn't have people to lean on in real life to the extent that I do, and I don't want to leave her waiting if she wants to talk, especially as there's no guarantee either of us will be here if we leave it too long. Today there are no messages from her, but there is one from a user whose advice I've come to value, and I wanted to thank her for suggesting the letter writing to me and to tell her where it's led. The message from @itsnotalloveryet2 is as thoughtful as always.

Hi there, I hope you don't mind the private message. I just wanted to say thank you for the support you're giving other users on their posts. I had a message from one of the forum users yesterday to say that talking to you is really helping her feel less alone. I hope the forum is doing the same for you, and that now we've blocked the person sending unkind messages, that you feel like this is a place where you can say whatever you need to say. I hope, too, that if you decided to write the letters, it's going the way you want it to. There are lots of charities, including Winston's Wish, that can help with supporting children when a parent is very ill, and I've put some links below. Don't ever hesitate to reach out to me if there's anything I can do to put you in touch with someone from one of the charities we work with xx

I've looked at some of the charities recommend by @itsnotalloveryet2 and other users of the forum, but I don't feel like I need to draw on their resources. As @ameliasmummy has shown me, I'm so lucky with the people I have around me, and if the children ever need someone to talk to, and don't feel like they can talk to Tom, I know Holly will be there for them. Even though I won't take her up on her offer, I want to thank @itsnotalloveryet2 for her support.

Of course I don't mind you getting in touch. You've been so incredibly kind and generous with your time. I was going to thank you for encouraging me to write letters to my children, it's making so much difference to me feeling like I'm not completely missing out on those milestone moments, and also knowing they'll feel that they have a part of me with them on those special days. I just wish I had more time, so I could say all the things I need to say to everyone I love. My husband and my twin sister are both going to have milestone moments and special days without me too, but those are much harder to anticipate and write about than my children's letters for some reason. You might remember my original post worrying about my husband meeting someone else, and I wonder if I should write him a letter for when he does eventually do that, letting him know that it's okay and that I want him to be happy. There's so much that I want to say and not enough time to do it all or to see everyone I want to see. I'm planning to try to address that last one at least, by throwing the mother of all parties to celebrate a big anniversary, as well as mine and my sister's birthdays and Christmas all rolled into one. It was your suggestion that helped me see I could still be at events I won't be around to experience, at least in some small way, and I'm so very grateful for your wisdom xx

It's a long response, but I need her to know that what she said made a difference. It means a lot to me that other forum users have said the same about me, because sometimes I feel like I'm not much good for anything these days. I don't expect her to respond any time soon, she probably has hundreds of messages as a site admin, so it's a surprise to see a reply pop up within the time it takes me to write responses to three of the other messages I've received.

Wow, that sounds like quite the party, what an amazing thing to do and I hope you have the best time. I think the letters to your other loved ones sound like a wonderful idea too, but I can understand why trying to predict the milestone moments might feel overwhelming. Maybe you shouldn't try, and perhaps instead write them something less specific, something where you say the things you feel it would be most important to say to them in any situation: that you love them, that you wish them happiness, or whatever you feel you'd

most regret not saying if it was left unsaid. You're an amazing
woman @worriedmum1982 and I'm sure the people you love
would value any kind of letter you are able to write xx

She's a wise woman, and she's right. There's no way I can
cover every base for Tom, Holly and my parents, or even for the
children. But I can make sure that the most important things
aren't left unsaid, and that they all know just how much I love
them and wish I didn't have to go.

# 25

## HOLLY

'I want you to come with us.' Lou made it sound like an order rather than a request when she told me she wanted me to be here this morning when Stan was dropped off for his first day of school.

'First days of school are for mums and dads, not fun aunties who are only supposed to be there to buy too many sweets at the end of the week.' I already knew Tom would be there because we'd talked about it a lot, about how Lou might react and whether she'd be strong enough to even go. Her last appointment with her consultant had gone about as badly as we'd all expected. Lou's kidneys haven't recovered from the first round of chemo, her neutrophil levels are through the roof, and she's not well enough to have any of the other treatments they might have tried. The scan also showed significant spread of tumours into her lungs, peritoneum and liver. Mr Whitelaw seemed amazed that she's still going, but he doesn't know my sister like I do; she's a force of nature and she's not going to let go until Stan and Flo start the new school year, and she's thrown the party to end all parties. We've worked hard to get everything in place, and it's less than two weeks away now. As much of a relief as it is that we're nearly there, I also don't want it to come, because I know it means we'll take a giant step closer to the day when we lose her and I'm not ready. I'll never be ready.

'Tom is coming, but so are you.' Lou's insistence I had to be here today didn't waver, and she's been so strong when she needs to be throughout this whole hellish experience. 'I want you to be there to meet Stan's teacher and for her to know who you are from day one. He's going to have so much to cope with in his first year of school, and his teacher needs someone she can call at any time when it gets too much for him. Tom might not always be around because of his work, and I know it's a lot to ask of you, but I need to know you will.'

'You don't even have to ask.' I'd hugged her then, feeling her bones protruding even through her clothes as the disease claims more and more of her.

'He's not going to have a mum soon, but he couldn't ask for a better auntie. He might not realise it for a long time, but that makes him lucky.' I don't know how many more pieces of my heart there are left, but as she whispered the words close to my ear, another part of it shattered.

So here I am now, walking towards the school gates pushing Lou in her wheelchair. Stan is sitting on her lap, wriggling almost nonstop to adjust his position, probably because there's so little flesh on her bones that sitting on her lap is uncomfortable. Flo is holding her right hand and Tom is on the far side of their daughter, holding Flo's other hand.

'I wish I could watch Stan going in to school, it's not fair that I have to go in first.' There's a note of petulance in Flo's voice and for the first time I have to suppress a smile. She's so like Lou at that age, which means I know just what to say.

'It's because you're so grown up, now that you're in juniors, you have to show the little ones the way.' I exchange a knowing look with my niece. Telling Stan he's a baby is her favourite way to put him in his place if he's playing the role of annoying little brother a bit too well, and he usually favours a karate chop in response. Mostly they get on brilliantly and I've been so proud of the efforts Flo has made to be more tolerant of him since her mum became ill, but she's still only seven and there are still only so many NERF bullets she can have fired at her head, or karate chops aimed at her arm, before it all gets a bit too much. I think she senses this is a big day both for Stan and her parents, so she doesn't resort to calling him a baby; instead, she straightens her shoulders and nods.

'Yes, when Stan goes to big school like me, he'll be able to walk into the classroom himself, but the little ones sometimes want to hold the teacher's hand.' Flo makes it sound as if she started school three decades ago instead of three years. I catch Lou's eye as she looks over her shoulder at me and we both smile.

'I want you to have the best day, sweetheart.' Lou pulls Flo closer to her as we reach the entrance to the junior school playground.

'I will, Mummy. Did you make my special sandwich?' Flo raises her eyebrows as she looks at her.

'Yes, and I showed Daddy and Auntie Holly how to make it too, in case there's ever a day when I can't do it.'

Flo's brow furrows as she processes the information. 'In case you're too poorly to do it?'

'Yes, or if I'm not here.' Lou kisses Flo, not leaving room for any more questions about where else she might be. Today is not the day for that kind of conversation, even though we all know it's coming. Or at least the adults do. I'm not sure my niece and nephew realise just how serious things are yet, and I hope they don't. The last days of innocence and unadulterated happiness are more precious than anything else I could imagine right now.

'Bye Mummy, bye Daddy, bye Auntie Holly.' Flo hugs each one of us in turn and then moves to face her little brother, who is still sitting on Lou's lap, just as Tom picks up his phone and starts to record. Leaning very close to him she lowers her voice just loud enough for me to hear. 'Remember what I said about being a good boy, Stan. Mummy needs us to be good.'

'I'm gonna be good, I promise.' Stan nods his head vigorously in response, nearly headbutting his sister as she plants a kiss on his face, and a lump the size of a tennis ball lodges itself in my throat. I might be biased, but these really are the most amazing children in the world and I'll happily karate chop anyone who says otherwise.

* * *

We all thought Stan might cry when the time came for us to leave him, but almost as soon as Tom gets his phone out to take a video of the moment, Stan notices the sandpit in the little covered area outside the Reception classroom and runs off without a backwards glance.

'Well, it shows how much kids can surprise you, doesn't it?' Lou tries to smile as we watch Stan disappear into a group of children, but I spot the quiver in her lips, and I lean down to put my arm around her shoulders.

'What it shows is just what a great job you've done of preparing him and making sure he's ready for this.'

'What if I'm not ready to leave him?' Anyone listening might assume she's talking about being ready to leave him at school for the first time ever, but Tom and I know it's more than that.

'No one's ever ready to leave someone they love, and vice

versa, but you got here. You got to today, and we've taken videos and photographs for Stan and Flo to look back on one day. It's another milestone moment you'll always be a part of.' I can see how hard Tom is trying to control his emotions, but he can't keep the catch from his voice, and he wipes his eyes with the back of his hand as Mrs Diggory, Stan's classroom teacher, approaches.

'Stan seems to have settled in straight away.' She's got a kind face, with a broad smile, and I know from what Lou has told me that she's already been briefed about the situation. She's the school's head of pastoral support, as well as being the Reception class teacher, so she was the best person to speak to about what was happening in both of the children's lives. I wonder whether it's crossed Mrs Diggory's mind that the little boy who just ran into the play area outside her classroom might be almost unrecognisable as the boy she'll encounter in the weeks and months to come. Losing a parent can change a child, Lou and I know that.

We might not have lost our parents in the physical sense, but neither of them were around for us the way we needed them to be. I forget my dream to become an artist, obsessing about exceling at school instead, thinking that if I did well enough Mum wouldn't have to worry about me, and there'd be no need for her to escape from her troubles by drinking too much, and Lou became the queen of the back-up plan, needing a safety net just to survive. Both of us were so shaped by the events of our childhoods, and I can't help wondering what losing Lou will do to Stan and Flo. It's up to me and Tom to make sure they never feel like they need to change to be noticed or praised, but we won't be able to stop if from affecting them altogether.

'I'm sure he'll love it in your class; Flo always did.' Lou smiles at Mrs Diggory and the older woman nods.

'Your children are an absolute credit to you.' She looks from

Lou and Tom to me, and then back again. 'And if any of you ever want to talk to me about any worries or concerns you have for either Stan or Flo, please don't hesitate.'

'Thank you.' Lou takes her hand, closing her eyes for a moment as she nods. 'It means a lot to me to know that you'll be with him every day at school and that if he has tough days you'll understand.'

'Oh Louisa, of course I will, we all will. You're an amazing woman, so brave.' Mrs Diggory hugs Lou, repeating the phrase she's heard countless times since her diagnosis. I know she hates hearing it, and she's ranted more than once about the fact she isn't brave at all, because bravery would indicate there was some kind of choice in all of this. But I know what Stan's teacher means, and the truth is I agree with her. My sister might not have a choice about this, but she has had a choice about how she handles it, and not once have I seen her do anything but prioritise Stan and Flo from the moment she got the news.

'Thank you.' Lou repeats herself, but there's not much more to say. Trusting her children to someone at any time would be a huge thing for my sister, but trusting them to someone else right now, and letting that person spend precious hours with her babies, because it's the right thing for them rather than her, takes a huge amount of selflessness and courage too. She's so much braver than she knows.

* * *

We got back to the house by 10 a.m. and Tom was due to travel up to London to meet with his producer to discuss a project for next year that they need to start the background work on very soon. Lou had to all but force him to go and when he tried to say he wasn't interested in thinking about work right now, she did what she does so well these days and gave him back a piece of his life, while managing to make him believe that he was doing her a favour.

'You'll need your work after I'm gone; it'll give you something to focus on.' The days when she used to take the edge off things, by saying something like 'if the worst comes to the worst', are over, because we already know they have. 'You'll be a better dad to Stan and Flo if you've got work to escape to, and there are going to be things that need paying for. The critical illness payout isn't going to last forever, and I'd be a lot less stressed if I knew you had some work lined up.'

The insurance payout has been one of the small mercies of this situation. Lou had taken out life insurance for both her and Tom as soon as she knew Flo was on the way, the ultimate Plan B in case the worst were to happen. The money has been something to be grateful for. So many of the people I encounter in my volunteering have to negotiate financial struggles on top of everything else. At least Lou and Tom haven't had that to deal with that, and it's a generous payout that means the pressure to return to work is nowhere near as great as Lou suggested. She was giving him the gift of something else to think about and as I watched her kiss him goodbye, my admiration for her rose even higher. When she was first diagnosed, there was a danger of her pushing us all away in her attempt to try and prepare us for life without her, but Lou has found a more balanced way of doing her best to ensure we all survive when she's gone. The trouble is, I still have no idea if I will.

'Mira will be here soon with the palliative care nurse; would you mind putting the kettle on please?' Lou is sitting in her favourite chair in the lounge. Once upon a time she'd never have sat down and rested like this, let alone asked someone else to make her a drink while she relaxed, but she's finally accepting that the more she rests, the more she's able to do. As I process her request, for a moment all I can do is grip the kitchen counter. *Palliative care*. I wish I didn't know what that meant, but I do.

I busy myself setting cups and saucers out on a tray and finding a teapot. I don't know why I'm making such a fuss, but every distraction seems to appeal these days, and I'm still faffing around looking for a milk jug when there's a knock at the door.

'I'll get it.' Calling through to the other room, I head towards the front door before Lou has a chance to respond. I open it to Mira and another woman, who looks to be in her early sixties, and who introduces herself as Judy.

'How are things, Holly?' Mira peers past me into the empty hallway, while they're still standing in the porch, and I shake my head.

'She's exhausted. She's desperately trying to pretend she isn't, but she hardly has the energy for anything. Did the latest test show any changes?' Lou has given permission for Tom and I to be told everything the medical team know, and I can tell by Mira's face, even before she speaks, that the news isn't good.

'The decline in Louisa's kidney function has progressed, despite stopping the chemotherapy and the secondary tumours are all growing quite rapidly. Things are progressing much more quickly than we'd hoped.'

'Will she make it to the party?'

'It's two weeks away, isn't it?' Mira's face gives her away again as I nod. 'I'm not sure she will. The cancer is everywhere now and almost anything could tip the balance. I'm so sorry.'

'I just don't want her to be in any pain.' My heart feels as though it's being ripped from my chest when I think about the prospect of Lou suffering. I hate the thought that she might not make it to her last hurrah, but none of that really matters. I just don't want her to know that Mira isn't expecting her to make it.

'Please don't tell her you don't think she's got that long; I think getting Stan to school and planning for the party is what's keeping her going.'

'I understand, and there's a lot we can do to manage her pain, but staying at home might not be the best option for that, and it's something Judy and I want to talk to her about.'

'She doesn't want to go to the hospital.' I can hear the fear in my own voice, because I know how much the idea of being taken to the hospital and never coming out again scares my sister, but Mira is shaking her head.

'Hospital isn't the best solution either, but we've managed to secure a space for Louisa at St Joseph's Hospice if she wants it. It's a wonderful place and Louisa will get all the care she needs right up to the end. Do you think it's something she might consider?'

'I don't know.' The word hospice sounds every bit as emotive as Judy's job title of palliative care nurse. They both suggest only one thing: we're reaching the end of the line. 'But if you think it's where she'll be cared for best, I'll do what I can to help persuade her. Has St Joseph's got a chapel?'

'Yes, it's beautiful too.' It's Judy who responds this time. 'Is Louisa religious?'

'Not really, but she's found peace since her diagnosis by visiting St Martin's, and it's where she was planning the vow renewal.'

'We could sort that out really quickly if needs be, we've done it before.' Judy makes it sound like a lunch order and it isn't the time to tell her that the party wasn't supposed to be just a vow renewal, there'll need to be Christmas trees, and a birthday cake at the very least. But if Lou does have to move to the hospice, maybe she can still get her last hurrah. It doesn't matter how hard we have to work and what it takes, I'm prepared to do it, if it means Lou holds on for a little bit longer, because right now every moment I have with my sister is precious.

I usher Mira and Judy down the hallway and into the lounge. Catching sight of Lou, my breath lodges in my throat. Sometimes I forget how much she's changed over the past few months, but leaving the room and walking in again is like seeing her properly for the first time in weeks. She looks so fragile now; her cheekbones are hollowed out and the skin looks almost translucent. Her wig seems too big for her now, as if her head has shrunk. It's like she's wasting away before our eyes, disappearing bit by bit. The thought makes tears sting my eyes, and I turn back to the kitchen as Mira introduces Judy. I take my time, re-boiling the kettle and moving with all the haste of a sloth. It's cowardly of me, but I'm not sure I can stand and watch my sister as she's forced to discuss her end-of-life plan. By the time I return with the tray I can tell they've mentioned the possibility of Lou going to the hospice even before she looks at me, her eyes glassy with unshed tears.

'They want me to go to St Joseph's.' She's shaking her head, and I move to her side, taking her hand.

'It's just an idea; no one is going to make you do anything you don't want to do.' Mira's tone is reassuring, and I squeeze my sister's hand, so that she knows I'm on her side too. We all are, but I can understand why she might not feel that way.

'These are difficult things to think about.' Judy tilts her head to one side, giving Lou a sympathetic look and a flash of irritation makes heat flood my cheeks. This woman has already lived two decades longer than my sister is going to get and she's not having to face leaving young children behind, so she's got no idea how difficult this is for Lou. But she carries on anyway. 'It can feel as if all your choices have been taken away from you, but that isn't true. You can decide where you want to spend the time you have left, and where you want to be when the end comes. Many people do choose to be at home, but sometimes that can have a big impact on other family members afterwards, and the hospice team are incredible. It's a lot to think about, and only you know what's right for you and your family.'

'I'm not ready. Not yet.' As she folds her arms across her chest, Lou's tone is resolute.

'And no one is going to force you to do anything; it's just an option to consider.'

'I'll think about it.' Lou turns to look at me and I nod, hoping she knows I'll support her whatever decision she makes. There's never been anything we wouldn't do for one another, and she's always had my back, just like I'll always have hers, but now always is being measured in days and hours, not the decades I'd assumed we had left.

* * *

Lou clearly isn't ready to talk more about the possibility of moving to the hospice when Mira and Judy leave. Instead, she takes out the notebook where she's been keeping lists of her plans for the party, and she turns to a clean page.

'I need to write some words for the renewal service, and I don't know where to start.'

'We could look online?' I pick up my phone and stare at it, so that Lou doesn't see my expression. There might not be a party if Mira is right about the likely decline in her health, and I've never had a poker face. These days I seem to cry more often than not, but if she asks me why I'm crying again, I'm not sure I could pass off a convincing lie. And I'm not going to take the party away from her before cancer gets the chance.

'I don't want my words to come from a website, I need them to come from me, and it's not just Tom I want to say something to, there are other people. I'm just worried about getting it right.'

'It will be right if it comes from you. Don't try to dress it up and make it fancy, just say what's in your heart; that way nothing important will be left unsaid.'

Lou holds my gaze for what feels like an eternity and it's almost as if I can feel the blood pumping through my veins. Have I said the wrong thing and gone too far? We've stopped dancing around the truth and pretending that time isn't running out, but I've made the renewal service sound like the last chance she'll have to say whatever needs to be said, and maybe she's not as ready to face that prospect as I thought she was. But then she nods.

'That's wise advice, thank you.' Reaching out, she squeezes my hand, just like I squeezed hers. 'For everything.'

I'm about to protest that I haven't done anything, but she's already released my hand and within seconds she's scribbling away with a biro, and the blank page is blank no more. This party is so important to her, and I can't let her leave before it happens. Lou has always been the master of the Plan B, but just this once it's my turn to ensure we've got one in place. I'll make sure she gets her farewell party, even if I wish with all my heart that she didn't need to have one.

# 26

## TOM

I remember when Lou and I got married like it was yesterday, but there have been more than three thousand five hundred days since then. That sounds like a hell of a lot, but it turns out that it's not enough. Not even close to it. The run up to the wedding was hectic, as these things often are, and when I broke my leg at the stag weekend, playing football in the garden of a pub of all things, it felt like a disaster. This was it, I'd ruined the wedding. My suit that had been agonised over for so long, would be accessorised with a boot cast and crutches, and there was no way of tying the colour of the cast into the sage green theme. I thought Lou was going to go mad when I told her, but she laughed. Actually laughed. Not a derisive snort of laughter, but a proper laugh, the kind where it takes a while to actually get any words out.

'Great, because that's our three things. All the bad luck being used up before the wedding must be a good thing.' She'd given me a rueful grin when she'd finally managed to speak. Our florist had already gone bankrupt, but far worse than that had been the loss of one of the earrings her grandmother had left her, which she'd been planning to wear on the day we got married. So the prospect of me having a cast in all the photos didn't faze her one little bit.

I realised then that she didn't care about things that didn't matter, when it came to our wedding. She wasn't marrying me for the perfect day, she was marrying me because she wanted to spend the rest of her life with me. I hadn't thought it was possible, but I loved her even more in that moment than I had before, and I didn't have one shred of doubt that I wanted to spend my life with her. I haven't regretted it for one day and even if I'd known that the time we'd have together was going to be cut so short and end so painfully, I wouldn't have missed it for the world.

I'm supposed to be writing some words for the wedding vow renewal and I want to say all of those things, but I don't want to make this about the fact that Lou is dying, I want to make it about the life we've lived together, and how grateful I am that Lou chose me of all people to share her life with. I'm terrified every day that this might be the one where Lou leaves us. She's getting more and more unwell, and the cocktail of medication she's on could restock the village pharmacy. There are nurses coming in and out, and we've put a bed down in the lounge so that Lou doesn't have to try and make it up the stairs.

The cancer has progressed so much more quickly than we expected and, as much as I can't bear the thought of losing her, part of me wonders whether the fact that Lou won't have to continue to suffer is one of the small mercies that Holly and I have tried to cling on to, in the face of losing the woman we both love most in the world. I couldn't have got through this without Holly; it's something I've thought about a lot during this whole nightmare. We've both been scared that Lou won't get the party she so desperately wants, and we've had to accept that it's not going to look how she originally planned. But Holly has worked so hard to make sure that, as long as Lou is still here and still wants to go ahead, she'll get to celebrate our anniversary, a milestone birthday and her final 'Christmas' in a meaningful way. Holly has met with the staff at St Joseph's, and the Plan B to hold the party there has quickly become our Plan A. We're just two days away now and as I take Lou's hand while she sleeps, I silently will her to hold on.

She's sleeping so much of the time now, but when Holly brings the children home from school in about an hour's time, Lou will use every ounce of energy she has to appear as normal as possible, and to make sure she soaks in every detail they're willing to share about the day they've spent without her. I try not to think about just how many more thousands of days of their childhood they'll have to spend without the best mother they could ever have asked for. If I let myself go there, I'm not sure there'll be any coming back.

## 27

I haven't told my family yet, but I won't be coming home from St Joseph's after the party. I've told Mira and she's made the arrangements. The room I'm getting ready in for the vow renewal, is the room where I'll spend most of the rest of my life and it's beautiful. There are French windows with a view out to a water fountain in the garden, and even this late in the morning there are still birds singing in the trees. I really thought I'd want to stay at home, but I feel at peace with the decision I've made, the ultimate contingency for the woman who has always needed a back-up plan to feel safe. I thought a lot about what Mira and Judy said on the day they visited, when they first raised the idea of me coming here, and I think it's the right decision for the children too. If I'm at home at the end, they'll always associate our house – their safe haven – with the place where their mummy died.

I don't know what the end is going to look like and being at the hospice means Tom can decide when the time is right for the children to say goodbye. I don't want them seeing me in my final days, if I can't talk to them, or hold them, and reassure them that it's going to be okay. It might sound like a ridiculous thing to say, but I know now that it's true. They will be okay, more than okay, because they've got Tom, Holly and a whole other army of people who care for them, right down to the staff at the school who've been so kind and supportive.

They're going to miss me, I don't doubt that any more, and it's going to hurt, not just in the immediate aftermath, but at different and sometimes unexpected moments throughout their lives. It will hurt because they know how good it feels to be loved, and to love in return, and there will be a gap where that love should be exchanged between me and my children. But the fact they know how much love matters is what makes them lucky, despite losing their mother at such a young age. Not everyone gets that, but there'll be no shortage of love for my children.

I chose the best man I've ever known to be my children's father, and fate gave them the most wonderful auntie they could have asked for too. So they're not just going to be okay, they're going to be so much more than that, and the thought of letting go hurts a tiny bit less with that knowledge.

'Are you ready?' Holly smiles as she comes into the room, the sight of her and the children making me gasp as another wave of love for them washes over me. Holly and Flo are in ruby red bridesmaid's dresses, and Stan has a little waistcoat to match, but it's covered in holly leaves too, which match the emerald green of my own dress. It had always been the plan to wear my original wedding dress, but despite not being able to zip it up since before I got pregnant with Flo, it now hangs off me like it was made for another woman altogether, and it was. That woman, the one I was before my diagnosis, has already gone.

'Yes, I'm ready.' I look over to Mum and she's clutching Dad's hand like her life depends upon it. There's no sign of either of them having had a drink; Dad's hands are shaky and I don't know how long he'll last before he caves in, but I'm still glad they're here and trying their best.

Jonathan and Billie will be at the ceremony with their children, although Jonathan has now been edged out of the best man role by Stan. He told Tom that Billie has cancelled their holiday away without the children, in favour of a trip to Disney and a weekend in Center Parcs, because she's realised how precious the time with them is. I still can't imagine Billie queuing to meet Mickey, or with her perfectly styled hair plastered to the side of her head as she hurtles down the rapids with her children, but the idea makes me smile for all the right reasons and I hope they make memories that will stay with them forever. I never needed a wakeup call to realise how important the chance to do that is, and I'm so glad we snatched every opportunity we got. I'm not thinking about today as being the last time I'll get to do that, it's just one more chance to make memories that will last forever, no matter how long or short that might be.

* * *

I've cried so much since my diagnosis, mostly the bitter, heart-rending, headache-inducing kind of tears that come with the knowledge you are losing something you desperately want to keep. The tears I have cried today have been very different. There have been moments of sadness, but what I've felt more than anything today is love. Everyone involved has put so much effort into the event. There are six Christmas trees all decorated in our red, green and gold theme in the room that St Joseph's have let us use for the party. Another big Christmas tree had been put in the chapel, and I spotted it as my father pushed my wheelchair down the aisle to meet Tom, while I gripped my mother's hand. There's an archway of balloons that leads into the reception room, and the centrepieces have been made to look like birthday cakes. Holly even had two gold brooches made, saying forty-three, which she pinned on to us after the vow renewal. It's definitely a step up from the sashes and deely-boppers I'd envisaged.

I loved every word Tom said in the vows he wrote for me, but one part in particular seemed to sum it all up.

'I don't think I ever really knew what love was until I met you, but that's because I was trying to define something that is never just one thing. It's about sharing the best times and the hardest and knowing that whatever the situation there's nowhere else you'd rather be, and no one else you'd rather share that moment with. It's as messy and ugly, as it is perfect and beautiful, but there is no one else I would have wanted to share my life with, and no place I've ever preferred to be than right by your side. We've made an amazing family and the love I had for you ten years ago has grown so much bigger. Whatever happens, it will continue to grow, through Flo and Stan, and that's the vow that I make you, because nothing can take away what we've built, and I wouldn't change it for the world. So I've had something made to mark the occasion.'

There wasn't a dry eye in the house even before he slipped the ring on to my finger that was set with the diamond from my grandmother's remaining earring, which I'd kept in a drawer for more than a decade and it meant so much that he'd done that. Then it was my turn.

'I know you're all expecting this to be about me making a vow to Tom, and celebrating the last ten years, and I'll get to that I promise, but today is also mine and Holly's birthday, and a kind of Christmas in September. Birthdays and Christmas are times when you share heartfelt words with people too and so there are some other things that I want to say, but I'll start with Tom.'

I turned to look directly at him, taking his hand, as he sat in a chair facing my wheelchair, a world away from how we exchanged our vows all those years before. 'Tom, I want to thank you for loving me from the first moment, right through to the last. For giving me the life I dreamt of ever since I can remember, and the best children in the world. I want to thank you for never asking anything of me, except to love you and our children, which was always so easy. It's been a blast, and I feel so lucky to have shared it all with you. I love you now more than ever, but there's one special vow I need to make to you today and it's this. If you ever think about trying to replace me, you'll never do better.' I paused then and a roar of laughter filled the room. 'But I want you to know that if she makes you even half as happy as you've made me, then she has my blessing.'

As I glanced towards Stan and Flo, after Tom and I had kissed, relief flooded my body that they were smiling. I'd been worried that saying this in front of them might upset them, but I'd thought long and hard about making it sound like a general what-if, rather than something that's very likely to happen one day. I'd also prepared Holly so she could reassure them if it made them worry more than they already were, but thankfully they seemed to be taking it in their stride.

'Now for my parents.' Tom stood up and turned my wheelchair, so that I was facing out towards where they sat, in the front row. They were probably nervous about what I was going to say, but they didn't need to be. This wasn't a time for recriminations, it was a time to make peace. 'We've been through some tough times, but I've always known that you love me. I want you to know that all of the bad times are forgiven, and all I ask in return is that you find a way to love yourselves as much as I love you.'

I wasn't sure at that point if I could carry on. I was already crying, but there was still so much I needed to say and I knew this might be my only chance. I could have said these things to the people I loved most in private, but I needed it to be imprinted on the memories of everyone sharing the day. That way, in years to come, when they talk about it with people who were there, they'll know how much I loved them and all the hopes I had for their future. They won't have to wonder if they've remembered what I said correctly, or what it felt like to be in that room, because everyone there will have experienced it and they'll be able to help the children fill in any gaps that might develop over time too.

'Holly, my other half. My partner in crime, confidante and lifelong best friend. You're the person who makes me laugh until I cry, knows my deepest secrets and has seen me at my worst, but has never once made me feel any less than loved. You're my rock and the person I trust most in the world, and I know that if I leave things in your hands, I'll be leaving them in the best possible place, but I want you to grab all that life has to offer. Do it for us and don't play it safe, because you deserve the world and I want you to experience it all. I love you in a way that only two people who met before they were even born can ever really love each other and I'm so incredibly grateful that you are my sister, and the best auntie ever.'

I'd almost got through it, but when Holly came up with Stan and Flo, it felt as if I was choking on the tears. I still had the hardest part to say, a public goodbye to my children that the videographer would record for them to watch back in the future, and I couldn't let them down.

'Don't worry everyone, I'm almost done. This isn't an Oscar speech, and I'm not going to list everyone from the postman to my hairdresser, I promise. Luckily, this comes ready done these days anyway.' I pointed to my wig and laughter spread around the room for a second time. I'm sure the guests were grateful that I'd lightened the mood, but it was more for me than them. It was the only way I could get through the last part. 'I want to thank all of you for coming today and for the role you've played in my wonderful life, because it really has been the best. But my final words are for my amazing children. Stan and Flo, you have been my everything in a way I never fully understood until recent months. Getting to be your mummy has been the best thing I've ever done and I'm so incredibly proud of how kind and thoughtful and loving you are. When I became your mummy, I got to be everything I ever wanted to be and I hope, when you grow up, that you remember you can be whatever you want to be too. It doesn't matter what that is, as long as you love and are loved in return, because that's all that really counts in the end.'

I don't know if they really understood, but when I held them both in turn, they clung on tight, and I think deep down they can sense that the end is approaching. We told them what we felt they could cope with, when I was first diagnosed, enough so the ending won't be a total shock, but not so much that they were unable to enjoy the time we had left. Things are changing quickly now and, once the party is over, we're going to have to tell them the truth. But for today there are still magical moments to be had, untainted for them by the knowledge that our time together has almost run out. And as I look at them now, charging towards me, I'm so grateful that I made it to this day and got to share all of this with them.

'You're the prettiest mummy here!' Flo presses her face against mine, her cheeks flushed from being chased around the room by her brother, as the DJ works his way through all my favourite songs.

'And you're the prettiest girl in the whole wide world.'

'Can I have this dance?' Tom suddenly appears beside our daughter, and gestures towards where Holly is now resting Stan on her hip, and spinning them both around in circles.

'Which one of us are you asking?' I look up at Tom and he smiles.

'Both of my girls.' Hoisting Flo on to my lap, he leans down so that he can hold my hands and gently pull us around in something that could pass for a slow dance shuffle. My parents join us on the dance floor, and Stan squeals with delight as his auntie dips her hip and tips him down towards the floor and back up again. I want to hold on to this perfect moment and never let go, but that's the thing about perfect moments, it's the knowledge that they will pass that makes them so beautiful, and all any of us can do is enjoy them while they last, and never, ever take them for granted.

# 28

## TOM

When Lou told me she wasn't coming home after that party, part of me wanted to try to persuade her to give us just one more night. But, when I looked at her, I realised just how much of herself she's already given us. Exhausted doesn't even cover it. She's been running on pure adrenaline to get through the party. We cut the timings down to just two hours from start to finish in the end, but it's still taken every ounce of strength she has left, and it would be selfish of me to try to persuade her to come home. But the idea of leaving her in St Joseph's alone terrifies me, in case she doesn't make it through the night. So I'm staying with her.

Holly has offered to look after the children, which is a huge weight off my mind, but we both know the time has come to be more honest with them about how Lou's cancer is progressing. We've agreed to talk to them tonight and I'm dreading it. Every conversation we've had with Lou's consultant has felt like the most difficult one of my life so far, but somehow I know this is going to be even worse.

The bag of stuff I need for St Joseph's is sitting at the bottom of the stairs and I can't put this off any longer. It's been a long and tiring day, and Stan and Flo are already in their pyjamas, courtesy of Auntie Holly. Stan's PJs are royal blue brushed cotton, with little green dinosaurs printed on them, and his sister's have got a tartan pattern. Flo's are from the set we all had last Christmas Eve, when we cosied up on the sofa together watching Disney movies until it was time to put out mince pies for Santa. I can't believe that was less than nine months ago, because it seems like another life entirely. A whole other world in fact. We had no idea what was to come and I'm grateful for that, but the speed with which everything has changed makes it even harder to believe it's real.

'She insisted on wearing her Christmas pyjamas to carry on with the celebrations.' It's clear Holly is exhausted too, when I look at her properly for the first time. I wonder how people cope when illness like this goes on for years. How do they keep living life and going to work, and carrying on with all the things that don't stop when someone they love has a terminal diagnosis? I have no idea, because I can feel us all running out of energy to keep putting one foot in front of the other, and we've been so lucky to be able to put work to one side. I guess they have no choice, and the truth is I'd keep going forever if it meant Lou could stay. That's how people do it, because nothing else matters as much as that does.

'Thank you.' I mouth the words to Holly and it's about so much more than getting the children into their pyjamas. I hope she knows that, but when all of this is over, I am going to tell her how grateful I am and just how much she means to me. Crouching slightly, I pull the children close, hugging them to my chest, until finally I'm forced to let them go when Stan starts trying to wriggle.

'Shall we all go and sit on the sofa? There's something Auntie Holly and I need to talk to you about.'

'What's wrong?' I catch my sister-in-law's eye as Flo asks the all-too-insightful question, and I feel like a deer in the headlights. How do I tell my seven-year-old daughter that everything's wrong, because she's about to lose her mum? I open my mouth to speak and nothing comes out, so it's Holly who has to save me from making this even worse.

'Nothing's happened, don't worry, we just need to talk to you about Mummy.' Before Flo can ask anything else, I scoop her into my arms, and Holly follows suit with Stan. We need to get to the sofa before everything comes out, somehow that feels incredibly important, as though being on the sofa when we give them this kind of news might in some way lessen the devastation we're about to unleash. It was a stupid idea, because the first thing I notice when we go into the lounge is Lou's empty bed.

'Where's Mummy? I want to see her.' Stan struggles free and runs over to the bed, looking underneath as if his mum might be hiding there.

'Come back here, sweetheart.' Holly gets to her feet and takes hold of his hand, bringing him back to the sofa. 'Mummy's stayed at St Joseph's where we had the party today.'

'Why?' Stan wrinkles his nose. 'Does she want some more cake?'

'No, darling.' I reach out and take his hand, my other arm wrapped around Flo's shoulders. 'They don't usually have parties at St Joseph's; they did it especially for us. It's a place where people usually go when they get really poorly, and they aren't going to get better. Do you remember we told you that the doctors can't make Mummy better?'

'Yes, but they can stop her getting more poorly.' Flo's eyes lock with mine and I know what she's thinking, that we made her a promise that she's been counting on us keeping. I just hope she can forgive me for letting her down.

'That's what we were hoping, but the medicine the doctors were giving her to do that stopped working, and that means...' Heaving a shuddering sigh, the rest of the words lodge in my throat. I know what I have to say, I just don't know how.

'It means Mummy is going to die.' Holly keeps it simple, just like we planned, but the wail that goes up from the children in response was something I could never have imagined. The sound is other worldly, and it physically hurts to hear it. I didn't want to cry, because this moment isn't about me, it's about them, but there's no way to control it and, when I look across at Holly, the tears are streaming down her face too.

'I don't want Mummy to die!' Flo hammers her tiny fists against my chest, but I barely even feel it.

'None of us do, baby. It's not fair and we all love Mummy so much.' I pull her closer, and Stan still hasn't spoken; he's cradled into the nook of Holly's arm, like the baby he was such a short time ago, and I ache for the parts of my children's childhood that cancer is stealing from them.

'Who's going to do my hair? You can't do it, you're rubbish at it.' I can almost feel the anger pulsating through my daughter's body. One of the things Lou has still managed right up to now, is doing Flo's hair for school, because even a ponytail ends up a lopsided mess on my watch. Flo's not really worried about her hair, that much I know. She's scared about who's going to take care of her and fill the gaps her mother is about to leave behind. Some of those gaps are unfillable, but I want her to know we'll do our best, and that she and Stan have people who love them and who'll be there for whatever they need. They're not just left with me.

'Auntie Holly will do it for special occasions, and I can learn to do it for school. She can teach me.'

'But I don't want Mummy to die!' Flo repeats her appeal, even more plaintively, and her little brother lets out a plea all of his own.

'I want my mummy.' It's such a simple request, one that should be so easily granted, but none of us can grant that wish for him or Flo, at least not for much longer, and I can't imagine anything more devastating because Lou's their whole world, and she's my everything too.

* * *

It's three days since the party and I haven't even shut my eyes, let alone slept, for the last twenty-four hours. Lou seems to be getting weaker with every passing hour and it won't be long now. For a moment when I looked at her earlier in the half light, I could have convinced myself her skin had the kind of sun-kissed glow it always gets when we have a holiday somewhere warm. Except I know it's not that; the nurses have said the tumour in her liver is taking it over, and her skin tone is changing far more noticeably as the liver begins to fail. I know I should make some phone calls, and bring people in, but I want her to myself for just a bit longer. She's mostly sleeping now, but when she wakes up, she's still lucid, and there are glimmers of the old Lou that I can't miss out on. She's already given me instructions on the list of places I need to try and take the children to see, before they outgrow wanting to go on holiday with their dad. She's also made me promise to go back to work properly as soon as I can and told me how proud she is of my career, and how she'll never forgive me if I let that become another casualty of her cancer.

It's only six o'clock in the morning, so I reason that I've got a couple of hours before I put in the call asking Holly to bring the children in and telling my in-laws that I think they need to come back too. The children have been in to visit once since the party, for less than half an hour, and Holly and I agreed afterwards that we'd only do it again when the time came to say goodbye. Holly got the hospice's permission to bring her cat, Tigs, along, when she brought the children in. It was the perfect distraction and gave them something to chat to their mum about, which didn't require much input from her. The cat was still stretched out alongside Lou when the time came for Holly and the children to leave, his loud purring almost like a lullaby.

'Could he stay, do you think?' Lou rested her hand on his body as she spoke, and Holly had nodded. She disappeared for less than five minutes, before coming back in to say she'd sorted it all out.

So now we're here, Lou and I, on her bed, with a large, ginger cat lying like a chaperone between us. And when she opens her eyes, she catches me watching her.

'Still creepy, watching me sleep.' She doesn't waste any words, now just being here is an effort, but there's a hint of a smile playing around her lips.

'I can't help it. I've never wanted to look elsewhere when there's a chance to look at you.' I repeat the line I've said many times before, and there's a glimmer in her eye that I thought I might never see again.

'Still cheesy, too.' She manages a small laugh this time and I savour the sound, trying not to wonder if it's the last time I'll ever hear it, and I entwine my fingers with hers instead. 'I trust you.'

'I should think so after all this time.' It's my turn to smile, but she's shaking her head.

'I trust you to pick the right person, for you and the children.'

'I don't want—'

'Stop.' Her tone is forceful, despite her voice being barely more than a whisper. 'I want you to be happy, not lonely, and I trust you.'

'Okay.' It's such an inadequate word when I want to say so much. That no one on earth could ever come close to Lou, and that the thought of ever trying to find someone to take her place is ridiculous, but I know she needs to believe I can be happy again without her, so *okay* is about all I can manage.

'But get it wrong and I'll come back to haunt you.' She laughs again and this time I do too. This awful disease has hit our lives like a wrecking ball, but my Lou is still here, finding humour until the last. Cancer was never a match for the love of my life.

# 29

## HOLLY

The palliative care team have told Tom that Lou will almost certainly die today and I've brought the children in to say goodbye. I spent some time this morning preparing them as best I can for what's to come, but I don't even know how to prepare myself. I've told Stan and Flo that Mummy might sleep a lot, and that the doctors are giving her medicine to make sure she's not in any pain, but there's a chance it will make her even sleepier. When Tom told me about the change to Lou's skin tone, I knew I had to prepare them for that too, and I explained that Mummy might look a bit different, because her body isn't working as well as it used to. They both cried then, and I did too, but it seemed to help the children more than me. I couldn't face eating, but when I offered to make them pancakes, they were much more enthusiastic than I expected.

I'm amazed at how resilient they're being, but I know their grief won't be a linear path. The reality of their mother being gone forever won't even begin to set in until it happens, and even then I suspect it won't fully sink in for quite a long time. The temptation to soften the edges for them has been so great, but all the advice from the various charities I've worked with is to keep things simple and avoid using confusing terms, like Mummy has gone to sleep, or she's up in the sky. Telling them that Lou is going to die is the worst thing I've ever had to do, but it would have been even worse to have to do it more than once. I don't think I could go through that again and yet even as we pull into the car park of St Joseph's, I know that very soon either me or Tom will have to tell them that their mother is dead.

'Okay guys, are you ready?' I turn to look at my niece and nephew, who both nod solemnly and, as I open the car door, I send up a silent prayer that today will be a good day for Lou, and that she'll be able to say a proper goodbye to her children.

'Hello babies.' Lou is propped up on pillows as we come into the room. She seems even smaller than she did at the party and there's no denying that she looks like someone who is dying. But she smiles at the children and holds out her arms to them. For a moment they hesitate, and I wonder if they're afraid, either of what Lou looks like now, or of somehow hurting her, but then they rush forward to give her a hug. Tom looks like he hasn't slept properly in weeks, and I suspect I do too, but we're here, and we're together, and somehow we'll get through this because of that.

'Do you know how much I love you both?' Even Lou's voice sounds different, and every word is clearly an effort, but the children nod.

'I love you too, Mummy.' Flo speaks first and then her brother responds too.

'I love you even more.' There's a flicker of a smile from my sister then, at the sibling rivalry. Having a twin sister has been the cornerstone of my life and I don't know who I'll be if I'm not Lou's other half any more.

'I'm going to miss you both so much, but if you ever miss me, you can give Daddy or Auntie Holly a great big hug, and they'll give you one back from me. I'm going to give them all my hugs to store up before I go, and they'll never run out.'

'I don't want you to die, Mummy.' Flo repeats her plea from the night of the party and Stan starts to cry.

'I don't want to die either, but my body has stopped working. I'll always love you, nothing can take that away. And if Daddy lifts you up on to the bed now, we can have a nice, long cuddle, and Tigs will squeeze in too. How about that?'

The children turn towards their father and urge him to lift them on to the bed, and he quickly obliges. Lou winces as little arms and legs thrash around until they all find a comfortable position, and then her face relaxes. I can hardly breathe for fear that the sobs that are caught in my throat might suddenly escape, and I marvel once more at what an amazing woman my sister is. It's only when I look at her face again a few moments later, that I realise how hard she's crying, silent tears sliding into the children's hair. She knows these are the last moments they'll ever share and the only way she'd have been able to stop herself from crying would be if she was already gone.

* * *

Flo and Stan hadn't wanted to go home and, in the end, Lou had whispered to Tom that she would pretend to be asleep, so he could tell them that Mummy needed to rest. Eventually they were persuaded to leave and I could see Lou's hands twitching as she pretended to sleep and fought the urge to reach out and hold them one final time.

Her friend, Joanna, came to pick the children up and my parents are on the way to say their final goodbyes too. But for now, it's Tom and me by the side of her bed, as I watch the rise and fall of her chest, and try not to hold my own breath.

'I want a mint Aero.' For a moment I think Lou is dreaming, but then she tugs on the sleeve of Tom's shirt and repeats her request. 'Mint Aero please. Holly can stay here.'

She's barely eaten in weeks and not at all since the party, but there's an urgency to her tone and Tom doesn't argue.

'Okay, I'll go to the shop. Do you want something, Holly?' He looks straight at me and widens his eyes, and it's then that I realise what it is that Lou really wants, and what he understood before I did. My sister wants some time on her own with me, while she still has the chance.

'I'll have the same as Lou.' It's something I must have said on thousands of occasions, because I've always wanted to be more like my sister. When I was a kid, it was probably more about not missing out on anything that I thought she was getting, but once we got older it was because I admired her so much and trusted her judgement.

When Tom disappears, I move to lie down next to Lou, face to face, and she takes hold of my hand.

'Thank you.' Her words are barely more than a whisper.

'What for?'

'For everything, for being you, and for your advice on the forum.' The length of the sentence seems to have her struggling for breath, and it makes me gasp too. I didn't know for a long time that the person I was corresponding with was my sister. She'd changed the details of her illness and kept other details vague. I wondered if it might be her when I realised she was asking the same question that seemed to be occupying a lot of Lou's concerns, about who might come into her children's lives after she'd gone. I figured it didn't matter whether it was Lou or not, I wanted to give this desperately scared women the same advice I would give my sister if I thought she was ready to listen.

I could tell @worriedmum1982 that all that mattered was making memories with her loved ones, that she needed to say all the things she thought were important, and that she had people she could trust to make sure her children would always be surrounded by love. Lou wasn't ready to hear any of those things from me, but it turned out she could listen to @itsnotallover2. As time went on, I had no doubt it was her, recognising Lou in the way she supported other people on the forum, long before she started talking about the party and having a twin sister. Part of me had wanted to tell Lou who I was, and that I knew it was her, but she'd made herself vulnerable and shared her innermost thoughts, in a place she'd assumed she was anonymous. I hadn't wanted to take that safe space away from her, so I kept it a secret, hoping she'd never find out.

'You knew?' She nods and I need to know when she worked it out. 'Right from the start?'

She shook her head. 'Not until I was writing my vows, when you told me not to leave anything unsaid...'

'I didn't know it was you either at first, it was the wrong type of cancer, but then I heard your voice in the words of encouragement you gave to other people and even on an anonymous forum you couldn't hide who you were. I thought about telling you, but I didn't know how you'd react and I didn't want you to lose the support of the forum, or for others to miss out on all the support you were giving them, despite what you were going through. You're the best person I've ever met Lou, and I'm so lucky I got to be your sister.'

'I love you.' She closes her eyes for a moment and if it wasn't for the flicker of her eyelids, I'd have been certain she was gone, but then she opens them again and looks straight at me.

'Look after the letters on my desk; they were your idea after all.' The hint of a smile is back for an instant and then her eyelids grow heavy, and I know that our last moments alone together have already passed. If we'd had forever, I could still never have told her all the things I need to say, so I just whisper that I'll always love her, and lie by her side until Tom comes back.

# 30

## LOUISA

The morphine driver has been a Godsend, despite how much it makes me sleep, and my last days and hours have been free from the physical pain that I feared so much. But no amount of morphine can deaden the heartache of saying goodbye to the people I love.

I can't believe I'll never see the children again. I won't accept it. I've never particularly believed in anything that comes after this, but I know that I'll meet them again, and I feel now as if I've met them before, in another life. Holly and Tom too. Our lives are so inextricably linked, it would take more than one lifetime to create that kind of bond, and a lot more than death to unravel it all. I don't know, maybe that's the morphine talking, but it suddenly feels so certain and it gives me comfort to cling to.

It's too much effort to talk now and I'm grateful that I took Holly's advice while I could and left nothing unsaid. I've told the people who made up my whole world just how much I love them and how important they've been to me and I hope my words will give them comfort. Not just the things I've said in the last few days, but in the letters I've left for Holly to distribute. I should have known it was her, guiding me online; after all, she works with lots of cancer charities and groups, and looking back it could only have been Holly.

I wasn't sure whether to be angry at first. But when I re-read her messages, I saw how perfect they were and how well she understood the situation, when I was still so confused. My attempts to push her and Tom together were ridiculous, and she knew that from the start, but if she'd told me that as Holly, I might never have listened. It was easier to take heed of my anonymous online friend, and acting on her advice has made my goodbyes far less agonising than they would have been otherwise.

When I open my eyes again, the light outside is fading fast, and I can feel my breathing growing shallower. Tom and Holly are holding my hands, and my parents are at the far end of the bed, all of them watching me and waiting. It must be torture, and I'm so glad the roles aren't reversed; I don't think I could bear it.

'You're the best thing that ever happened to me, and I promise I'll love the children enough for both of us.' Tom's voice is so familiar, but it feels like he's drifting further away and I try to nod to let him know I've heard what he's said.

'We love you, sweetheart, and we're so proud of you.' Mum's voice is thick with emotion.

'Sleep tight, darling girl, I—' That's as far as Dad gets before he lets out a sob, and I watch Mum fold him into her arms.

'I love you, Lou, and I'll miss you forever, but it's okay if you go now. Nan and Gramps will be waiting.' My sister's sweet voice is the last thing I hear, and even though I battle to keep my eyes open, I know I can't keep fighting to stay awake. When I close my eyes, I won't be coming back, but it's okay because I've lived the most beautiful life. My eyelids are getting so heavy now and I know it's time, so I take a deep breath and let them close.

# 31

## HOLLY

I keep waiting for Lou to breathe again and, when she doesn't, the urge to shake her almost overwhelms me. I thought I was ready, but I'm not. She can't be gone; all the light that was my sister cannot just be extinguished. I'm already aching to hear her laugh again, or to reminisce about something only the two of us can remember, but she's so still. For a moment the only sound is Mum sobbing. Emotion is choking in my throat, but I can't cry, because that would make it real, and when I accept that this is it and I'll never get to talk to my sister again, I don't know if I'll be able to function. Instead I try to focus on the practicalities, hoping that they'll stop the emotion from completely over-whelming me.

There's so much to do; so many people loved Lou and organ-ising the funeral is going to be a major task. Before anything else, Stan and Flo will need to be told. Tom has asked me to be there when that happens, but we'd already agreed that if Lou died before the children were due back from Joanna's he wouldn't pick them up to tell them any sooner. That will give them one more day of not knowing she's gone. I don't know if an expert on these things would say that's the right thing to do, but all I know is that I'd give anything right now to have one more day of believing that Lou is still around.

I finally let go of my sister's hand as one of the nurses comes into the room. She's talking about next steps, but I don't take it in. Kissing Lou's still-warm forehead, I turn to my parents and allow myself to be wrapped in their arms as they whisper their gratitude that they've still got me. It hits me all over again, that I'm just half of a pair, an only child now, who was born to be one of two. And despite my fears that giving in to tears would be a lifelong commitment, I can't stop them coming. I haven't just lost my sister and my best friend, it feels like I've lost myself too.

# 32

## TOM

The staff at the hospice were wonderful. They took as much care of Lou in death as they had in life. She'd only been there for a few days after the party, but some of the staff were clearly moved by her death, and spoke about her as though they knew her far better than that, just because of the brief exchanges they'd had, or the way Lou acted. She had that effect on people, but I don't think she ever realised it. They say that people might not remember what you said to them, but they will remember how they made you feel, and Lou just had this knack of making people feel good. That's not to say she was perfect; I've got to try to avoid putting her on a pedestal, because the void in my life without her is already so vast, and if I re-paint her as perfect, it will swallow me whole. She lost patience with people at times, and there were those who irritated her, but her heart was always so good, and she gave second chances far more easily than most. Holly's the same; for twins they were incredibly different in some ways, but that good-heartedness ran through both of them like words through a stick of rock.

All the paperwork that made Lou's death official was

processed quickly, but it still doesn't feel real, and I don't think it will until Holly and I tell the children.

'Did you have a nice time?' It's the first thing I say to them, after Joanna drops them back home, but my daughter's no fool and she cuts to the chase.

'Is Mummy okay?'

'Come here, sweetheart.' I pull my daughter on to my lap, and Holly picks up Stan. Even before I say anything else, Flo starts to cry. 'Mummy died yesterday.'

'Is she coming back?' Stan looks so confused and despite the ways we tried to prepare them, the enormity of the truth still hasn't hit him.

'No, darling, she's not. Her body got really tired and it just stopped working. She really wanted to stay here with you and Flo, because she loved you both so much, but she just couldn't.' Holly holds him tight as he starts to cry too.

'What if you die too, Daddy?' Flo looks at me through the tears and my stomach turns to concrete. 'Or Auntie Holly.'

'We're not going to die, I promise you that we'll always be here to look after you.' Lou and I made a pact years ago never to make the children promises we weren't certain we could keep, but just this once I think she'd forgive me, because our children desperately need to hear that they won't lose anyone else.

'Mummy loved the two of you more than anything in the world. I do too, and so does Auntie Holly. We promised Mummy that we'd make our love even bigger than it was already, because she isn't here any more to give you her share, and you don't need to worry about anything. We're going to be here, and whenever you want to talk about Mummy, or you're missing her hugs, all you have to do is say.'

'Is she in heaven?' Flo's eyes are still round with concern, but some of the tension seems to have left her face, and I nod my head. I don't know if I believe in any of that, and the truth is until Lou died I'd have said it was a fairy tale to make loss more bearable. But what else was my life with Lou, if it wasn't a fairy tale? We should never have got together after the way we met, or had such amazing children with incredible ease, when Holly fought like mad and never got the chance to be a mother. Okay, so our happy ever after might have been cut far too short, but as I look at our children, I realise our story isn't over, even without Lou.

'Does Mummy live on a cloud?' For a moment Flo's question takes me by surprise, but what shocks me even more is that there's a bubble of laughter trying to get past the lump in my throat that I thought might stop me from ever laughing again. And when I look across at Holly, her lips are twitching too, but it's Holly who regains her composure first to answer Flo's question.

'I don't know, darling, but whatever it's like in heaven, Mummy will be happy. She'll miss you and Stan like mad, but she'll be with our grandparents, so she won't be alone. Best of all she's not poorly any more, and she'll be so proud of you both and never stop loving you.'

I hope with all my heart that Holly's description of where Lou is now is true, but even if it's not I'm certain it was the right thing to say. The smile on Flo's face and the calming of Stan's tears are enough to convince me of that. Maybe I was wrong about what happens after someone dies, I don't know. But there's something else I know I was wrong about, when I said Holly had never got the chance to be a mother. She's been like a second mother to the children from the moment they arrived. It can't make up for losing their mum, nothing ever could, but they really do have the next best thing and it's the closest to a happy ever after my children could ask for, in a life without Lou.

# 33

## HOLLY

Today is my sister's funeral. Those are not words I should be saying. She didn't want everyone to wear black, because she thought it would make the children even more sad. Her favourite colour was green, but she didn't dictate that everyone should wear that, because she wasn't that kind of person. It was me who asked that people wear a splash of green if they have it, a necklace or some socks, but I told them, if not, whatever they want would have been just fine with Lou.

Lou drew people to her like a magnet, although she never really saw that herself. Even the people who acted as if they didn't like her, reacted that way because they wanted to be like her in some way. Lou was confident in her decisions, happily walking away from a career with a level of prestige because she wanted to focus on being a mother. She didn't let it worry her what other people thought, or take any notice of the barbed comments she'd get about stay-at-home mothers somehow having less worth. Equally she didn't try to pretend her choices were for everyone, and she understood why so many of her friends either wanted to work, or had to, sometimes both. But it was that assurance in who she was that sometimes made people envy her. I knew the other side, though; how hard won that apparent confidence was, and just how many Plan Bs there had been along the way to give her that assurance. It was why she'd kept a tiny bit of freelance work going, in case it turned out that full-time parenting wasn't for her, or if hers and Tom's financial situation ever drastically changed and she no longer had the privilege of choice. She was only confident because the Plan B was in place; it was who she was, but only those closest to her ever really saw that side of Lou.

That magnetic charm explains why there's not enough room in St Martin's for everyone who wants to say goodbye, and why the doors have been left open so those in the churchyard can still hear. Kate has been given special permission to lead the service, and I'm so glad that's the case. She's known Lou a long time, getting far closer to her over recent weeks, and that's clear in how she talks about her as the service begins.

My parents are at the far end of the pew, next to me, with Flo and Stan sitting between me and Tom. The children have been amazing, since we told them the news. Of course there have been tears, lots of them, and a couple of meltdowns, but there have been times when they've come to comfort me, or Tom. Those are the moments when I know that Lou isn't really gone; she's here in her children and I'm really grateful that Tom wants me to be so involved. I'm not living in the house with them, but I visit every day. And sometimes Tom drops the children to me, to give him some time on his own. Things will change over time and at some point I'll need to step back a bit, but just as Lou knew her raison d'être was to be their mother, I know mine is to help the space she left behind feel a little less empty.

Tom and I are both speaking today, and I hope I can do Lou justice. When he gets up to speak and stands next to the wicker coffin, topped with yellow and white roses, I wrap my arm around both children and take a deep breath.

'It's a testament to how loved Lou was that there are so many of you here today. She'd have been incredibly touched that so many of you have given up your time to be here.' Tom's swallow is caught by the microphone and I can see in his eyes that this is every bit as hard as we'd both suspected it would be. It doesn't matter that he's a seasoned journalist who regularly appears on screen, these words are the ones he most wants to get right and they're also the hardest he's ever had to say.

'I never thought this day would come. I know it comes for us all, but I'd always assumed I would go first. No one wants to imagine dying, but that thought gave me comfort, because a life without Lou felt like no life at all. And yet it turns out I was wrong on so many counts, most of all that there is any such thing as a life without Lou. She's still here in every conversation I have with friends, the great things they remember about her, or what she did to make them feel welcome as a part of our lives. She's in every corner of our house, with the things she did to make it feel like home. I thought I knew everything I was ever going to know about Lou, and that now she's not here, there would never be another chance for me to discover something wonderful about her, and my God I've discovered so many wonderful things about my wife over the years. But it turns out I was wrong about that too, because Lou's parents and most of all, her twin sister, Holly, are still helping me to discover wonderful things that I never knew about my wife. That gives me more comfort than I could ever have imagined. The relationship with someone you love doesn't end when they die, it just changes, and whenever it feels like Lou's further away, all I have to do is look at our wonderful children to know for sure that there's no such thing as a life without her, because my life has been all about Lou from the day we met, and not even death can take that away.'

I don't know if Tom originally planned to say more than that, but he steps back as emotion threatens to overwhelm him. Whatever he originally planned, it doesn't matter, because the words he has just delivered are perfect. As he moves back towards his seat, I thank Kate's foresight for suggesting that we have a hymn in between Tom's eulogy and mine. A big part of me wants to hand the words I have written to Kate and just ask her to read them on my behalf, but I can't let Lou down. Although even my silent mouthing of 'Amazing Grace' is a pitiful effort, as I try to gather myself together.

Moving past the children and Tom, I concentrate on breathing in and out, but just as I reach the lectern, I freeze, more uncertain than ever that I can do this. And that's when I feel it, the strangest sensation, like a hand on the small of my back urging me on. I know it's just my imagination, but I allow the feeling to take over, and keep walking, setting down the piece of paper in front of me. Except, after the things Tom has just said, I know I'm going to be going slightly off script.

'Tom has already said it all, far better than I ever could, but as hard as this is, I could not let this moment pass without telling you all just how much Lou meant to me.' I look down for a moment, and then turn towards the wicker coffin and try not to picture my sister lying inside it. Instead, I think of us together, Lou throwing her head back as she so often did when she found something funny, and how often that would escalate to us crying with laughter in a way I've never quite done with anyone else. 'Lou, lots of people are born with gifts. Some people can paint, or dance, or sing, or play a musical instrument so beautifully it can bring people to tears. You were born with so many gifts, like your ability to love fiercely and freely, to make people feel comfortable and to find laughter in the toughest of situations. You also had the gift of crafting words in a way that could paint a picture of a place you'd visited, more vividly than any photograph or video could ever hope to convey. You were never short of gifts, but I often wondered what mine was. What was the greatest gift I was born with, if indeed there were any? I've realised in the last few months what that gift was, and what I should always have known. I had the greatest gift anyone could ever have been born with, and that gift was you. So I can't feel bitter that forty-three years wasn't long enough, and I'll try not to feel as terribly sad as I do right now that you're no longer here, because Tom was right, you're not really gone. I can still feel that fierce love you had for the people who meant the most to you, and I can hear the echo of your laughter when Stan starts to giggle, and your brilliant way with words that Flo is already showing. Thank you for the gift you gave me of being my sister, of sharing your life and your family with me. I will love you forever and I'll never stop missing you, but nothing can take away the bond we had.'

I should be walking back to my seat, but I can hardly see for my tears, and I'm frozen to the spot for a second time. Only now there's no hand at my back. Twenty seconds later, I'm still facing the congregation. I can't walk away and leave Lou behind, this time forever. My legs just won't cooperate. I look at Tom, silently begging him to help me, but before he can react, Flo pushes past him, with Stan hot on her heels. And in seconds they are with me, placing their tiny hands in mine, and my whole body relaxes, like a taut wire that's been about to snap and is suddenly released instead. I'm not half of a whole, forever incomplete without my sister. I'm part of a jigsaw, and even though there's a piece missing, which means the picture will never be quite as perfect as it used to be, it's still beautiful in its own unique way and that's all because of Lou.

\* \* \*

The wake has been beautiful in its own way too. It's being held in a marquee in the grounds of St Martin's, on the side that over-looks the woods and fields behind the church, just like we'd orig-inally planned to do for Lou's party. Drinks and food were served following the church service, and most of the mourners stayed in the marquee while Lou's body was taken for a private cremation at a crematorium ten miles away, with just the closest of family attending. Now we're all back. It's one of those stunning autumn days, where the dappled sunlight of late afternoon perfectly highlights the kaleidoscope of changing colours, ambers, golds and russet reds all competing for attention. Laughter is the soundtrack of the afternoon, as people share memories of Lou. There have been tears too, but she'd have been so happy that there's been more of a focus on the joy she brought to all of our lives.

My parents are sitting with Kate and her dad and stepmum. It's been a tough day for all of us, but I know they have felt as wrapped in the love from the community of Castlebourne as I have. I hope it's something they can take forward with them to finally find the help Lou so desperately wanted them to get.

Tom has been circulating amongst the guests, doing what Lou would have done and making sure no one feels left out. Last night I gave him the first of the letters, as Lou's note inside the box on her desk had instructed me to do. There was one for him and one for each of the children, to be read on the eve of her funeral. I'm aching to know what the letters said, and as I look up and see Tom heading towards me, I wonder if he'll tell me, or if it's some-thing he wants to keep to himself. I feel a little bit envious that Tom and the children have been able to hear Lou's voice via her letters, but I understand why she only wrote to them. The rest of the letters in the box were all for Stan and Flo, so I've no right to feel envious of Tom, but grief isn't a logical thing.

'Hey you.' Tom kisses my cheek, wrapping his arms around me and holding me so tightly for a moment that it's difficult to breathe. Then he pulls away, letting me go. 'Thank you for today, and for everything. Not just these past few months, but from the moment I met Lou. I've always felt so lucky that meeting the love of my life meant that I got to have you in my life too.'

'Even when I was always around, like the third wheel no one needs.'

'You were never that, not even for a second, but it turns out that a third wheel is the best thing you could have, when one of the other wheels is gone. You're the most wonderful auntie Stan and Flo could ever have been given.' Tom sighs. 'But you're so much more than that. You're the sister I never had. I always wanted a sibling and, when I met Lou, I finally got one. I really hope that's not going to change, because I couldn't bear to lose you too.'

'There's no chance of that. Whatever happens, and whoever else might one day come into your family, you have to remember that a bonus sister is for life, not just for Christmas.' I smile and Tom does too. I'm so glad he feels the same way I do. All the notions Lou got into her head at one point about trying to control who Tom might one day have a relationship with, and even the idea that that someone could be me, were crazy. She knew that in the end; it was just a symptom of her trying to have some kind of influence over a situation that had completely spiralled out of her control. But she made this happen, this brother and sisterly bond between me and Tom, and I know she'd be delighted at how just strong it's become. 'I had the best sister ever, and because of that a friend could never be "like a sister" to me, the way some people's friends are to them. A friendship could never compare to what

Lou and I shared. But you're the only brother I've ever had, and you're stuck with me now, like it or not.'

'I like it, I like it a lot.' Tom hugs me again, and then reaches down into his pocket and holds out an envelope.

'Is that the letter Lou wrote you?'

'No. This was inside my letter, with very strict instructions to give it to you today.'

I don't know how to feel. Part of me wants to grab the letter and rip it straight open, but this is the last time I'm ever going to hear from Lou and I'm not sure I can bear it. I miss her so much already, and my eyes are filling with tears for what feels like the hundredth time in the last few hours alone. I wonder if it would be easier to face if Tom told me what was in it.

'Have you read it?'

'Of course not; this is between you and Lou.' Tom kisses my cheek for a second time, before briefly touching my hand and then turning away.

As he disappears back into the crowd of mourners, I head out of the marquee, clutching the letter as if it was a priceless artefact, which is exactly what it is. The path outside meanders around the church, to the spot at the back where our grandparents' ashes are buried, and where Lou's will be interred too. There's a bench close by, beneath a huge oak tree, and I crunch across a carpet of fallen acorn husks to reach it.

'Well, you got me, Lou, I didn't think I was getting a letter from you.' I whisper the words on the breeze that is gently stirring the branches above me and a huge oak leaf flutters to the ground. More gifts from Lou, or just the changing of the season? I don't know, but I pick it up anyway and set it down on the bench next to me. I hesitate for a moment, savouring this moment, the last time we'll 'speak', and then I open the envelope and pull out the letter. I want to savour every word, but at the same time there's a voracious greed to read what she's written almost more quickly than I can take it in, so I force myself to slow down and read the words out loud, not caring whether someone else might suddenly appear. My voice and Lou's were always the most similar thing about us, so it'll be almost as if I can hear her speaking again.

My big sister, the best big sister there ever was,

You might only have arrived first by twenty-three minutes, an accident of fate based on who'd jostled nearest the exit at the crucial time, but you fulfilled that big sister role from the first moments I can remember. You always stood up for me, and fought my corner, encouraged me and stepped forward whenever I needed help. You were more than just a sister, you were like a second mum – often the only mum I had – and you were my best friend too.

You understood me like no other person ever really did, not even Tom, as wonderful as he is. You knew why I always had to have a Plan B, and you never once got irritated by it, no matter how infuriating it must have sometimes been. When I knew my Plan A for life had been shredded to bits by my diagnosis, I came up with a Plan B as usual, but this time it was a ridiculous one, and one that would never have worked. You found a way to get me to see that, without coming out and saying it directly, because you knew if you did that I'd just dig my heels in even harder. When I first worked out you were @itsnotalloveryet2 I felt angry and hurt, but it only lasted minutes. As soon as I looked at your messages again, I could see what you were doing, and I knew how right you were. You and Tom together was a crazy idea, not because I don't think he'd be incredibly lucky to have you, but because you don't deserve to be anyone's Plan B.

For so long you've fitted around my life, and I've been so lucky and so grateful to have you all to myself, but it's time you found your own Plan A for a change. I know you'll be there for Stan and Flo and Tom, but please don't make that your everything. I don't know what that Plan A will look like, maybe another relationship isn't what you want. All I know is that you deserve to be loved by someone who knows that nothing could replace you. I've known that my whole life, and it gives me to comfort to think that someone might just fill my shoes in that respect. Whatever you want most make that your Plan A, make room in your life to let it in, and for once put yourself first.

I'm so glad the children have you in their life and, whatever the future brings, I know Tom will make the right decisions for them. I should have trusted him from the start and left the Plan B to fate, but you know what I'm like!

Well, I suppose this is it, the last, last goodbye. I miss you already, but I've had the most amazing life and through all the ups and downs, the one constant in it has always been you.

All my love forever, Lou xx

I haven't stopped crying since halfway through the first line and I'm not even going to try. I let the tears slide down my face as I re-read the letter again and silently make one final promise to the sister I adored to find my own Plan A.

## 34

It's been four months since Lou died and we've somehow survived a series of firsts without her. The tenth wedding anniversary that should have been such a celebration, and a family Christmas filled with love and tears in almost equal measure. It's January now and I promised myself this will be the year I fulfil my final promise to Lou.

Tom has gone back to work part-time, and we're managing the children between us, with support from some of Lou's most trusted friends. There's someone new in Tom and the children's lives already, a beautiful little Jack Russell called Molly, who we all adore. Even Tigs is learning to tolerate her.

My working life has changed significantly and I'm going back to university to study part time, on a campus twenty minutes' drive from Castlebourne. My old firm were making some redundancies after a change of direction. I shouldn't have been one of them, but I put my name forward and, I think because of what I'd told them about needing to be there for Flo and Stan, they agreed. I got a healthy payout after almost twenty years of unbroken service, apart from extended sick leave during my treatment for breast cancer, and it was more than enough to pay off the last of my mortgage. The rest will see me through until I finish my studies. I'm finally following my heart and retraining as an art therapist, so that I can turn my passion into a career, and I think Lou would have approved. The charity work I've done since my own brush with cancer has always been important to me, but it's taken on a whole new dimension since losing Lou. I only need to be in university two days a week and I wanted to do something to honour my sister, something that would make a much bigger difference than helping out at fundraisers, or monitoring online cancer support forums. All of those things are great, but they weren't quite enough to be a legacy for Lou, and that's the other half of my Plan A, just like Lou was the other half of me. She'd probably pull a face at that, me putting her right at the centre of my plans, but we were always indivisible and her death hasn't changed that.

I've thought of little else in any windows of spare time I've had over the last four months, and I suppose I might be accused of burying myself in this project, but I know that's not true. I spend so much time with the people I love most, and I've made sure to reciprocate when friends have reached out, because every time I'm in danger of getting tunnel vision about this, it's almost as if I can hear my sister telling me not to let the project swallow me up. All of the research I've done to try and find a way of helping people like Lou kept coming back to one thing: when she was diagnosed, she felt lost. She had no one to talk to about her greatest fears except strangers on an anonymous forum. There was nowhere she could be honest about the terror of a faceless woman – some other mother – one day raising her children. It sent her into a kind of madness at first, and it got me thinking that creating a real place to go, where those kinds of conversations aren't taboo, would be the best possible legacy I could create for my sister.

I read all about Maggie's centres, which provide a place where cancer patients and others affected by the disease can go for support, as well as information and advice. The trouble is, there's nothing even vaguely similar within sixty miles of our home, and a journey like that would have been too much for Lou quite quickly after her diagnosis. So I came up with the idea of fundraising to create something similar, on a much smaller scale, and closer to home, specifically for those affected by an incurable diagnosis. I've approached some of my current and existing clients about funding, selling them the angle that their donations can be written off against tax, and I think I've got enough to get the project off the ground.

The next thing I need to do is to locate a venue, where we could site a cabin initially, to house a drop-in centre, or even just a space for people to meet and chat. Lou's Lodge, that's the idea I've got in my head, but I'm a long way from pinning down the specifics of it yet. The grounds of St Joseph's are stunning, and there'd certainly be room to accommodate a lodge, but when the idea first popped into my head I had no idea if they'd turn me down flat.

I spoke to some of the staff who helped set up a meeting with the CEO, Alison Jefferies, and the new operational director, who hadn't even been appointed to the role when the meeting was arranged, but today's the day I get to meet them both and finally put forward my pitch.

Pulling into the car park of St Joseph's brings back so many memories. The trees are bare now and it looks so different from when Lou was here, yet as I get out of the car and see a sign for the chapel, I almost expect to see her.

Taking a deep breath, I head through the doors into reception. The man behind the counter smiles and asks how he can help me. I'm almost tempted to enquire whether he's got any idea how I can stop my legs from shaking, as my nerves about being here start to kick in. You've got to have a lot of confidence to turn up somewhere like this and make the kind of request I'm about to make, but Lou was always the more assured of the two of us. I just need to think about how she'd have handled it and I'll be okay. I know what she'd have done, she'd already have been thinking through a Plan B, in case the pitch got turned down, and just knowing she had one would have made her more confident. I'll start thinking about that while I'm waiting, in the hope that it can help me calm my nerves too. I smile at the receptionist and announce why I'm here.

'Hi, I'm Holly Champion. I've got a meeting with Alison Jefferies and the new operational director.'

'Ah yes.' The receptionist looks at his computer. 'Dan said to give him a call when you were here.'

'Thank you.' I busy myself with reading some of the posters on the noticeboard in the reception area, too nervous to sit down, while I wait to be collected.

'Good to see you again, Holly.' Even before I look up, I recognise the voice. This isn't any Dan, it's Dan Kingston, the last person I went on a date with. Well, I call it a date, I'm not quite sure if that's what it was. I know it was supposed to be. I'd liked him right from the start, but we never made it to dinner or drinks, because it was the day that Tom turned up outside the cinema, desperate to talk to me, when Lou's cancer had started to escalate at a pace that had knocked us all off our feet. Colour floods my cheeks at the way I treated Dan, just disappearing with a man he knew nothing about and barely apologising for the fact that I'd bailed on our date. He was very understanding at the time, but I didn't keep the promise I made to get in touch again when I was ready, because Lou's illness consumed us all. If he holds that against me, any chance I might have had of trying to persuade St Joseph's to site Lou's Lodge in their grounds might be gone, but at least my nerves have evaporated, All I can do is try my best, and I know that would have been enough for my sister.

* * *

'I think that was really positive.' Dan smiles as we walk out together to the car park and all I can do is murmur my agreement, as I try not to notice how nice his aftershave is. I pitched the idea flawlessly because I had nothing to lose, having convinced myself that it was already a lost cause. When Alison asked me why the project was so important to me and said she'd heard a little bit about Lou, I filled her in on the rest. I even found myself telling her that I'd left Dan high and dry, heat colouring my cheeks all over again as I gave him a belated apology for not getting back in touch again once things had calmed down, like I'd promised to. He'd said it was nothing and that there was no need to apologise, which should have been a relief to hear, but I found myself feeling disappointed that it hadn't mattered to him at all that he didn't hear from me again and that he'd clearly meant every word when he'd said it was nothing.

'You and Alison were very kind; you made it easy for me. Thank you.' I return Dan's smile, and he tilts his head slightly as he looks at me.

'I wish you'd told me about how bad things were with Lou at the time. The volunteer coordinator mentioned it a couple of days later, when she told us you wouldn't be able to return for the foreseeable future. I picked up the phone to call you or text you God knows how many times, but I had no idea if you'd want to hear from me and the last thing I wanted to do was to intrude when you were going through so much. I was preparing for this job and tying things up at the old one. I should have texted to tell you how sorry I was to hear about Lou, but I put my own worries about whether you'd want to hear from me above doing the right thing and I really am sorry.' Dan has the most open face I think I've ever seen, and the kindest eyes too. And suddenly I feel it again, that force urging me forward, like a hand in the small of my back.

'I'm the one who should be sorry. I didn't explain things properly at the time.' I clench the muscles in my jaw for a moment, wrestling with whether to clamp my mouth shut, or let go of the words that seem to be bubbling up inside me. But I know what it is Lou would have wanted me to do. 'If it's not too late and it doesn't muddy the waters too much with you and Alison considering my proposal for the lodge, maybe I could make it up to you? Dinner, as my treat?'

I've never in my life been this bold, and the second or two of silence before he responds seems to stretch on for days.

'I'd absolutely love that.' Dan smiles that lovely warm smile of his again and I remember how to breathe. 'I'll speak to Alison and if she thinks there's any potential conflict of interest, I'm sure we can get the Director of Finance involved instead of me, before it's taken to the board. I don't think she'll have any issues with it, but I've only been here a couple of weeks, and I can't say for sure. Either way, dinner sounds great.'

'If there's a particular restaurant you fancy, just let me know. From what Alison said, I know you've got a lot of evening fundraisers coming up, so I could always cook Sunday lunch at mine, if that's easier?'

'I really don't mind, either Plan A or B works for me. It's the company that matters.'

'It really is.' I can't stop a slow smile from creeping across my face at Dan's words, which he couldn't have chosen more perfectly if he'd tried. 'I'll text you some dates when I get home and you can let me know which works best, as well as if there's anything that you don't eat.'

'I can't wait.'

'Me neither, see you soon.' Leaning forward, I kiss his cheek before getting into my car and driving away. It's far too early to say whether Dan will be a part of my future, but I know Lou would have approved that I'm open to the possibility. It turns out fate can come up with Plan Bs of its own when you give it enough space. I think, in the end, my sister must have realised that too and it was what allowed her to spend the time she had left cherishing every moment, instead of planning for a future she couldn't control. Everyone could learn a valuable lesson from that and I'm going to carry it with me whatever the future might bring. Having a plan is all well and good, but being open to new possibilities brings a joy of its own and, for the first time in a long time, I'm excited to discover what lies ahead.

# ACKNOWLEDGEMENTS

I wanted to start by giving you a little bit of insight into why I wrote *A Mother's Last Wish*. I have written over thirty books, but this is probably my most personal story. I was inspired to write the novel after my own diagnosis with kidney cancer when I was in my late thirties. I was given the news on my daughter's ninth birthday, when my son was just five. I'll never forget the abject terror I felt about the prospect of leaving my children, when I knew just how much they still needed me, and that terrified me far more than the diagnosis.

Thanks to my fantastic consultant, Mr Choi, I made a full recovery, but I never forgot how it felt to face the prospect of having to leave my children, when all I wanted to do was stay. I know how lucky I am to have been given that chance, but sadly I've had friends and family who've also been affected by cancer, some of whom tragically left young children behind when they lost their lives to this awful disease. These amazing women demonstrated the incredible love they had for their children, even in the midst of their darkest days, and the strength of that love left a legacy that is somehow uplifting, despite how badly they are missed. I wanted to reflect that in Lou and Holly's story, to pay tribute to these wonderful women, and I hope with all my heart that I've succeeded.

If you've been affected by any of the themes in this novel, please reach out for support at one of the sources below:

www.macmillan.org.uk

www.cruse.org.uk

www.winstonswish.org

I'm incredibly grateful to the amazing team at Boldwood Books for giving me the opportunity to tell this story. Primarily the thanks for this lies with my fantastic editor, Emily Ruston, and my brilliant copy editor, Candida Bradford, and proof reader, Rachel Sargeant, for helping to shape this story into something I can be proud of. I also want to thank the entire team at Boldwood Books who are now too numerous to mention individually, but whose work I'm eternally thankful for. A special shout out goes to my marketing lead, Marcela Torres, who works tirelessly to help my books reach readers all over the world.

I have to say thanks as always to my friends and family, who put up with me constantly seeming to be buried under deadlines, and sometimes being very slow at replying to messages as a result. A special thanks to my husband for bringing endless cups of tea out to my writing room in the garden, and to my very good friend Jennie for her help with the final read through of the story.

My deep gratitude as always goes to all the reviewers who support the launch of my books and help get the word out. If you read my series novels, you'll know I usually thank reviewers by name, but for my standalone stories, the list of book bloggers organised by the brilliant Rachel Gilbey tends to change more frequently and I'd hate to accidentally leave anyone out. So, I'll just say a huge thank you to you all instead.

My biggest thanks, as always, goes to my readers. You have changed my life and given me a platform to tell stories like this which mean so much to me. Thank you all from the bottom of my heart.

Finally, I want to say thank you to my children, Anna and

Harry, to whom this book is dedicated. Being your mum has been the biggest joy and the greatest adventure of my life. I will always be grateful that I got the chance to watch you both grow into the incredible adults you have become, and I love you more than you will ever know.

# ABOUT THE AUTHOR

**Jo Bartlett** is the bestselling author of over nineteen women's fiction titles. She fits her writing in between her two day jobs as an educational consultant and university lecturer and lives with her family and three dogs on the Kent coast.

Sign up to Jo Bartlett's mailing list for news, competitions and updates on future books.

Follow Jo on social media here:

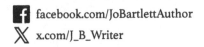 facebook.com/JoBartlettAuthor

x.com/J_B_Writer

# ALSO BY JO BARTLETT

**The Cornish Midwife Series**

The Cornish Midwife

A Summer Wedding For The Cornish Midwife

A Winter's Wish For The Cornish Midwife

A Spring Surprise For The Cornish Midwife

A Leap of Faith For The Cornish Midwife

Mistletoe and Magic for the Cornish Midwife

A Change of Heart for the Cornish Midwife

Happy Ever After for the Cornish Midwife

**Seabreeze Farm**

Welcome to Seabreeze Farm

Finding Family at Seabreeze Farm

One Last Summer at Seabreeze Farm

**Cornish Country Hospital Series**

Welcome to the Cornish Country Hospital

Finding Friends at the Cornish Country Hospital

A Found Family at the Cornish Country Hospital

Lessons in Love at the Cornish Country Hospital

**Standalone**

Second Changes at Cherry Tree Cottage

A Cornish Summer's Kiss

Meet Me in Central Park

The Girl She Left Behind

A Mother's Last Wish

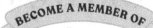

# Boldwood

Boldwood Books is an award-winning fiction publishing company seeking out the best stories from around the world.

**Find out more at www.boldwoodbooks.com**

Join our reader community for brilliant books, competitions and offers!

Follow us
@BoldwoodBooks
@TheBoldBookClub

Sign up to our weekly deals newsletter

https://bit.ly/BoldwoodBNewsletter